THIS IS B.S.

THIS IS B.S.

CRYPTID ASSASSIN™ BOOK SIX

MICHAEL ANDERLE

DISRUPTIVE IMAGINATION®

Copyright © 2020 Michael Anderle
Cover Art by Jake @ J Caleb Design
http://jcalebdesign.com / jcalebdesign@gmail.com
Cover copyright © LMBPN Publishing
A Michael Anderle Production

LMBPN Publishing
PMB 196, 2540 South Maryland Pkwy
Las Vegas, NV 89109

First US edition, May, 2020
eBook ISBN: 978-1-64202-920-8
Print ISBN: 978-1-64202-921-5

THE THIS IS B.S. TEAM

Thanks to our Beta Readers

Jeff Eaton, John Ashmore, and Kelly O'Donnell

Thanks to the JIT Readers

Deb Mader
Dorothy Lloyd
Kerry Mortimer
Diane L. Smith
Jeff Eaton
John Ashmore
Peter Manis
Jeff Goode

If we've missed anyone, please let us know!

Editor
Skyhunter Editing Team

CHAPTER ONE

A part of her relished the chance to get back to work again. For Vickie, it meant things were returning to normal and it surprised her a little how appealing that thought was. She certainly didn't mind participating in the adventures Taylor, Bobby, and Tanya found themselves in, and the other part of her that had tasted the excitement wasn't entirely sold on the idea of normal. Still, at that moment, she hoped everyone would get back so they could do what she thought of as real work.

Aside from all this, the distractions were killer for her grades. While she could certainly apply herself and get those up, it inevitably meant more work—the kind she didn't appreciate since she had a full-time job.

With things returning to their usual routine again, there was less stress. The downside, of course, was that everything was boring and she would soon ache for something more exciting to do. She was aware of the apparently contradictory demands that always seemed to be in conflict within her, but it wasn't necessarily a problem.

She'd made an early start after an uncommonly good night's rest. Traffic hadn't yet reached a peak with most of the people still struggling to get up after a weekend of partying on the Strip.

Of course, there was any number of those who started early, but by this time, they were already at work. She pulled up to the strip mall and turned the security system off as she pulled her Tesla in to make sure Taylor knew she had arrived. By her estimation, there wouldn't be much for her to do for the day. A couple of new suits were due in for repairs, but that had always been Taylor and Bobby's realm in the shop, and Tanya now learned the ropes and picked up tasks from them.

Vickie wasn't entirely sure how it was happening—maybe spending all the extra time with the mechanic paid off in more ways than one—but the woman learned the details of working on the suits faster than any of them had anticipated. She was still behind Taylor and Bobby, of course, but she was catching up quickly. It wouldn't be long before they didn't need their boss to be on the work floor and they would have to find something else for him to do.

Or maybe it simply meant they could take on more work than before. Taylor seemed like the type who wouldn't simply rest on his laurels when his business did well. Hard economic times were always around the corner, it seemed, and they wouldn't wait around for things to go badly when there were other possibilities.

He was already up and in the shop when she pulled in. He didn't look like he had been doing any work, though. His attention was focused on his laptop, which rested on the desk, and she could see very little sign of the usual grease stains that covered his hands when he started work early.

"Hey, Taylor," she called from the car as she closed the door and made her way to him. "What are you doing up this early? I thought you would sleep in today."

The man narrowed his eyes at her as she approached. "Why did you think that?"

"I don't know. You own the place, so there's no reason for you to be up this early. That's what you pay us to do, right?"

Vickie watched him carefully and expected some kind of witty retort. It was one of the things she liked about him, although certainly not the only thing. He had a sharp mind for conversation and it was fun to keep him on his toes.

But something was different today. His eyes seemed vacant and unfocused, the vagueness emphasized by the way his gaze flicked constantly toward the screen of his laptop even though there wasn't anything open in the display.

He realized that she had asked him something and snapped his head around, trying to recall what it was. "I... yeah, I guess. I wasn't able to sleep much last night, so it was a matter of sitting around upstairs or down here. I flipped a coin and came down here."

She sat in the seat beside him, powered her work computer up, and studied him closely. "Is everything okay with you? You seem much less...obtrusive than usual."

Taylor scowled at her. "And what's that supposed to mean?"

"Well, if you want me to tell you that I don't look forward to a little banter in the mornings when I come in here, it would be an outright lie. You're usually a little more alert and talkative, so the fact that you're not means something might be wrong. Or off. Or whatever terminology you'd prefer to use to describe the fact that you're simply not yourself."

He stared at her for a few seconds, and she realized he was at a loss as to what to say next. Maybe he was trying to think of a response. Then again, maybe he wasn't sure what was happening himself and he was distracted by looking for the answer to that. Either way, Taylor without a quick retort wasn't very common, which made it interesting enough in its own right.

He was saved from having to think of a decent response, though, when the shop door began to open again and Bobby's truck drew in. He and Tanya had car-pooled often lately, and Vickie wasn't sure if the woman spent that much time at his apartment, if they had moved in together, or if she had moved into a place of her own.

Taylor had offered her accommodation in the strip mall and while not the best, it was better than not having a roof over her head at all. It was also better than many different apartment complexes she had seen around Vegas, but not by much.

The high Internet speed was what put it head and shoulders above the competition, but Tanya didn't seem like the kind of person who would fully appreciate having full-speed Internet.

The vehicle stopped and the couple slid out, clearly

eager to get to work. Bobby brought his traditional offering of donuts and coffee, enough for four.

"You know, you should think about paying Bobby for these deliveries he makes," Vickie noted. She pulled up the scheduling software she had started working on once it became clear that she would work more from the desk than on the suits that were being delivered. "The dude brings food and coffee every day so you might as well make it worth his while, right?"

Taylor snapped out of being lost in thought again and focused his gaze on her. "Oh...yeah, that's probably a good idea. He's brought me the receipts for the purchases, though, and I've added it to his salary every month already. That...that's what you meant, right?"

"Wow, you really are out of it today. What the hell is going on in that red-crowned head of yours, Tay-Tay?"

His scowl over the nickname was what she most wanted to see, and it was enough to lift her spirits a little more. For his part, he ignored her question and made his way to the improvised break room where Bobby and Tanya began to get ready for the day.

Vickie wasn't about to let him off that easily and followed him quickly to the other side of the shop to snag her coffee and one of the chocolate-sprinkled donuts.

"Is the delivery still coming in today?" Bobby asked, blissfully unaware of his boss' current mood.

She intended to change that, but there was time to fit business talk in too. "The truck's scheduled to arrive in a couple of hours. It should give us enough time to get the shop cleaned and ready before they get here, but it'll also mean enough time in the day to get the suits set up and put work into them before we close for the day. What do you think, Taylor?"

The man took a bite from one of the vanilla-glazed confectionaries before he realized she had spoken to him. "Oh…uh, yeah, that would be great. We do need to get some of the tools and parts squared away and make this place ready for action again. Simply because we've been out of the country doesn't give us an excuse to leave our workplace looking like a pigsty."

Bobby had known Taylor longer than she had, and she could tell that the stout mechanic was now a little suspicious. It wasn't glaringly obvious since Tanya didn't react in the same manner, but something was going on with Taylor and Vickie was determined to get to the bottom of it.

"What kind of priorities will we set?" Bobby asked, most likely in an attempt to glean more information about what was plaguing his boss.

She doubted they would get more than a typical response from the man. The fact that he continued to glance at the laptop every few seconds meant there was something there he wanted to get back to and he didn't want them to see it.

The hacker convinced herself this was a mystery that needed her to solve it. If necessary, that was what she would do all day today. While there was work to be done, this was one hell of a lot more important. She would peek into her boss' personal life, intrude, and make a general nuisance of herself.

For his own good, of course.

"Tay-Tay," Vickie grumbled as he started to walk to the

desk and the laptop he watched like a mama hawk. "Do you really think we won't notice that something's going on with you? Seriously?"

Tanya looked surprised but it disappeared quickly. Bobby's expression remained unchanged and he shook his head gently as he took another sip of his coffee.

Taylor looked at her with a hint of defensiveness in his posture. It was probably the first time she'd seen him like this and it was a little disconcerting. "In private. Come on."

She followed him quickly up the stairs to his living quarters. He dropped into a seat and gestured for her to do the same. "I think I'm going crazy."

"What? You only realized this now? You're fucking nuts, Taylor. This isn't news. Can we get back to work now?"

His scowl was deeper than usual, and she stopped herself from saying anything else.

"Crazier than usual, I mean." His voice was a little calmer but far from relaxed. He sounded more intense the lower his tone became. "I chatted to your cousin over dinner the other night when we got back from the Zoo and... I think she was hitting on me."

Vickie stared blankly at him and needed a moment to process that. "You're right. You're crazier than usual."

"Right?" Taylor agreed and extended a hand to her. "Right? I thought that was a little too far out there too. She said something like...uh, I would have to take her somewhere nicer than Il Fornaio on our first date, and I couldn't tell if she was joking or not."

She shook her head. Hitting on Taylor didn't sound like the Niki she knew. Of course, joking about him taking her out on a date wasn't like her either. Nothing about this made sense.

The only rational deduction was that she was probably missing something—a part of the story that wasn't there.

"I mean..." Taylor continued, "she knows me and isn't the kind of woman to go for the kind of guy I am, right?"

The hacker dragged her hand through her hair and tilted her head curiously. "Do...do you want her to have meant something by it more than a throwaway joke?"

He finally looked into her eyes and she didn't like the feeling she got from him. It had a desperate feel to it and coming from a man who usually didn't appear to give a shit about what was happening around him, it felt uncomfortable to see him so vulnerable.

"I don't know. She and I work together well enough and I wouldn't want to mess with that."

Vickie nodded. She had her answer, even if he wasn't willing to admit it to himself. "Well, now that you got that off your chest, do you think you can put your head into the shop and work without us having to worry about you losing a hand while operating the machinery?"

Taylor smirked and that was the most like himself he had appeared all day. "Yeah, I think so. Let's get to work."

Elisa couldn't quite believe that she had reached this particular point. People fantasized about quitting their jobs and made a big deal out of it—a statement of some kind. They were usually those who hated their lives while trapped in a cubicle doing meaningless work. Many dreamed about the day when they would have the leverage to leave.

While she didn't think she had the leverage, there wasn't any choice for her at this point. After the shit she'd seen, merely being a reporter in the middle of it all was not appealing.

The secretary looked up from her desk when the intercom buzzed and waved to grab her attention where she sat and waited as patiently as she could.

"Cas will see you now," she said with a small, polite smile.

Karen had worked at the Crypto-Inquirer almost as long as Elisa had and knew more about the ins and outs of the company than Cas probably did. The man was the creative type but he never admitted to knowing much about running a business like this, even though he had been to business school. He was content to let others more inclined and qualified manage what they could on his behalf.

She stepped inside the office and detected the faint hit of cigarette smoke that told her he was probably about ten minutes away from lighting another one of those cancer-cylinders. It also meant she had almost the same length of time to talk to him while he was in a good mood.

"Morning, Elisa," Cas called and gestured for her to take a seat across from him. "I hope you're not feeling too jet-lagged since I do want to know what you found out during your time in Vegas. Learning the truth about who committed that robbery would put our little operation on the map, and it's about time people noticed us."

Elisa fought back the feeling that made her want to help

him. Of course, he hadn't been responsible for any of the hardships she had gone through and she didn't intend to hold anyone at the Crypto-Inquirer to blame.

Her time with them was at an end, however, and there was no good way to break it to him.

"Cas…I'm here to tender my resignation."

Well, that was much simpler than she thought it would be. There was no way better than simple and direct, she decided.

He laughed, probably thinking she would say she was joking or retract her statement. After a few seconds, he realized she was completely serious. He leaned forward on his desk and stared intently at her.

"Is there a reason why you've suddenly decided to leave us? Is it money? Did someone offer you more money? Is that why you're ducking out on us? Because I can tell you right now, I can give you a raise. It probably won't match whatever you've been promised, but you have to know the loyalty we've shown you over the years you've been with us—"

Elisa knew he would go on for a while about that and she had no desire to listen to his speech about loyalty. She had heard it fifteen times by now and she had the entire discourse down by heart.

Instead, she raised her hand and brought his speech to a halt. "It's not about the money, Cas. It's…these things were much more fun to write about when…"

She couldn't tell him about what she had seen during her adventures, so all she could do was shake her head and hope that was sufficient to add weight to her words.

"What? What is it?"

"Well, I did discover things when I was in the middle of it, but while I was there, the people who got me out of the trouble I landed in made me sign an NDA that would keep me from legally sharing virtually anything I discovered while I was in Vegas."

Cas looked confused. There was some disappointment involved as he sensed there was a story hidden in what she tried to hide. Even so, she wouldn't try to convince him otherwise. If he wanted to go out there and deal with the Vegas mob, that was his call to make.

"Well…shit. Is there anything about what happened you could share?"

Elisa considered his question for a moment. "Well, I can tell you that I wasn't in Vegas the whole time. Which… yeah, you don't need to worry about the costs of the trip. I won't submit the receipts for reimbursement. The only cost relevant to you is for the flight over there, of course, since you guys bought that for me before I had a chance to do it myself."

He nodded. "That's fair, I guess. I really hate to see you go, El."

She stood from her seat and placed her letter of resignation on his desk. "Yeah, me too."

With her usual efficiency, she had emailed him a copy as well to make sure it wasn't lost in the pile of paperwork. Given the way he looked anxiously at the bottom drawer of his desk, she had a feeling he would have a smoke before returning to work. The chances were something would be lost before the paperwork could get to HR.

With nothing left to be said, she stepped out of the

office, closed the door behind her, and headed toward the elevators.

Once the metal doors closed and she could feel the car moving down, she released a long sigh.

"That went about as well as I could have hoped," she muttered to no one in particular.

CHAPTER TWO

It was unquestionably an exceptionally pleasant morning.

Niki Banks wasn't the kind of woman to enjoy things like that. People who had the time to smell the roses were those who tended to look around and enjoy the view of the sun coming up in the sky on a cloudless day. The busy people never had the time to notice or talk about how it was evidence of one deity or another painting a picture.

Even then, Nevada didn't have much in the way of picturesque landscapes to enjoy unless one happened to like a shit-ton of desert with a view of mountains in the distance.

Jansen and Maxwell stood nearby and poured over a selection of files while she spent time on the other side of the hangar. While she didn't have the time for the grand vista, she did enjoy the cooler temperatures that came with early morning near Vegas.

She moved to where the two were busy and nursed a warm cup of coffee as she inspected their work.

"Did you know," she said to break the silence that hung over them, "that the State of Nevada is the fourth-largest producer of gold in the world?"

Maxwell looked up from his work and removed a pair of reading glasses. "No shit."

"Yeah, I read that somewhere. Nevada, if it were its own country, would be the fourth-largest gold producer in the world behind China, Australia, and Russia. Apparently, it also has the world's second-largest gold deposit behind some unpronounceable place in South Africa. And people kind of stepped right over it on their way to California during the Gold Rush. How the hell did that many people miss that much gold when that was all they were looking for?"

Jansen didn't even look up from reading through the files to answer her. "The gold around here is low-grade, mixed in, and hard to find. They didn't realize there was any around here until 1962, as I recall. It takes a very technical process to leach it from the rest of the bullshit."

Niki scowled and took another sip of her coffee. "Still, though. I can't imagine San Francisco would be that big a place if people had stopped here instead of there."

"Nevada would probably not be the same place either," he pointed out. "Do you have some ideas about where we'll head next?"

She placed her cup on the table. "I thought you guys had more of a connection with Speare than I did."

"We report to Mr. Speare about what you do when you're out and about and wandering the Earth, looking for monsters to kill. It's a one-way street, though. He doesn't tell us anything about what we're supposed to do. That's all on you."

"Well, since it's all on me, I guess we do have a couple of inklings of people doing the wrong thing with shit they pulled out of the Zoo. But we're still in the process of building a team, so inklings won't cut it until we have a proper, bonafide emergency on our hands."

"In that case…"

"Yeah, we call in Taylor McFadden. Until then, can you at least tell me we have a hacker on our list who can help us?"

Maxwell frowned. "I thought you'd arranged for your old AI to be transferred?"

Nicki sighed. "Speare has signed off on it and the FBI have told us they don't want it and prefer to use their own —dumb choice and they're shooting themselves in the foot by sticking with their inferior software, but it's their call. The problem is that until the creator has run a full integrity scan on the software to make sure it's not corrupted, DOD won't authorize the upload. We can't sit around with our fingers up our asses until they reach consensus, so we need a hacker."

Jansen pushed a couple of the files to her. "We have a couple of candidates, but it's tough to validate them. People don't exactly put 'hacker' on their resumes. We can look into software engineers and the like, but they probably won't have the skill set we need. More importantly, it's unlikely that they'll be willing to do what we need them to do. We've looked into people who might have criminal records that they've concealed and that kind of thing.

Sometimes, they don't even need to have them concealed as long as we can find out what they did."

"So we're simply picking cyber-criminals up off the street?" She raised an eyebrow in disapproval.

"Of course not. There are extensive procedures we've followed to find the people who might be prime candidates for your team. That's why there are only two files."

She scowled as she looked at the manila folders in front of her. The entire process irritated her because she knew she already had the people she wanted on the team—the very, very best and people she could trust. Vickie and Jennie were both the best available.

Except, of course, for the small problem that both were currently employed by the private sector in jobs they probably infinitely preferred to working for the DOD. Her sister had established herself as quite the juggernaut in her company and Vickie was going through the motions of college while she worked with Taylor in his business. While she could probably make more money with the DOD, Niki doubted the girl would want to be involved with working for the government. She was too much of a free spirit.

Besides, working with Taylor had been a positive influence in her life and she didn't want to remove her from it.

"Banks?"

She looked up from the files and realized that Jansen was speaking to her.

"What?"

"Your phone's ringing."

So it was. She took the device from her pocket and

checked the number to make sure it was who she thought it was before she pressed the button to answer the call.

"Good morning, Mr. Speare. I...assume it's still morning where you are."

"That's a reasonable assumption. I'm pleased to see you're already at work. As it happens, I have work for you. Our intelligence has been rigorously focused on their efforts to gather substantiated intel on a particular company. This information is, of course, concerned with the unofficial and below the radar operations of a company that has worked with assets imported from the Zoo. It is interesting to know that there are a limited number of people who have access to what has been taken from that fucking jungle and that so many of them fail miserably in their processes to contain it."

"If Taylor is to be believed, that shit is as alive as the monsters he ends up having to kill. It's like it's alive and trying to get loose."

"It doesn't help that the contracts are passed through on political affiliations rather than actual competence."

"Yeah, I can see how that would make things a little more complicated than they'd need to be."

"Either way, we do have a couple of people in place to investigate the work of a firm that goes by the name of Gottfried and Gottfried, a family-owned business."

"How does a family-owned business get a government contract?"

"I should mention that the Gottfried family has worked in the realm of pharmaceuticals since the time when people got cocaine in their cough syrup."

"Oh."

"Yeah. But moving on, the people we have looking into their projects have discovered very real signs that hinky shit is in progress. They'll dig a little deeper, but we need you to go in and be enough of a pain to draw the CEO in, which should provide an opportunity for you to investigate whether these people have fucked up enough on their contract to warrant your intervention. So, what do you think? Are you up for it?"

Niki thought the man was merely yanking her chain, but there was something to be said for professionalism in the workplace, even if it happened to be a hangar out in the middle of Nevada.

"Of course. That's what you hired me for, right?"

Speare laughed over the line. "Of course it is. I'm merely glad you still feel like it's a job you can do. I'll send you the details—or rather, I'll send the details to your team."

The call ended abruptly. He was never one for goodbyes, it seemed, and Niki no longer expected him to be polite over the phone.

Maybe that was simply the way he was.

Either way, it had little relevance to the matter at hand. Niki turned her attention to Maxwell and Jansen, who had stopped their perusal of the files that had been provided and stared expectantly at her. They had done so ever since she picked the phone up.

"Well, it looks like we have something to do after all," she said and grinned as she stated the obvious. "Jansen, you should receive the details via email in a couple of minutes. Once that's done, you can probably go ahead and file a flight plan since I have a feeling that whenever things get bad to the point where we have to be involved, it means they are about to spiral out of control and take the term 'shit hitting the fan' to a whole new level."

The two men immediately began to clear the paperwork from the table. They could continue working on it while on the plane.

"Will do, boss," the smaller of the two assured her as Niki scowled at the now lukewarm mug of coffee in her hand. If they had to constantly jump whenever Speare had something on the docket for them, she would need a more complete team than merely whoever was still alive from her time with the FBI.

Until then, though, putting out fires and jumping from one emergency to the other necessitated improvised solutions, and this was the best she could do for the moment.

After a few years of focused work, things had finally begun to look up.

The pressure that resulted when people were put in charge with the expectation of rapid results would always end badly. Richard Albert Torrance had been put in a position where immediate success was the only option available to him.

While he could return to teaching at Harvard, that had always been intended as a part-time gig. Tenured professors were never those at the forefront of biological discoveries. This was especially the case when there were all kinds of new fronts to explore and an alien force made the advances for them. All they needed to do was discover them and document them for future use.

Two options were available to him if he wanted to be at the cutting edge of this opportunity. The first was that he could go to the middle of the desert and study everything up close, which didn't feel like an option at all in his mind. Or he needed to work at one of the labs that picked up the biological material sent out of the jungle for testing and study.

The latter seemed like the better choice and would still ensure that he could be ahead of the pack and put his name on some of the discoveries that came from the Zoo.

It was what had led him to be recruited by Gottfried and Gottfried, and it didn't take him long to realize that many other people had come to the same conclusion he had. Too many other people, he thought with a grimace.

Aside from the basic irritation of such a long drive to reach the lab, it also provided too much time to consider a situation he often thought of as impossible. He had purchased a small house in the suburbs, and even though there was very little traffic on the road to the isolated facility, it still took almost three hours to get there and back.

Of course, being research director did have a few perks. He had his own office with a small room and a cot where he could spend the night if he wasn't willing to drive all the way home when he had worked a particularly long shift. That mitigated some of the negatives but it still wasn't ideal.

Although, he reminded himself, it was better than heading out to the middle of the nightmare jungle—barely but still better.

He pulled up to the front entrance and waited for one of the guards to approach and check his identification. The higher-ups had sent warnings about corporate espionage and had become more and more paranoid about security. This had already reached the point where they put all the resources possible into securing the hell out of the building. Surprisingly, it included having all the security guards meeting every single member of staff so they didn't rely only on electronic systems that could be broken into and hacked.

There were still problems with their decision to focus on only low-tech security. On top of the guards being able to recognize everyone, an additional system of ID cards with tracking chips in them made sure that not only were they tagged coming in, but every step they took through the facility was tracked.

This second layer was because there was a problem with human error too. Terrance had read somewhere that most people who were called hackers by the media were mostly grifters who knew how to talk themselves through the high-tech security systems that had been put in place.

The practical result of the precautionary measures was that they extended the three-hour drive from his home by a fifteen-minute wait while people checked and double-checked whether he was allowed to enter the building or not.

Finally, one of the smaller doors on the perimeter opened and an older guard ambled toward his Lincoln. Terrance already knew to lower the window as he approached.

"Good morning, Dr. Terrance," the man said with a small smile as Terrance passed him his ID card. "I hope you had a nice weekend."

"Not too bad, not too bad. Brock, right?"

He smiled. "Yep, that's me."

"These security checks are more and more invasive by the day. Do you think I'll have to ready myself for cavity searches before this whole paranoia comes to a head?"

Brock laughed and handed him his ID card. "Hell, I hope not. No offense to the very skilled and intelligent people who work here, but between you and me, I'd rather not see what they have going on under their lab coats. But nah, these are merely a few more precautions. The CEO was alerted that we had a couple of visitors from the DOD and he wanted to make sure everything was secure just in case. He talked about contracts being reliant on the added security or something like that."

Terrance kept his pleasant smile in place but alarm bells rang in the back of his head. DOD visitors? At the lab? Why hadn't he been alerted about this? He was the research director and had run the entire lab for the past three years and provided the CEOs with all the results they had demanded.

Many people had vied for the job when it was thrown out there, and the board had wanted assurances from those who took over the facility that it would give them a leg up on the competition.

He'd promised them that and more. They tended to believe whatever a Harvard professor told them was possible and didn't question whether what he intended to do was legal or not.

For the most part, of course, it was legal. It was also the kind of thing that was frowned upon in the community of supercilious pricks he had dealt with most of his life. A significant number of papers had been written on the dangers of testing the goop that was pulled out of the jungle on biological subjects, much less live ones. This meant most of the people in Washington would get nervous if someone from the DOD told them about what was happening in the lab.

But what was the point of having all this security if they couldn't take risks to stay ahead?

Of course, the CEO would claim all kinds of ignorance over what was happening, fire him, prosecute him, and then turn and hire someone else to do the same thing.

He grasped his wheel a little tighter as the gate began to move. Terrance didn't wait for it to be fully open before he eased his car through and drove it into the underground parking lot. Too many people forgot where they were supposed to park, but no one would pull into the spot that was the closest to the elevators.

That was the one with his name on it and he halted so abruptly that his tires squealed slightly. Many people might have tried but they would be the ones who were fired. There were literally thousands of biology masters and PhD students who would have killed for a job in his lab and that fact alone was enough to keep the others in line.

He stepped out and into the elevator, pressed the close-door button, and scowled as it took him to the second floor. Having a corner office wasn't quite as great when it didn't overlook a city with a great view, but it was still a corner office. He wouldn't complain about it.

And there was a view, of course. Looking out into nature was still a pleasant way to achieve Zen while he drank his morning coffee and prepared for the day ahead.

It was a good start to be able to sit for a moment and appreciate the view.

But not today. There were more important matters to attend to.

"Get Jerry on the phone," Terrance told his secretary before she even had a chance to get a word in edgewise. Niceties would have to come later. "On a secured line."

"Of course, Dr. Terrance."

He stepped into his office, closed the door, and made sure to lock it before he moved to his desk where his land-line was already ringing. He picked it up off the cradle and waited for the line to secure itself before it connected with his second-in-command's phone number.

"This is Dr. Greer."

"Jerry, it's Rich. Look, were you here when those DOD guys came over? The guard at the front says they came but it wasn't when I checked out on Friday, so I assume it was over the weekend. You were in charge then, right?"

"Hey, Rich. Yeah...yeah, there were a couple of guys from the DOD. They said they were checking for contract violations regarding the security stipulated. They weren't around for long, though, and only talked to the guards, checked their stations, and made sure our electronic security was on point. They didn't come down to the lower levels."

"They didn't see what we are doing there, right?"

"Of course not." Greer didn't sound too concerned, and Terrance certainly respected the man's judgment. "Most of the servers there are isolated anyway, so they didn't even see a hint of what takes place. Believe me, I had the computer people run checks on all the systems they looked at, and it was only about the security. There's nothing to worry about, I promise."

"Okay, thanks, Jerry. I'll be down shortly."

Despite his friend's assurances, he didn't feel completely reassured. People sniffing around his place of business meant that either it was simply a routine audit or someone was suspicious. While logic said the former, a deep unease suggested the latter and that it was only a matter of time before they needed to do some cleaning.

He needed to get a cleanup procedure on paper. Just in case.

CHAPTER THREE

The information came in quickly. Niki didn't like these kinds of jobs to come out of the blue, but she obviously had little say in it. When they had a whiff of a situation that might turn bad, they needed to act on it quickly or people would die.

"Give me the rundown again, Jansen," she grumbled and leaned back in her seat. They were about an hour away from the airfield in Virginia, which gave them more than enough time to work with.

Jansen pulled the file up on his laptop for what felt like the hundredth time. She had the file herself and had read it dozens of times, but there was something about hearing it that made it easier to commit the details to memory. She was one of those people who remembered what she heard better than what she read.

"There was a routine inspection on one of the facilities of a contracted company, Gottfried & Gottfried, working under the shell name All Spaces Above Horizon Ltd. All companies that accept contracts from the DOD have to go through routine and random inspections from time to time to make sure they're not selling military secrets or putting any of their findings on a website or something.

"Anyway, G & G are given contracts to process and test goop taken out of the Zoo and the security inspectors saw that sections of the lab were restricted and the research director had to be contacted before they were allowed access into the lower levels."

"How isn't that standard operations, especially for a company that deals with as much classified material as this one does?" Niki asked. "That's what I don't get. These people have called us in on an operation that's fucking working for them."

Jansen shrugged. "It is standard operations, but there were some other red flags involved."

"This is where I still have questions, despite how many times I've read those damn documents. What other red flags? Did they see something? Anything that'll tell us that it's our kind of operation?"

"It doesn't say. For all we know, it could have been a gut instinct. That's why Speare wants us to go in as a DOD inspection unit, cover ground they weren't able to, and make sure nothing's going wrong."

"And that's the part I don't like. We're doing intelligence work."

"Yeah," Jansen muttered. "That's what Speare indicated in his file. His team wouldn't have been able to get in deep enough without raising alarms if something bad is going on."

Something had niggled at her from the beginning, and it

was almost a relief to put it into words and face the source of her disquiet. She wasn't DOD intelligence. Those guys knew what to look for in this particular situation. She didn't know what might constitute a red flag and in all likelihood, wouldn't be able to identify them even if they were there.

"I need to remind you that I'm not the intelligence operative on this team," she said finally and folded her arms.

"Well, it's lucky for you that you have me on your team." Jansen smirked like he knew something she didn't, although he knew she was familiar with his file. Still, it was an attempt at a joke, even though it wasn't all that funny in the circumstances. "Anyway, you're the lead on the inspection, so you need to bluff your way through the security and get us inside. And keep in mind that if they resist us breaching their security like that, it doesn't necessarily mean they're guilty. It merely means they have something to hide."

"Wait—them hiding something doesn't mean that they're guilty?"

"Well…it does, obviously, but it could be something the Trade Commission or Health and Safety doesn't approve of or something like that. We also report on everything we find—or, rather, I report on everything we find. But our job is to make sure they're not doing something that'll endanger American lives down the road through messing with that bullshit goop."

Niki nodded slowly but her expression suggested distaste. "So I simply…bluff my way through."

"You know how to intimidate the rich pricks who run

these labs. I saw you do it and in fact, I'd go so far as to say you like it too."

She looked at Maxwell. "Do you believe this shit?"

The larger man stared at her for a few seconds. "Do you not enjoy putting those rich assholes in their place?"

Not entirely comfortable with this unexpected challenge, she shrugged. "It's not a terrible feeling," she conceded reluctantly and hated the truth of it. This remained one of her points of inner conflict and raising it openly like this stirred feelings of guilt and vulnerability she couldn't afford.

Jansen grinned. "Oh, yeah, you enjoy it. Anyway, getting us in the door is step one. From there, we can bullshit, intimidate, and otherwise talk these people into allowing us into the lower levels where they hide their dirty little secrets. After that—"

Niki leaned forward. "Do you know what we're looking for? Honestly, I'm no scientist and I don't know jack about what these fucking assholes do that creates the monsters we have to deal with. It could be fucking magic for all I could tell."

He tilted his head in thought. "No, I can't say that I do."

"Then get me someone who does," she instructed and leaned back in her seat. The plane began to tilt into its descent, indicating that they would land soon.

"I have the perfect guy," Jansen replied and snapped his seatbelt on before he returned to work. "Dr. Salinger Jacobs. He has written the book on most things regarding the Zoo—and I mean that literally. He has publications out explaining his adventures in the Zoo. They make for interesting reading if you're...uh, into that kind of shit."

"Biology or simply a collection of alien plants and animals?"

"Either or."

"And who the fuck calls their kid Salinger? What kind of name is that?"

"I'm fairly sure it's the name of the writer for Catcher in the Rye. J. D. Salinger."

Niki shook her head and waited for Jansen to make contact with the doctor in question. The chances were that someone called Salinger had intellectual parents and ended up being one himself. Still, she couldn't imagine an old, stuffy lecturer going into the Zoo enough to catch the attention of someone like her bodyguard.

The call finally went through as the plane began to land. Jansen was calling someone in the Sahara—in or near the Zoo, by the looks of it—and she had no idea what time it was there. Maybe they were lucky and had managed to catch him between trips. For all she knew, they caught him while he was in the fucking jungle.

The first connection showed that he certainly wasn't in the Zoo although it wasn't any kind of office that she had ever seen before. In fact, it looked like a living room with an open plan that revealed a kitchen behind him.

The biggest surprise on the screen was the man— although man wasn't quite the right word. He looked like a kid, barely into his twenties although he was built far better than most athletes. If she had met him on the street, she would have guessed he was about a year, maybe a year and a half into a college football scholarship. He had tanned skin, mopey black hair, and dark eyes.

Apparently, her surprise was more obvious than she

had intended it to be and the man on the other side of the connection laughed.

Niki shook her head. "I'm sorry, I didn't—"

He raised his hand. "There's no need to apologize. I know I don't look like what most people imagine when they hear the name Dr. Salinger Jacobs. Seriously, my parents didn't realize how much that would get me bullied. You can call me Sal, though."

"I think I'll call you Dr. Jacobs," she stated firmly.

"No problem. That sounds good to me."

She smirked. "Anyway, I'm Agent Niki Banks and I work with the Department of Defense. If you're on our list of approved consultants Jansen can call, I'll go ahead and assume all the legal rigmarole has already been taken care of." She paused and looked from her bodyguard to the scientist and both men nodded.

"Right. With that covered, I remind you that this discussion and any others in this matter are covered by all the classified information and non-disclosure legalese. Okay, back to business. I work with a specialized branch of the DOD that deals with people here who make mistakes with the goop that's sent back. We're dealing with a potential infestation and the DOD, as amazing and unbelievable as it sounds, is the first line of defense. We're more than happy to compensate you for this consultation, obviously."

"And what's the last line of defense?"

"A group of freelancers—former Zoo operatives we brought in to deal with the infestations when they begin to claim lives."

"Who do you operate with? I assume you have a team of your own on the front line against Zoo infestations."

"Oh. Well, not a team per se."

"You might want to think about getting one."

"I have a man I usually call in. He has a team."

"What's his name?"

"Taylor McFadden."

"Oh. Well, I guess I can erase the thought I had that you were woefully unprepared for the task you gave yourself that I never said aloud and should have kept to myself. You have that crazy sonofabitch on your side? Now that's something impressive."

"If you mean because I'm able to work with the sono-fabitch, you might be right."

Jacobs laughed again. "Well, that crazy son of a bitch has saved my skin once and the members of my team no less than thirteen times. You can forget what you said about the compensation for my consulting on this. I think your bosses at the DOD will be happy to hear that I'll do this pro bono."

"My bosses don't care about budgetary matters."

"Well, now I feel like an asshole for wanting to waive the consultation fees. There's nothing I like more than being paid with my tax dollars."

"Do you even pay taxes in the Zoo?"

"That's not the point. Anyway, I'll move right along and assume that you won't add an invoice from me in whatever budget you file for this situation. Why don't you go ahead and explain exactly what this situation is? I have been known for being able to talk fast and say a lot without actually saying anything, so anytime you want to chime in here..."

His voice trailed off and he waited for her to do

precisely that. Niki was not sure what she had been talking about. He wasn't wrong, though. He could talk fast and say absolutely nothing without so much as taking a breath.

She shook her head to clear her head. "Right. We'll have to talk about when Taylor might have learned social graces another time, I guess."

"Good luck with that." Jacobs laughed. "The guy may be willing to take a knife, bullet, or alien monster bite for people, but getting him to dress his asshole-ishness up as anything else...now that would be a neat trick."

"Getting him to dress up at all is a feat of magic I've never seen before," Niki muttered. "You know, now that I think about it, Taylor has mentioned you before, although we were a little tipsy by that point in the conversation. I always thought Salinger Jacobs was some stuffy-shirted professor somewhere, but he did say you were the preeminent non-governmental scientist."

"Wow, so he eventually did graduate from monosyllabic words. I have to give him credit. He did put enough time into it."

"Don't get me wrong. I absolutely agree with you," Niki conceded. "But he has always found ways to surprise me."

A small smile crept onto his face. "Yeah, he has that ability going for him. Tell me, did he really drop a fucking helicopter on himself?"

Niki narrowed her eyes. "That is supposed to be classified information."

He chuckled. "We operate next to an alien-infested, DOD-classified, jungle war zone in the middle of the Sahara. I'm fairly sure we have a higher clearance than most of the people in congress."

She folded her arms in front of her chest and tilted her head. "What makes you say that?"

"Because the fact that we operate at the front line means we need to have all the information possible available to us. Going into that fucking jungle with anything other than everything that is known about it is tantamount to suicide."

"I...think I follow that logic." She nodded her head slowly.

"Anyway, if you do something incredibly stupid in the Zoo, that's only a back-hoe and your ass is forgotten. Whether you're killed by a human or a Zoo monster, no one will go in there to track a potential idiot. Hell, the only reason we have idiots in the jungle is because when push comes to shove, idiots who can point their guns in the right direction when told to are the useful kind and you can plan around them being idiots."

Niki shook her head. "And...right there, you lost me. What...what are you talking about?"

"Did he actually drop a helicopter on himself? I know Taylor is not a fucking idiot, so if he did, he probably had a good reason. I'm not sure what reason one might have to drop a helicopter on oneself, hence my interest."

If there was one thing she didn't want to talk about, this was it. Without a doubt, it wasn't a pleasant memory, but in reality, who was she protecting in this instance? She was no longer in the FBI and the people she was protecting weren't those who could be hurt with the information.

Besides, she was making her own rules at this point.

She sighed deeply and shook her head. "Well, for starters, he didn't drop a helicopter on himself. I'm not sure how that would have been done given that he was on the ground at the time. No, what he did was much worse. We were dealing with a large number of cryptids at the time—hundreds really—so he made the call to have the Army bomb his location before it was completely overrun. The only thing that saved him was when an already downed helicopter was overturned and crunched on top of him."

"I'll go ahead and guess that didn't end as well as he hoped."

"Talking to him later, I think he kind of expected to be killed and he thought taking the monsters with him while he was at it was a good enough trade, so… I guess that depends. It did get him sent to the hospital for a couple of months and another few months in rehabilitation. He hasn't gotten all the muscle back, but he's working on it if the stories I hear about him are correct."

Jacobs leaned back in his seat. "Yeah, that sounds like him."

Niki realized that the plane had already been immobile for a few minutes and the crew waited for them to disembark if they intended to do so. She wanted to get the conversation with Jacobs over first, which meant it was time to get down to brass tacks. It irritated her that she'd allowed herself to be diverted into talking about Taylor.

"Well, enough chewing the fat for now," she stated and focused her attention on Jansen. "It's time we start talking about what we need your help with. Jansen, as you're more familiar with Dr. Jacobs' work than I am, I'll let you fill him in."

"Right," the man responded immediately. "We've been

dealing with situations where companies that run the labs and get the goop from the Zoo don't treat it with the respect it deserves. There has been an increase of instances of containment breaches and monsters attacking innocent civilians over the past few months, which is why this task force was created. There were also updates within the legislation to allow for punishment of these companies if they're caught experimenting with the goop on live biological subjects."

"Well, that all sounds fantastic," the scientist responded. "It sounds like you guys have it handled over there. Of course, if that were the case, you wouldn't call me in to consult."

"That is exactly right, Dr. Jacobs," Jansen admitted. "We have all the legal power available to bring to bear on people who break the law and stop them from creating an infestation the likes of which could endanger the lives of the American people. What we lack is the expertise to pinpoint the cases in which they use the goop in a way that would cause those infestations. The idea of this task force is to catch these instances before they blow up and get people injured."

Jacobs nodded slowly. "So, to be clear, you need me to be able to pinpoint the situations where their testing will blow up in their faces in a spectacular manner?"

"Yep," Niki confirmed crisply.

"Well, I'll save you all considerable time and simply point out that any time they test the goop on live biological subjects is a time when it'll blow up in their faces. It's not a matter of if, it's when. You'll be able to note any changes that occur since they are fairly obvious. The goop has a unique interaction with DNA. It forges through it, picks out proteins, and transforms them by way of the enzymes—"

"Okay, a quick note before we go down that rabbit hole," Niki interrupted. "We'll probably not be able to follow roughly ninety percent of what you're saying."

"The cliff notes is that you'll see mutations—changes— once it interacts with the biomass that it's exposed to and transforms it. These aren't always obvious, but they will always be there. You merely need to pay attention."

"I have a feeling we'll be able to know it when we see it," Jansen added. "But we'd still appreciate your ongoing expertise in the matter, Dr. Jacobs."

The man shrugged. "I can't promise I'll always be here to help you guys since I do have a company of my own to run. But I'll be damned if I don't do all I can to stop these fuckers from spreading anywhere else in the world."

"Now, where have I heard that before?" Niki mumbled under her breath.

CHAPTER FOUR

Vickie had been right. There was considerable work to do.

The days they had spent away from it wouldn't alter the fact. Taylor realized he did have problems that involved not wanting to tackle a mountain of issues because it all looked insurmountable. The result was that he procrastinated far too much, which inevitably made the mountain simply grow bigger.

Thankfully, he had a team with him that was willing to put up with his idiosyncrasies and somehow got the job done. Vickie was already at her desk, tracking the new clients who were coming in as well as the invoices being sent to those they already had.

He really did want her on those since they would track Freddie's laundering of their illegal funds. From what she'd said, the money was already being paid but some automatic red flags had been raised that needed to be resolved. Based on her explanation, the money had already passed through the red flag restrictions as there was no way for the banks or the IRS to prove that it wasn't paying for services rendered.

And, of course, all of that was taxable income anyway.

She reminded him that she and her teammates were a little more motivated to get the money cleared since that was where their pay for the heist would come from. He'd promised them that they would receive their 'bonuses' before he did, although it wouldn't be based on the exact amount that had been stolen. Some would go to Freddie, even with his substantial discount, for his efforts to help them launder the cash.

Bobby and Tanya were involved in the more physical side of the work to be done. Cleaning the shop was more of a job than Taylor had realized, but they tackled it well and, sure enough, seeing other people putting the effort in was enough to get him involved as well.

The housekeeping and cleaning of the workspace were accomplished quickly when conducted by all three of them, and it wasn't long until they stepped back and declared it a job well done.

Tanya took Bobby's car to get more supplies, both for cleaning as well as restocking the break room, which left the job of now setting the shop up for the new arrivals to Taylor and Bobby.

The truck came at more or less the time it was scheduled for. Taylor generally liked it when their deliveries were on time but in this case, it was much more satisfying.

"I've had my fill of deliveries going wrong," he muttered as they helped the delivery men haul the crates off the truck and over to the harnesses. "Having one go right is so much better."

Bobby scowled at him. "You know there was only one delivery that went wrong, right? Only one, and we fixed it without too much muss and fuss."

"We had to fly all the way to fucking Africa to resolve it and even then, we had to pry our delivery from the cold dead fingers of the people who tried to rob us, all while getting a damn reporter out who had managed to stash herself in one of the suits. If that's not what you call too much muss or fuss, I don't know what to tell you."

The mechanic paused for a second and nodded. "Okay, point taken, but it was still only the one delivery that went wrong. You're acting like this is a common occurrence."

"One time is enough for me, thanks."

It was a fair point, and the mechanic had to concede it. The chances were that no one would be stupid enough to try to steal any more of their shipments now that they had routed them to a better-defended airfield. The price had gone up as well but given the kind of cash he'd had to drop to get them to Nigeria on the drop of a dime, the tradeoff would be in his favor.

Taylor had made the calculations and realized there was no point in raising prices, at least not until the end of the quarter. Once they had a good idea of what their profit margin would be, they could think about price adjustments.

The delivery men left as soon as they'd offloaded, and he began to pull the crate away from the suits they would work on.

The individual pieces themselves told a story that probably hadn't ended well for the person inside the suit. The damage appeared to have been mostly restricted to the external armor.

"Shit," he muttered and nudged the helmet gently. Claw marks had scarred most of the armor and a couple of scratches had sheared completely through. "What the hell do you figure did this?"

Bobby studied the damage without response, picked the hand up, and tested the hydraulics inside. The fluid had all leaked out or maybe been drained after they'd removed the man.

Whether or not he had been retrieved alive was a question no one wanted answered.

"It looks like a killerpillar," the mechanic noted finally and pointed out abrasions around the side. "I used to see this kind of damage to the external armor when those fuckers jumped and brushed over it with the carapaces. They have a kind of sandpaper quality that makes it wear the steel down even in a quick brushing motion."

"I don't see any of the puncture marks," Taylor added. "It doesn't look like it attacked this guy but tried to move somewhere else and he got a little close."

"Or gal," Vickie interjected. "I've seen that more and more female combatants go into the Zoo too."

He nodded in agreement. "Right, or gal. The point is… what did all this damage to the suit? Seriously, there aren't many creatures that would be capable of this."

"Maybe not intentionally." Bobby pulled a couple of sections of armor apart and removed what looked like chunks of wood that had been embedded inside. Those seemed to have penetrated a little deeper and massive splinters had been driven in through the sheer weight of whatever had fallen on the man.

"Yeah…" Taylor shook his head. "It looks like someone shot it out of the trees, it fell and brought pieces of wood with it, and landed directly on top of the sucker. But why he stood there and took it is the question. Did he not notice that something that big was wandering around on top of him or did he think his suit could take the punishment?"

Bobby shook his head. "It's more likely that the guy was pinned down already and couldn't move away. The team-mates who shot it out of the trees would have warned him about it. You still can't account for when these guys are idiots who don't know when to duck out of a fight and regroup."

He couldn't help but agree. With that said, though, it did look like the man inside had managed to survive the drop, although he wouldn't have been much good to his team for the rest of the trip into the Zoo. The hydraulic system displayed all kinds of damage, most of the weapons systems were down, and the guy had probably taken a beating himself. He'd needed to be dragged out.

It was a good sign, though. If his team had been in a tough, difficult fight, he wouldn't have been recovered. In a life-or-death situation, a team leader would make the decision to leave him there, hope the animals thought he was dead, and attempt to come back for him later or to collect the tags.

This appeared to be a single struggle with one creature, though, before they managed to get the wounded out.

Alive, hopefully. No matter what he happened to think

about someone's skills while in the Zoo, that wasn't the entirety of their life. If they weren't the best fighters in the world, they might end up being great in others' ways—great fathers, teachers, or intelligence operatives. There were a hundred different ways to judge them, and so it felt a little unfair to measure them solely by their ability to kill alien monsters.

Bobby nudged him in the shoulder. "Are you okay there?"

Taylor realized that his hands were shaking as he stared at the wood splinters in his hands. He put them on the table and tucked his hands quickly into his pockets. "Yeah, I'm fine."

Bobby picked the chunks up but still eyed him narrowly before he inspected them. "Well, on the bright side, we now have a couple of souvenirs from the piece of shit jungle across the world and we didn't even need to dive in there ourselves."

"Ooh, what will we do with them?" Vickie asked as she rolled her chair closer to them, pushed to her feet when she got as far as the chair would go, and hurried to where Bobby inspected the pieces. "I know, we can make little trees with them and use them as decoration—because Tay-Tay, you know I love you, but this place does need sprucing up. I'd say it needs a woman's touch, but I think we're beyond that point now. We need the Gordon Ramsey of decorators to come in and make it livable for human beings."

Bobby looked confused and Taylor leaned in a little closer. "He was a celebrity chef back in the day and became famous for yelling at people in a British accent.

And for being a great chef too, but that wasn't the main draw."

"It's always good TV to be yelled at by a Brit," the mechanic conceded.

"Agreed," Vickie added. "Oh, I know what we can do with them. We can make them into little chips—like casino chips but out of wood instead of plastic—and all five of us can wear them on chains around our necks."

"Four, you mean," Taylor corrected her.

She shifted her gaze away. "Sure. Anyway, we could wear them and they could be, like, the signature of our team. Everyone with McFadden's Mechs and McFadden's Mercs would be known for wearing a little wooden chip cut from a tree from the Zoo."

"Stick them in the incinerator," he muttered and folded his arms.

"What?" she protested. "No, we had the perfect little thing going. Did you not understand the concept? You know…the chips because we operate out of Vegas and the wood cut from the Zoo, because—come on, don't harsh my mellow!"

"Harsh your mellow?" Bobby interrupted. "Did you smoke something before you came into work today? Something one of your fellow college students gave you and you don't want us to know about?"

"No, I'm not high, Dad," Vickie replied in an exasperated tone. "It's only a goddamn saying. Chill the fuck out."

"It's biological material from the Zoo," Taylor reminded her, took the piece from her hand, and put it on the table. "As of right now, there's no way to know or tell what the hell something like that is capable of. For all we know, it could be able to turn other animals into monsters simply by touch. Hell, it could start affecting us if we keep them close for long enough."

Vickie rolled her eyes and sighed deeply but she did have to admit that he knew more about whatever they were dealing with than she did. She didn't have to like it but he obviously didn't intend to have Zoo shit permanently decorate either his team or his place of business.

"Do you think you could have been a little softer on her?" Bobby asked once she had returned to her computer. " I know you have all kinds of reasons to mistrust the shit that comes out of the Zoo, but…like, it was a good idea. Team building and that kind of thing is never a bad idea."

Taylor scratched his beard idly. "Yeah, I guess you're right. It wasn't my best moment, I'll admit. Do you think there's something I can do to make it up for her?"

"I'm fairly sure she'll forget all about it if her account gets all the zeroes on it first," the mechanic suggested.

"Are you sure about that? You have been with me the longest."

"Which means I'm more financially stable. Besides, you're keeping it in a trust or something for when she graduates college, right? So it gives her something to work toward."

He rolled his shoulders and took a deep breath. "Yeah, I guess. Maybe we could still do her little chip chain idea but not with something out of the Zoo."

"We could always say it's from the Zoo. How the hell would she know the difference?"

Taylor considered the idea for a moment but shook his head. "No, I don't think so. If there's something in the world I don't want to do, it's underestimate what that girl can find out about me when she puts her mind to it. The chances are, we wouldn't be able to keep the subterfuge up for long."

"But the chip idea?"

"Sure."

The shop doors began to open and the two men turned as Tanya returned with Bobby's truck.

"Do you think I should tell her to continue the cleaning while I get to work on the suits?" the mechanic asked.

Taylor laughed aloud. "Yeah, you should totally do that. Not because it'll end well for you, because it won't, but because it'll be hilarious to watch."

"Fuck you."

He grinned and flipped the man off. "Get those pieces of wood in the incinerator before you talk your girlfriend into cleaning what's already been cleaned."

Taylor ducked away before Bobby could smack him across the head. He was barely fast enough and the man's fingers brushed his hair. Still, he managed to beat a hasty retreat and moved to where Vickie worked on her computer.

"Hey," he said and placed a hand on her shoulder. "Are you okay?"

"Yeah," she replied quickly and turned to look at him. "What's in that big red head of yours?"

"I wanted to apologize. I may have shut your idea down a little too harshly. It wasn't a bad idea, mind you, and I was a little too curt in my response to you."

Vickie laughed and hugged him awkwardly while she

remained in her seat. "So you came all the way here to apologize?"

He thought about it and could not come up with any other reason. "Yep, that's it, I guess. It's only…if there was anyone who should learn not to fuck around with goop shit, it would be us, right? But we could probably get those chip necklaces, maybe as a bonus for the team at the end of the quarter."

"Oh, that's cool. I didn't even think you were being that bad."

"Really?"

"Well, it could have been the case a couple of minutes ago, but I had a call from one of our clients and I managed a huge upsell. I estimate my commission will be somewhere around two grand, so you could say I'm in a fairly good mood."

Taylor laughed. "Holy shit. What the hell did you sell them on?"

"I convinced them to send in two more of their reserve suits for the upgrades we're offering as well as a top-up, and I pushed the same on the other two they were already sending. All told and all calculated, I made two thousand big ones in the past two minutes. Call me…I don't know, Jeff Bezos or something."

"Well, I could not be prouder of you." He chuckled and patted her gently on the shoulder.

"Oh, speaking of…well, not pride, necessarily, but while you're here, there was something I wanted to talk to you about."

"Is it urgent?"

"Not really, but time is more or less of the essence."

"Can it wait, though? I have to go out and pick up the new parts we need for these suits. I'll be an hour, maybe an hour and a half, tops."

Vickie sighed in an overly dramatic fashion and rolled eyes. "Fine. But you now owe me. Remember that."

"Will do," he muttered, stepped away from the desk, and retrieved his keys from his pocket. The four-by-four would be easier to maneuver through Vegas at this time of day but it wouldn't be able to move the parts he needed without some kind of trailer, which fucked the maneuverability anyway.

He needed to use Liz and then, hopefully, hear what Vickie had to tell him.

CHAPTER FIVE

N iki scowled at the clothes she wore. While her time in the FBI inured her to the concept of the inevitable pantsuits, she'd already adjusted to wearing a coat over a polo or dress shirt and jeans, which were equally as effective and far more comfortable.

The more informal attire had become the norm in her life. Having to go back into the stuffy, official look already grated on her nerves.

"Why the hell do all these labs have to be out in the middle of goddamn nowhere?" she asked the two men in the car with her. Both were seated in the front of the SUV and looked the part of the muscle that would accompany a ranking inspector of the DOD.

She wasn't sure how a ranking inspector of the DOD was supposed to act but had a feeling it could be more or less explained as acting like a bitch and assuming the people around her would be too intimidated to object.

That was something she could do.

Jansen looked at her through the rearview mirror as he answered her question. "Mostly because the more recent health and safety requirements for facilities like this recommend that they be as far away from major population centers as possible. The logic is that if something goes wrong, it happens way the fuck out here and not where it can kill thousands or millions.

"That said, there are labs in built-up areas—most of them established early on—but I'm inclined to think it has a fair amount to do with accessibility. If any of them have anything to hide, it's easier to do so off the beaten track, as it were. I'm sure the comfort and convenience of the people coming to visit and work here were considered but disregarded considering the larger threat—whichever one you buy into."

Niki could tell the man was being sarcastic with her, but his delivery was in a complete deadpan and she couldn't help herself when she looked out the window and cracked a smile.

"Well, they could have found a way to make it all work," Niki continued and tried to keep a straight face when she turned to focus on him. "I'm sure they could find a way to make it safe for the larger populations and still keep it within a convenient distance. Maybe burying the labs hundreds of feet under the ground can serve both purposes. It makes it more isolated and easier to defend, and the chances of anyone stumbling on what you're trying to hide are minimal. There's only one way in and one way out."

"There are problems with that, of course," Jansen countered, his expression completely neutral as he held her gaze. "For one thing, it means you need to transport dangerous materials close to larger population centers. There's also the situation of there being a fire or some kind of gas leak and having only one way out, which would give every firefighter in the country an aneurysm. Oh, and the fact that there are still possibilities for containment breaches. If there's anything we've learned while working with you, it's that these monsters will find a way out no matter what kind of security you have in place."

"It seems like the best way to work it is to simply not bring the goop into the country in the first place," Maxwell added, his gaze fixed on the road as he was the designated driver.

"Well, yeah, there is that," Niki admitted. "But the US government won't be willing to risk letting the Chinese or the Russians get a leg up and somehow stumble their way into some kind of biological weapon. Not because we're actually at war with them but because...well, they have big egos in Washington."

It was one of the more annoying realities they faced and one she didn't want to think about. It was only a matter of time before people decided to start using this as a weapon instead of a youth juice. Someone would choose to bomb their enemies with the goop and let the inevitable monster infestation overwhelm their enemy's defenses. It seemed especially possible if they operated out of somewhere in Southeast Asia, South or Central America, or anywhere that had enough biomass to fuel the infestation and spread it quickly.

With only a single event like that, the Zoo would be worldwide and would spread faster than it could be contained from dozens of infestations across the planet.

She shook the feeling of impending doom away and settled into her seat again as the lab came into her view. The facility didn't look any different than those she'd visited in the past. It was like they were all constructed in a similar block-like architecture with an external wall for security and to keep anyone from seeing what was happening inside.

The structure did have a couple of windows, even though they were essentially one-way mirrors to ensure that people could see out but not in.

The SUV pulled up to the heavy steel gate, and from the calm look of her team, it was safe to assume that something was happening inside that they needed to wait for. She assumed someone who had access to the cameras was checking their plates to make sure they were allowed entry.

Maxwell used the almost two full minutes to check his phone, while Jansen rubbed his temples like he was nursing a headache.

Niki could feel something like a headache begin to plague her as the seconds ticked past until finally, a smaller door opened in the middle of the massive gate and one of the security guards stepped out. He wore a full uniform, complete with a bulletproof vest, a cap with the company logo, a pistol holstered on his belt, and a selection of other weapons close at hand. She identified pepper spray, a stun gun, and a baton as his non-lethal options, as well as a pair of handcuffs in case it became necessary to take someone into custody.

"It looks like these guys don't fuck around," she commented as the guard moved closer and tapped lightly on the driver's window. Maxwell rolled the glass down and pulled up his DOD credentials.

Jansen had his out too, and Niki retrieved hers from her coat.

The security guard didn't bother to look into the back seat and waved them toward the gate that had already begun to swing open slowly for them to drive inside.

Apparently, they were expected. A small team had already been assembled outside the building. That was what the delay was, she realized and focused on a tall, portly man who stood at the front. It was always difficult to fit a suit around a man that large, even for a talented tailor, but whoever had made it had done a decent job of it. She waited until the car had stopped completely before she slid out and stepped forward like she had done this every day of her life.

Jansen and Maxwell fell into formation behind her. Niki directed her attention toward the door of the lab and moved forward but the large man stepped in front of her, along with a small group in lab coats. There appeared to be a couple of lawyers present as well, although they remained well back like they had only been called in because they were required to be there.

"Hi. You must be Niki Banks from the DOD." The man's voice was thick and carried a resonance like he was an opera singer or had been a singer at some point. "I'm Jeffrey Gottfried, CEO of G & G and owner of this facility.

I was informed that you were coming in for a follow-up inspection and I wanted to make sure you were well-received."

Niki forced a polite smile as she shook the man's hand. "Yes, I'm Niki Banks, and I wasn't aware there would be a greeting party. I honestly would have preferred there to not have been any warning. People who prepare for their inspections tend to cover up what they don't want people like me to find. Not that I'm saying you are hiding anything, of course. It's merely the general feeling I get when people greet me like this."

Jeffrey laughed loudly, a bellow from his stomach. "Your honesty is refreshing, I have to say. A guy like me is always surrounded by annoying yes-men, which can be bad for your ego if it has a problem inflating and staying inflated."

She focused on him and tried not to look as annoyed as she felt. "Well, that's...great for you, I guess. I still need to inspect your building, however, and I'm still annoyed by the fact that I need to play politician about it. So why don't we simply get this over with? Who's your entourage?"

"These two are my attorneys, Jameson and Yuri, my representatives in this," Jeffrey explained and indicated the two men in expensive suits. "This is Dr. Richard Terrance—he's the research director and runs this entire installation—and this is Dr. Jeremy Greer, who is his second in command."

"I think the proper terminology is project manager," Terrance interrupted quickly, stepped forward, and extended his hand to her. "I was sad to hear your team needed to vacate before they were able to complete their inspection. I do hope you'll be able to do a more thorough job this time around. We can't afford to have our projects interrupted on a whim."

"This whim you mention..." she muttered and sensed the doctor's clear hostility. "It wouldn't have anything to do with the fact that your projects are funded by taxpayer money, would it? We wouldn't want US citizens to fund something that could end up being a waste of time—or, heaven forbid, cause damage to their quality of life—would we, Dr. Terrance?"

"Of course not—"

"And the citizens of the United States would not want their money to be squandered on dangerous projects involving imported goods that have been used and tested without proper consideration for the dangers and consequences involved."

She could almost see the moment when his blood began to run cold. His gaze twitched toward the building. To her, that alone was enough evidence to have the entire facility locked down and inspected since she was certain they would find monsters in the lower, hidden levels of the lab.

There were lawyers present, however, and she needed to at least make a show of finding the truth instead of making assumptions.

Terrance gathered his composure once more. "We understand the risks and have more than prepared for them, which is why the DOD deemed us the right installation to hand these projects to. I think you'll find we have nothing to hide here."

Niki nodded and gestured for Jansen and Maxwell to join her as she strode toward the main entrance.

Gottfried's entourage rushed to keep pace. "You know, I would be inclined to believe you if the last couple of installations we visited didn't try to peddle the same kind of bullshit. So if you don't mind, why don't we go ahead and step inside and get this over with?"

She could tell that the man wasn't used to being spoken to like that and he looked on the verge of losing his temper. Not that she expected anything different. PhDs were already in a position to be more arrogant than they needed to be, and when you put them in a position of power, that kind of thing went to their heads more often than not. She had seen it happen dozens of times with people from all walks of life. Some deserved to be in the positions they occupied and others didn't.

In the end, if there was nothing to check them, they would simply continue the push to become the biggest asshole they could be.

The doors were pulled open and she shook her head as she touched her pocket lightly, where her phone vibrated. Jennie had told her to expect that since it was how the software she had installed in the phone alerted her to confirm that the process of mining the local servers for data had started.

The rest of the group followed close behind as Niki headed toward the server rooms themselves. She tried to keep herself moving and so avoid distractions from the group.

Gottfried wasn't the kind of man who liked being held on the edge for too long, and he was already rushing in to take control of the situation.

"We should probably go to my office," he suggested and

seemed a little out of breath even from the slight increase in pace required to catch up with her. "We can discuss what your people were concerned about and hopefully settle this speedily."

Niki turned to Jansen and Maxwell. Neither evidenced much of a reaction but they carried the tablets that would be used for the data transfer. She didn't understand the full concept of what Jennie had offered to help them with from afar, but maybe that was for the best. For now, at least.

She grasped her phone a little tighter and forced a smile. "That sounds fine. I'd like to run over their findings with you to make sure the items that raised the red flags and involved me aren't something to be worried about."

"Of course. There's nothing we would love more than to make sure that the DOD is happy with our work here."

Niki indicated for her team to join her. They took the elevator and once on the correct level, walked into one of the larger offices. It occupied almost half the floor and comprised a number of sections that seemed to suggest the man had little intention of doing much work while he was in the office. One of these was a bathroom with a shower and another room where he could spend the night was larger than many New York apartments.

A large window looked over the landscape, perfectly placed to be visible from a massive desk of marble and wood. The piece of furniture was clearly created to fit the theme of another room and was conspicuously out of place in this particular office.

Her scowl deepened at the pretentiousness of it all and she shook her head slowly. It all seemed designed to ensure that anyone who stepped inside knew that the person who owned the office was rich and powerful in the company and didn't care how the message came across. It was obvious that Gottfried didn't spend much time on location.

Why would he? The man likely had an office somewhere and didn't need to deal with this kind of commute.

Dr. Terrance joined them and immediately moved to a large screen that filled almost an entire wall of the office. "Why don't we go over the sections your team looked at before they needed to leave. Perhaps that would—"

"Actually, I think I can handle that," Niki interrupted as her phone vibrated again. She turned to Jansen, who nodded, took a tablet from his briefcase, and handed it to her.

None of those present in the room knew what she intended until she unlocked the device and pulled what had been uploaded onto the huge screen. It displayed the entirety of the research that had been conducted in the facility, including the sections that were supposed to be walled off and isolated.

"I'm sure none of you need me or my team to explain and that you'll know exactly what we are talking about," Niki stated while she pulled the files up on the screen. "In the interests of avoiding confusion, though, I'll clarify. The idea is that people connect to the Wi-Fi in the building and they pull the files up on their computers, laptops, and shit like that. Of course, that wouldn't show on the files that were shared on the servers, but with the network of what's shared and then deleted, we were able to put together considerable interesting information. For instance, Dr. Terrance, would you care to explain what Project G-6662 entails?"

The surprise on the doctor's face was clear and very palpable, which left her little to think about other than his possible guilt. She doubted that he would do anything to stop them, but she could almost see the gears turning in the man's head about how he could explain this in front of a board of directors.

"I don't personally know much about the possibilities of gene splicing, but I do have people I know who could probably give us a decent idea of what we're dealing with here," she added coldly.

"Of course," Terrance responded quickly, "we would be willing to share anything you find with specialists of your choosing at a time of your choosing."

"Well, it's funny you should mention that because the time I choose is now."

He looked confused for a few seconds as she turned to Jansen, who nodded and retrieved his tablet.

"I don't understand," the scientist muttered.

"You will in a second," Niki stated and tried not to seem like she was gloating. "I don't know if you've ever heard of a certain Dr. Salinger Jacobs. Honestly, I didn't know much about him until I started working with people from the Zoo, and they tell me he is the leading expert in the field of crypto-biology. Yes, I didn't think that was a word either, but you know how it goes. You never stop learning in life."

Terrance narrowed his eyes. "Do you—Salinger Jacobs? Where have I heard that name before?"

"Well, if you're interested in the field of biology and what has been happening in Northern Africa over the past few years, you might have heard of him. Jansen, do we have a connection yet?"

The man nodded and pulled the call up to the screen as well to reveal the young man she had met before. He had managed to change since their last communication, although it was only a dress shirt. She didn't know what he would look like in a coat or even a full suit. From what she'd heard, he was difficult to predict at the best of times. Of course, he had gone through the process of getting his doctorate, which might or might not have required him to dress up. She honestly didn't have a clue.

She wasn't sure what it fully entailed, but she had a vague recollection that Jennie had to face an entire lecture theatre full of older men who questioned her unmercifully regarding her dissertation and seemed determined to find fault. That was what had stuck in her head, and whether her sister had dressed up or not didn't seem all that important.

Jacobs did look a little more comfortable than she thought he would. The kid was cool under pressure, she had to give him that.

"Dr. Jacobs, thank you for joining us," Niki said.

"What the hell is going on here?" Jeffrey asked and glared at his team. They seemed equally as lost as he was.

Terrance, on the other hand, appeared panicked, and he sweated profusely. Almost without thought, he dabbed his forehead quickly with a small handkerchief.

"Hi. I've been asked to consult for the DOD on this matter," Jacobs stated and waved awkwardly at all the people present in the office. "I was told there would be no issues with my looking at your projects to make sure no laws were being broken."

Niki glanced at the CEO. "That won't be a problem, will it?"

The man appeared to be caught between a rock and a hard place. He didn't want to piss the DOD off but he did have reservations about a random person looking over his company's proprietary research.

Jacobs didn't intend to wait around for their permission and he had already begun to study the projects that had been shared with him. Something sank in Niki's stomach when he reached the G-6662 project she had mentioned a little earlier. It was the one the other team had tried to look into before they had been stonewalled.

"Are you shitting me?" he asked and peered more intently at his laptop. "Are you...goddammit—who approved this project?"

She checked and gestured to Dr. Terrance. "That would be this gentleman here. I don't see any other signatures on this, although I can't say if it means there was no one else involved or if no one else wanted their names on it."

"I don't remember a project like that crossing my desk," Jeffrey muttered and drew closer. Niki knew the man was likely to lie in this kind of situation, but he did look like he was seeing it for the first time.

"You...motherfucking cocksucker!" Jacobs snarled with sudden outrage through the video chat, clearly speaking to Terrance. "What the hell did you think you were doing? Have you even looked at the research that has come out of the Zoo? Or did you assume your purely theoretical knowledge gives you the insight and the right to screw with other people's lives?"

"I don't need to listen to this—" the man announced and tried to sound offended.

"Yes, you do, you useless, arrogant, self-serving prick." Jacobs cut him off quickly. "What did you think? That you could splice animal genes to create super-intelligent mutants and there wouldn't be consequences? That you could take what the Zoo has already all but perfected and hone them into killing machines capable of anticipating and countering every defense known to man far better than they already do?"

Niki's heart dropped into her stomach, and she could see the shock in Jeffrey's face as well as all those present and turned to Terrance. He tried to pretend that he was shocked as well, but it was clear that while he was not the head of the company, he had more than enough time and opportunity to report what was happening to his superiors and had neglected to do so.

"Wait," Jeffrey interjected as Jacobs paused in his tirade to take a deep breath. "Are you the Dr. Salinger Jacobs? *Alien Beasts: An Introduction to Crypto-Biology?* That Salinger Jacobs?"

The young man nodded slowly. "I'm...surprised you've heard of me."

"I didn't think that you would be so...young. Interesting. Are you currently—"

"I'm running my own company at the moment," he snapped before the man could continue. "I'm not looking for any other job prospects at the moment unless you're interested in Heavy Metal doing consulting for you."

"We might at that. I'll be in touch."

"Can we get back on topic, please?" Niki snapped but

made an effort to not sound too hostile. "The gene-splicing that occurred in the project—is that something to be worried about?"

"Well, yes, unless you're the kind of person who thought the Spanish Flu was a common cold. In fact, the Spanish Flu is something of a misnomer that was created by wartime propaganda during the first World War, but... that's not important right now." Niki realized it was common for him to go off on tangents as his mind had a tendency to move quickly and his mouth simply followed where it led. "What is important is that you, Dr. Terrance, are a fucking asshole. The kind that's...you know, gaping—"

"Gaping, prolapsed anus is my preferred description," Niki suggested.

"Yes. That. You know, I think I'll steal that from you."

"Be my guest."

"The purpose of our research—if you took the time to examine it in more detail—has been to eliminate the aggression in the animals, which we have largely achieved by increasing their intelligence." Terrance made a stiff effort to take control of the situation. "I'm sure your input will be taken into account but the documented results speak for themselves. Your insults and personal attack are not necessary, Mr. Jacobs."

"It's Dr. Jacobs, and when you come to the Zoo and study the creatures you're trying to create in a lab, we can discuss the questionable accuracy of your results. Aggression against mankind is the fundamental nature of these beasts. No amount of clever scientific tweaking will ever eliminate that because the Zoo doesn't follow natural laws.

All you've done is create a super-breed that has the intelligence and instinct to let you think you've won. Right now, they're simply waiting for the right moment, and you're too focused on your personal agenda and illusions of grandeur to see it. Honestly, there are no words to describe the magnitude of your error, you...you..."

"Gaping, prolapsed anus," Niki supplied.

"It'll do, but I wanted to think of something on my own that defined something that truly deserves to be shat out of a fucking killerpillar."

"Be sure to send your bill for your efforts, Dr. Jacobs," Jeffrey stated quickly in an effort to move the topic away from the discussion of the best insults to use.

Jacobs nodded. "Anytime. I need to get back to work. Nice to hear from you again, Agent Banks."

The line disconnected and Niki turned to see that Terrance had inched slowly toward the door. Too late, she realized that in all the excitement, neither of her two bodyguards had remained at the exit—something they'd need to discuss when this was over. It was a rookie mistake, and she kicked herself for not noticing.

When he realized she was watching him, he turned fully and his body language suggested that he intended to sprint toward the door.

She wasn't sure what he thought he would accomplish. If he managed to escape the room, all they had to do was lock the building down and drag him back.

Unless he had a bolt hole no one was aware of. Indignation surged, perhaps triggered by Jacobs' virulent response, and it fed a rapid marquee of those lost to these infestations through her mind. When it culminated in an image of an all but dead Taylor in the hospital, she'd had about enough of this asshat as she could take.

In that room, about to attempt to flee, was someone responsible—a visible enemy she could pin her rage onto. She drew her sidearm before she had time to think about it. Her thumb touched the safety off as he took a small step toward his intended freedom. The desire to simply blow his head off clamored but she forced herself to aim low and squeezed the trigger.

The whole room resonated and left her ears ringing as the weapon kicked into her hand. Her aim was decent enough and the bullet punched into the man's pants and out the other side. It caught him low in the calf but he screamed in pain, crumpled, and clutched his leg.

"Fuck!" he roared in agony. "You fucking bitch!"

She pushed aside a brief surge of guilt and focused on the mission. The DOD had hired a bitch, and that was exactly what they'd get. The fact that it fed into a growing need for retribution was a temporary advantage. She'd deal with the conflict and questions in her head later.

"The only reason the janitor staff will clean up a little blood from a through-and-through flesh wound and not blood, brains, and itty-bitty pieces of skull is because we still need answers from you." She made sure to keep her voice calm as she thumbed the safety on and slid the sidearm carefully into her holster. "Now, get him the hell up. We have an inspection to continue."

Maxwell and Jansen exchanged a hasty glance before the former moved to where Terrance still squirmed on the floor. Niki locked gazes with Jeffrey, and the man uttered a soft chuckle that suggested shock.

"Like a breath of fresh fucking air," he muttered as they all headed out of the office. She chose to not give him the opportunity for that to blossom into outrage and noticed that the attorneys hung back, obviously wishing they were elsewhere. They might make trouble, but she'd deal with it if and when it happened. For now, everyone was cowed enough to hopefully put up little resistance.

CHAPTER SIX

Niki could hear the man struggling to catch up to her. In fact, it was almost like she could feel it, as every step the large CEO took made the floor shiver.

He must have been a wrestler or maybe a football player in college. People didn't get large in the way he did by overeating and not exercising. She imagined that despite Jeffrey's severe lack of shape, he was stronger than she was, at least in terms of sheer power.

"Agent Banks," the man rumbled once he was close enough for him to speak to her without everyone else in their party listening, "I'm as much for putting the arrogant intellectuals in their place as the next guy, but don't you think that was a little too much?"

She shook her head firmly once they reached the elevators. "Maybe shooting him was a little over the top, but I don't have either the time or the patience for the inevitable song and dance with your building's security if he managed to escape the room. Not that it was the most logical response —more like his fight or flight instinct realized it had no fight in it. But I also don't know which of your security staff, if any, he has in his pocket."

Her expression grim, she stared boldly at him and dared him to deny the possibility. "Either way, it's now irrelevant. He will have a field dressing put on the flesh wound and while he'll be in pain, I think he's earned that. I might not know much about biology, but it makes sense that there's no real medical or scientific use for gene splicing animals in the way it's detailed in the report. To my mind, the only logical outcome is to create some kind of animal weapon."

"Who would be interested in something like that?" Jansen asked as they stepped into the elevator and ignored Terrance's groans of pain. Maxwell took the opportunity to bind his leg to stop the bleeding.

"I think there are still laws in place to prohibit bio-engineering animals as weapons, right?" Niki countered. "So it would be someone or an organization that deliberately flouts the laws against biological warfare?"

"Not really," Jansen replied and shook his head. "The existing laws are against germ warfare and that kind of thing. Those currently in place prohibit the use of Zoo goop in genetic splicing since the dangers aren't known."

"Still, I imagine there's a market for that in countries like North Korea and maybe China," Niki suggested. "They wouldn't care about the consequences as much as they would the results. At least, that's the assumption these days. Mr. Gottfried, if you weren't involved in this at all you should think about investigating Dr. Terrance's personal communications to make sure he didn't plan to sell his research to foreign entities."

"I will do that," the CEO muttered once they began the descent to the lower levels. The elevator stopped when their movements were challenged by the security system, and the man had his retina and thumbprint scanned. He turned his attention to her once the elevator moved again. Niki noted the numbers that scrolled to show how many sub-levels there were in the facility. "It should be noted that I would have very little to gain and everything to lose if I were to find myself involved in any of this."

"Well, there would be a hefty financial return in it if you find the right kind of buyer," she pointed out.

"They wouldn't want to buy it the way the US military would be forced to," Gottfried countered smoothly. "They would pay a couple of million to get their hands on the technology and reverse-engineer it so they could do it themselves. On the other hand, G & G is worth over three hundred and seventy billion dollars according to our last assessment. If I were found to be selling technology to a foreign entity, we would lose all our defense contracts, and stocks would instantly take a massive nosedive. I would lose my position in the company and so would most of the board of directors, and that's before all the legal issues that would arise. Believe me when I say it would not be worth our time to attempt this at a corporate level."

"You sound like you've given this considerable thought," Niki said after a moment of silence.

"Market research is a funny beast. They dig up all kinds of things you didn't know you wanted to find out about. There's nothing in the business that keeps us from researching certain things."

She shrugged. The guy had a point. She could be as

suspicious as she wanted, but until she could prove he was involved, everything he knew about it was pure speculation.

None of the lawyers had made a fuss, she realized with a flash of insight. They weren't there to defend Dr. Terrance or even the lab. They were present only to make sure Gottfried wasn't held liable for any of what might be found inside, which was enough to tell her the man at least knew something hinky was happening. While he might not be an active and willing participant, he knew enough to think he would need legal representation.

The elevator dinged to tell them they had arrived at the lowest levels. They were almost a hundred meters below ground and the only way in and out of it was the elevator they had used. A stairwell nearby would remain locked until the alarms in the building activated for a fire or some other kind of emergency.

Niki looked around the labs and noted how few people were present. Less than a dozen worked an entire floor and they appeared as paranoid as Terrance had been. All stopped their tasks when the group stepped out of the elevator. They had probably been assured that their efforts in this section of the facility would not be general knowledge.

She could feel something watching her almost immediately when they approached the testing sections of the area. Her instincts told her it went beyond the human eyes that monitored her to something considerably more terrifying. Monsters were housed there and they knew she had arrived. Maybe they already knew there was the blood of their fellow creatures on her hands.

They couldn't know she had killed other cryptids, she reminded herself sharply, but the way their focus seemed to have settled on her made the far-fetched notion seem too real to be comfortable.

"They're always kept under armed guard," Terrance explained, the words strained as if delivered through clenched teeth. "No testing is performed on them while they are alive, of course. They are only studied while alive. Their genetics are tinkered with before and biopsies are conducted post-mortem. While alive, cameras watch them twenty-four hours a day with kill switches on all enclosures. They're kept behind three-inch-thick titanium-reinforced glass, double-paned and completely sealed so that if the kill switches don't work, we can suck the oxygen out of their cells in seconds. Effectively, we can kill them if they try to attack the glass even once. Our purpose is an attempt to breed the aggression out of them and so far, it's working."

Niki narrowed her eyes. "What do you mean? That they haven't tried to attack the glass at all? Any monsters I've seen have no sense of self-preservation at all. They throw themselves at bullets like they hope to absorb as many as possible so those coming in behind have the opportunity to kill whoever is shooting them. Those I've seen personally would fling themselves at the glass until they die or it breaks."

"Well, after a couple of attempts ended in failure, they haven't tried since. Our geneticists discovered a few possible predispositions toward aggressiveness that have since vanished along with the attempts to escape. The increased intelligence has offset the primitive urge to attack, although we obviously take every precaution until this has been empirically proven through a series of studies."

It was far more likely that the creatures had realized that they died if they tried to escape. Jacobs had warned of the dangers of increased intelligence and damned if he wasn't right. Something about the way the mutants watched her and the group indicated a sly and canny mental capability she wouldn't have believed possible if she hadn't seen it with her own eyes.

She didn't move closer to any of the containment cells and maintained her distance while a couple of the monsters watched her intently.

"Are you sure they aren't simply biding their time?" Niki asked and registered that she felt a little breathless. "They've realized that escape through sheer force won't end well for them and they're trying to find a new way. Have you studied the genetic changes and tracked them after death? The goop has been known to alter a creature's genetic makeup even during its life."

That was a line that she remembered Taylor using, and Terrance nodded slowly.

"Of course, but there have been no signs of alterations that we need to worry about," he replied and shifted to keep his balance but also rest his wounded leg. "Security was always at the forefront of our minds and in doing these studies, our understanding of the goop's effect on the genetic structure of the DNA it encounters has increased by leaps and bounds. This new knowledge has already helped the people on the front lines and given them a fighting chance against the monsters they face. You have to understand that I wasn't doing any of this for the money. No one approached me and offered me anything. I'm doing this to save lives."

"And I'm sure you never let anything as cold as cash influence your decisions, right?" she mumbled and shook her head. "You stepped over the line into matters you don't understand because you simply want to save lives, right?"

He knew what she meant and could sense the sarcasm in her voice. "As much as you might hate me, don't think my intentions were anything other than saving lives, Agent. You do it on the front lines and may despise people like me, but don't forget that it's the work of people like me that provides you with the weapons to stay alive and well and with whatever edges we can give you."

She stared silently at him for a moment rather than respond. There were ways to get what was needed without having to step into research that was taboo for a reason. Besides, he hadn't taken the risks into consideration. While he'd put everything in place to make sure regular animals wouldn't be able to escape, they weren't dealing with regular animals. Or, she thought acidly, even with regular Zoo animals. If Jacobs was right, these were super-Zoo and no one had a clue what they were capable of.

When she turned, she moved her hand instinctively to the weapon at her hip. One of the creatures watched her intently. It resembled a panther and its thick, muscular body seemed to roll under the lights. Its tail flicked with a little too much agility, and the dexterity of it seemed to suggest that it might be prehensile. The creature's black eyes stared at her, its whole body impossibly still.

It wasn't, she registered, even breathing.

With her hand still on her weapon, she returned the focus and held her breath as well as she waited for something to happen. She did not intend to be caught unprepared if...well, she wasn't sure what might happen, only that something could.

Its ears flicked and she realized they were much longer than they'd first appeared and stretched almost to its shoulders.

In the next moment, it moved impossibly quickly, darted forward, and stopped just shy of the glass before it retreated again. It reached the back of its cell and surged forward again. This time, it showed no signs of stopping.

Niki drew her weapon almost before she knew what would happen and the creature impacted with the glass. The structure showed no sign of damage. In fact, the collision barely made a sound but a splash of red blood was visible across the surface as the creature dropped back, apparently dazed.

Alarms blared and vents on the far side of the enclosure opened. Fan blades whirred to draw the air out of the room. The monster shuddered and its jaws opened like it was trying to breathe and sucked in air that had no oxygen. It trembled and sagged slowly onto the floor of its enclosure. Blood dripped from its head as its eyes closed.

She dragged in a breath and realized that her weapon was still in her hand as if her instincts compelled her to wait for something to happen. Something else, she clarified mentally. It seemed impossible that a creature like this would see her, charge, and die so easily. Given even her limited experience with Zoo creatures, it simply didn't make sense and seemed to contradict everything she knew or had come to expect.

Then again, maybe seeing someone or something new in the area was enough to prompt it to try to react, hoping for a way out. How the hell would she know what was logical or not? She simply wasn't qualified to provide a definitive answer.

"Like I said," the doctor stated, his stare a little challenging when she still refused to holster her weapon, "security here is as tight as anywhere in the world, and you should have no concerns. Believe me, we've considered far, far worse than anything you can imagine and have already planned and prepared for it."

"People keep asking me to believe them," Niki replied acidly. "It makes me wonder if they're trying to convince me or themselves."

"Specimen fifty-seven," a voice said through the speakers. "Pulse is gone. Asphyxiation. Should we remove the specimen to the autopsy chamber?"

"Yes," Terrance responded and a couple of guards stepped out of a chamber on the far side of the hallway and strode to the dead creature's cell.

One or more men remained in the guardhouse, and the locks were slowly disengaged from the enclosure. It took thirty seconds before they were able to pry the door open and step inside. Niki noted one of them checking something that had been stabbed into the back of the creature's neck. It was likely a monitoring device as well as the kill switch that had been mentioned, just in case.

She scowled and maintained her distance as they began to drag the body out.

"Make sure to collect the blood from inside as well," the doctor instructed once the two security guards finished their inspection of the cell. A group of three researchers wearing crisp white lab coats stepped in with a burnished steel trolly to ferry the body to one of the other rooms.

The mutant was dead and evidenced not even a sign of a twitch when it was lifted with a fair amount of effort by the five who gathered around it. Niki hadn't realized how massive the creature was until she saw all of them struggle to lift what was much larger than a panther or even a lion. It was maybe smaller than a very large tiger.

"Why would they stop trying to break through the glass after a couple of times and now, they try again for the first time in...I'll say months?" Jansen asked no one in particular.

"Maybe the change in personnel was enough to set them off," she suggested. She pulled away to let the people work unimpeded but still grasped her weapon and watched closely. Even hearing herself say it didn't make sense. She had to get to the bottom of this because every voice of caution within her was rampant.

She was about to turn to discuss it with the people around her when a flicker of movement caught her eye. At first, she thought she'd imagined it, but a second quiver made her turn fully to focus on the mutant. The ears definitely moved and not only because the creature was pushed around.

It could have simply been an involuntary response. The monster had died suddenly and reflexes embedded in its nervous system might explain it.

The eyes opened and locked onto her almost immediately.

"Shit!" Niki yelled and raised her weapon. "Get away from the trolley! Now!"

Her warning was met with confused skepticism at first, although she was a little gratified to see out of the corners of her eyes that Maxwell and Jansen both reacted immediately and drew their weapons. The guards and the researchers gaped at her in bewilderment and shook their heads rather than paying attention to the creature.

That changed almost instantly when it uttered a low, guttural roar and flashed its claws at the five who stood around the trolley. She could see the sheer power in the creature as it hooked its claws into the people around it and dragged them aside. The motion made the trolley spin on its wheels and the beast bounded to its feet, off the surface, and into the room.

The powerful jaws turned to attack the five, who still sprawled stunned and confused. She couldn't wait for anyone else to be slaughtered and had to act immediately.

Niki stepped forward and assumed the familiar stance she'd spent so many hours practicing at the Quantico academy. She grasped her weapon with both hands and bent her knees lightly before she squeezed the trigger while she focused down the sights.

The bullet impacted and forced the creature back, but it was far from dead. It bared its teeth at her and responded with another powerful roar. Thankfully, the distraction was enough to enable the workers to scuttle away from it and she felt comfortable with resuming fire without the fear of wounding them.

The mutant spun and prowled as it tried to find a way to attack her in the tight confines of the lab.

Maxwell and Jansen fired a barrage as well. She followed their lead and delivered a concerted volley at the creature. They had been trained to aim for center mass, but that didn't appear to do enough damage. She wasn't sure how many rounds she had left in her magazine and hadn't counted her shots, which meant that if she suddenly needed to reload, the monster would have the time it needed to attack her.

Without a moment's hesitation, she altered her aim to target its head as it launched itself across the narrow distance between them. She pulled the trigger.

The first shot went a little wide and caught an ear, but the second and third struck the forehead, where blood still seeped from when it had charged the glass only minutes earlier.

She wasn't sure whether it was the first or second round that felled it, but it collapsed with enough force to slide a few more feet along the slick surface. After a moment, she realized she was still pulling the trigger despite the soft clicks that told her it was empty.

Niki fumbled in her coat pocket for a replacement magazine. She released the empty one and tried to push another one in but it took three attempts before it finally clicked in the way it was meant to.

"Fucking...goddammit," she whispered, stepped over the creature, and pulled the trigger three times. The whole body jolted each time she did so and brought a measure of grim satisfaction. They could never be too careful, especially not in these situations.

"Are you all right?" Jansen asked as he stepped beside her.

"Yeah." She nodded slowly. "We'll...we'll need help on this. I'm fairly sure there's a military base not too far from here. Could you go to the ground level and let them know we could use assistance down here?"

"Will do, boss."

Maxwell stood beside her and she didn't mind much. The monster had played dead before and—in her mind, at least—there wasn't much to prevent it from trying again.

"Is everyone okay?" Niki called to the guards and researchers. Blood stained the white lab coats, but nothing seemed serious. They were already applying first aid and indicated that they were fine for the moment. It took a while for her to wrap her head around that as she'd fully expected them to be slaughtered, given the easy prey they presented. Then again, the mutant had seemed fixated on her from the beginning. Perhaps it had identified her as the primary threat that should be eliminated first. With her out of the equation, the others would offer no resistance.

Satisfied that there were no mortal injuries, she turned her attention to where Jeffrey, Terrance, and the rest of their group cowered in fear.

"You'll need to bring medics down here," Niki asserted and gestured toward those who had tried to move the dead monster. "You should probably think about running tests for any kind of venom that big baddie over there might have carried in its claws, just in case. You never know what surprises you might have in store when you mess around with these monsters."

All Jeffrey could do was nod, although he was slowly regaining his composure.

"As for the other people here... Well, I'm calling in the cavalry, so you have two options at the moment. You call security and incinerate everything on these lower floors that might have had contact with the goop."

The CEO paused and waited for her to continue. "What...what's the second option?" he ventured after a moment.

"I take control of this facility and assume your position in the company pending a full investigation into your practices, everything is incinerated anyway, and you find yourself penniless when we take Gottfried and Gottfried public. Do you have any questions?"

"Yes," he muttered and straightened his tie. "What do you think we should do about Dr. Terrance?"

Niki looked at the doctor who still nursed the wound in his leg and tried to ignore the conversation. "I honestly don't give a continental, but if you're looking for a scapegoat, he's it. Fire him and make a show of it for all your people to see, and you walk away from this place—for good. We'll arrest him, throw every charge we can at him, and make sure he never has the chance for this kind of fuckery again."

CHAPTER SEVEN

Vickie didn't like the fact that Taylor had been out and about more now than he had been when he'd come from the hospital. They wouldn't talk about what exactly had changed but she could see something in him. She didn't want to call it fear but it was something a little manic.

Still, it was healthier than merely moping around the strip mall, waiting for something to happen like a call from Niki or more work to come in from outside.

He had told her they would talk after he'd delivered the parts, and the asshole forgot. Bobby and Tanya finished with their day at work and in fairness, she spent most of the day busy with her job. But when everything was finished and they were closing the shop for the day, she remembered she did have something she critically needed to talk to Taylor about.

She didn't feel right leaving her other two colleagues with all the cleanup work, but they didn't seem to notice her absence.

There was only one place where he would be at this time of day. Unless someone was due to call him, he would be at the little gym they'd set up.

He used it more than anyone else and she would never tell him he spent too much time working out. The man had been in the hospital for long enough to lose much of the muscle mass he was generally known for, and he was more than entitled to work it all on again.

Vickie moved toward the gym and nodded when she heard the light, rhythmic clinking from inside. As she stepped through the door, she could see him prone on the bench, pushing a weighted bar. He was breathing deeply, and a sheen of sweat touched his skin and caught the light.

She dropped onto the bench next to his and waited for him to finish. While she didn't know how far into his set he was, she knew better than to interrupt him. He pushed himself hard and went past ten even after she'd sat. It was more weight than she could carry, that much she knew, but he continued until she lost count.

The routine had become almost mechanical—push and lower in a slow repetition while breathing slowly and evenly each time.

Finally, he pushed the bar up a little higher than before and settled it into the little hook above him. He checked to make sure it was secure before he released it and pushed up, scratching his beard lightly.

She gave him a moment to take a sip of water from the bottle beside him before she spoke. "You know, I always heard that if you try to build muscle, you're supposed to put as much weight on as you can stand for shorter sets."

Taylor nodded and took another swig from his bottle.

"Sure, I guess. I've never been a bodybuilder, though. My intention has never been to be as big as possible but as strong as possible. There are a couple of ways to measure that. One is to be able to lift a much heavier weight in one go, which leads men to be much bulkier—strongmen, you know the type. Another is to be able to last forever like the slim people who run marathons for fun. My ideal is to find some point between them. That is the kind of body type that most militaries prefer since those guys are able to survive the longest."

Vickie nodded slowly. She wasn't the person to ask about workout routines. Despite her lean build, she wasn't into exercising. Taylor had talked to her about getting self-defense training and he had delivered on it too, but over the months he had been in the hospital, she hadn't kept up with the lessons and she hadn't thought to approach him with the idea since he returned.

She simply assumed he'd forgotten and given that they had been very busy ever since he'd come out of the hospital, she didn't blame him. There was so much shit going on that they still needed to deal with.

"I wanted to talk to you about something," she stated finally and spoke firmly so he didn't think he had the option to back out of it now. He seemed willing to accept it, which made it easier.

"Fine, but you have to spot me." He rumbled a chuckle and eased onto the bench to slide under the weights as she moved to stand at his head.

"Do you really think I can lift this much weight if you run into a problem?" she asked dubiously. "Because I have to say you have far more faith in me than I do."

"There's some psychology to it," Taylor muttered and raised his hands to grasp the bar above his head. "Or something, anyway. I never understood it, but if I struggle, you could put one finger's worth of weight on top and that would finish me. On the flip side, you could help me by lifting with one finger. I'm not sure where it comes from. Maybe the body summons a little more power when it realizes it has help on its side. You know that the human body has self-limiting psychology, which keeps you from injuring yourself. Did you know, for instance..." He paused, grunted, and lifted the bar from its hook to lower it slowly. "Biting through a finger takes less power than it would take to bite through a carrot. But put your finger in your mouth and you suddenly won't be able to bite that hard."

"That seems kind of an odd thing to know about offhand," Vickie commented as he settled into his breathing rhythm and began to lift and lower the bar again. "Do you know it takes that much strength to bite through a human finger because you've done it before?"

"Nope." He grunted. "But someone else has and they recorded it."

"And you'll take the word of someone who's snacked on human fingers?"

Taylor glared at her. "You did have something you wanted to talk with me about, right?"

Vickie grimaced. "Oh...shit, right. Anyway, I wanted to talk to you about some negotiations. You know, salary and the like. I feel confident about how they'll go because if I don't like how the negotiations go, I'll simply start pushing on the weights until you see things from my point of view."

He grinned at her and his pace didn't waver. "Fair enough. What do you want, exactly? Because I feel you're compensated fairly for the work you do."

"That's my point," she said. "I don't think I want to be in sales anymore."

That made him pause and he left his arms extended for a second as he looked at her. "Okay. Does that mean you want to work more on the suits? Get into mechanical work?"

"No, not really."

"Well, it's not like we have many other branches available, you know. We're still a small company. Do you want to work reception at the gym?"

Vickie couldn't help a small smirk. "Well, no, not that either. I thought that...well, the operations you inevitably get in the middle of. You need an operator, a woman in the van, as it were."

"Is there any particular reason why you want this change in vocation?" Taylor mumbled, once again in rhythm with the weight routine. "Or are you merely bored by sassing the pants and wallets off our clients?"

"Don't get me wrong, it's still the best part of the job. But that's not the point. My point is...well, I worked with you guys and it was more fun than I've ever had. No, fun isn't quite the word. I felt compelled, you know? Like I worked at my peak and pushed myself to the limit. And unlike many people I know, I like that feeling. I enjoy being pushed to reach the best of my abilities and seeing what I'm able to do when under stress."

Taylor said nothing as he continued his set and she could understand that. This was the kind of thing that was best discussed when they were both not lifting heavy weights. Aside from that, it looked like he was a little out of breath and had to suck it in a little deeper. The sweat on his skin grew a little heavier, and it wasn't long until his arms shook with the last push and he slid the bar into the hooks.

"Are you okay?" Vickie asked, moved away, and sat across from him again as he straightened to a seated position.

"Yeah, the third set is always the toughest," he muttered and snagged his bottle again. "Anyway, you were saying? About your abilities being tested? We could probably bring something like that into your work."

"There was more to it than that, though. I mean…like, working with a team and being a part of the group was something new, something special that I've never experienced before. I've always been the lone ranger kind of operator, always working on my own and getting the job done myself without having to rely on anyone."

"I don't think that would particularly change."

"Sure," she grumbled and shrugged. "But the point is… well, having someone rely on me was a new experience too —and not necessarily a bad one. Knowing you guys were relying on me being at the top of my game was what drew that out of me, you know? It pushed me farther than I'd ever gone before. It wasn't even about how what we were doing was…well, not strictly illegal but definitely clandestine and maybe even a little illicit."

Taylor smirked as he took a sip from his bottle. "Are you sure that's not what attracts you to it? The fact that what you did was outside the law?"

Vickie laughed. "Okay, I've broken the law since I was a teenager. As soon as I knew how to operate a computer, there was the appeal of being able to break the law from afar. I won't even try to deny that it's certainly a turn-on."

He winced physically in response to that description. "That's...uh, more of a mental picture than I needed there, Vickie."

"Suck it up, boss-dad. Are you telling me you aren't able to picture worse in that dirty mind of yours?"

"No, I'm not telling you that, but it's still not something I want to think about. Anyway, back on topic..."

She nodded as his voice trailed off, which indicated that he was waiting for more from her. "Anyway...yeah. Being part of a team. Maybe doing what's not legal but doing the right thing...it felt right, you know?"

The man nodded, picked a towel up, and wiped his face with it. "You know that simply means you're growing up, right? Maturing and shit."

Vickie had a feeling he had hoped for a laugh from her. He probably wanted to defuse the tension as he was clearly not that comfortable having this conversation with her. Neither of them was used to being this vulnerable.

"I've never helped to save lives before, Taylor," she whispered and shook her head.

"Is that something you want to do full time? For instance, look at me and Bobby. We race around like chickens with our heads cut off, then we come here and settle in. This is the anchor. I'm not speaking for the big man, of course, but for me, coming here and having something to work at and build is a good thing."

"I know and I get that," she replied. "But we're simply

cogs in the wheel. Here, we're merely pieces and that's how I feel every time I come into work here or even turn up for one of my classes. But when I help to run operations like when Elisa called me from the plane and needed my help, and I was there for her and you guys... I don't know. It felt like a drug."

"Have you ever tried drugs?"

Vickie shook her head. "Not really, no."

Taylor narrowed his eyes, not sure whether to believe her, but he moved on quickly. "Well, whether you have or not is irrelevant. The big draw of drugs is the release of endorphins—the feel-good chemicals in your body, basically. Using drugs is a way to do that artificially, but another way to do it... Well, your body treats it as a reward system to encourage behavior that helps with your consistent survival. It usually comes after a release of adrenaline too."

"Thanks, I know about basic anatomy too, Taylor."

He grinned at her. "Well, so you know, when someone says something is 'like crack' or some other drug, they are describing the way it feels, which is the release of endorphins or whatever. Anyway, that's the same reason why you enjoyed working as an operator so much, I think."

Vickie thought he might have a point in there somewhere and waited for him to finally reach it.

Taylor leaned forward and rested his elbows on his knees. "Do you want training? Do you want to be taught how to run the suits and be ready for combat in them?"

Vickie shrugged. "Would it be so crazy if I did?"

"Of course not," he was quick to reply. "On the other hand, though, you have to realize that I'd have to clear it with your cousin first. I wouldn't want to wake up one day with her finding out, taking offense, and sticking a.45 up my ass and emptying the magazine."

She chuckled. "Well, yeah, I guess that would be a shitty morning for everyone involved. I'll clear it with her first. And…thanks."

He raised an eyebrow. "What for?"

"You know, giving a shit. For showing me what an actual dad is supposed to do—care but let me make my own decisions."

Taylor chuckled, but his gaze shifted quickly to the entrance of the gym. She immediately looked to where Bobby stood at the door with the silhouette of someone beside him. Vickie knew immediately who it was, although Taylor needed a few extra seconds to recognize the woman.

"Elisa?" he asked and stood slowly. "What the hell is she doing here?"

"What—did you think I would leave you hanging without a sales expert?" the hacker countered hastily and patted him on the shoulder. "She and I had a chat about her changing vocations too, and she expressed interest in working here with us."

"Well…shit." Taylor growled in annoyance and turned to face her. "You have to explain this to your cousin too. I won't have my balls roasted in a hibachi for something I had nothing to do with."

Vickie snickered. "Way to stand up for yourself there, Taylor."

"This is another one of those dad things," he retorted

and grinned as he flipped his towel over his shoulder. "I'll allow you to accept responsibility for your actions."

She tried to roll her eyes but he laughed and slapped her lightly on her back, a good demonstration that he didn't lack for power. It felt like she would feel that mark for a while.

"I'll finish my workout," he called to Bobby. "Get her… situated or something and I'll be there after I've had a shower."

CHAPTER EIGHT

Niki sealed herself away mentally from the activity around her. She didn't want to think about what was happening in the lab and to the people who worked there. There were dozens of different reasons for them to have walked away from the facility before and they hadn't taken them.

Now, they all spilled out and looked confused as they asked questions while the alarms continued to blare inside the facility. It was impossible that no one knew what was happening in the lower levels, and she wouldn't buy the word of anyone who said they were ignorant. They were all scientists and researchers. The very nature of their job was to question everything and push the boundaries of what was known.

Taylor would have had a few very choice words to share with them about it, but he would also make sure they were all brought out alive to be properly berated.

She groaned aloud and hated the fact that he was her inspiration for moments like this. Of course, she would be dead before she admitted it to the man. But if she needed any inspiration for dealing with anything Zoo-related, he was probably one of the best examples. Him and that Dr. Jacobs fellow. Both appeared to have vastly different and yet complementing experiences of the jungle.

It didn't take long for word to come back from the Army garrison nearby. They hadn't had any word from the DOD to alert them to the emergency, and Niki didn't want any kind of a panic to result in the area. There was still a fair number of civilians nearby—something like a township with a population of almost three thousand, she'd been told—and by the looks of it, they had barely nipped the problem in the bud.

Thankfully, they had stepped in before it erupted and turned into a real issue. Niki didn't want anything to interfere with the work of clearing the lab.

Jansen intercepted her as she helped to pull the last of the researchers from inside. "I've had word from the garrison. Apparently, they needed someone with higher standing with the DOD to affect any kind of mobilization, so I contacted Speare and let him know. The guy's connected, I have to say that for him."

"How long until we can get a first-response unit in?" she asked.

"I'm not sure how he did it." Her bodyguard continued with his narrative. "He probably got a couple of Army generals on the line. Anyway, I heard from the garrison about five minutes ago. They're sending a first-response team via helicopter, which should arrive in an hour or so. The rest of the troops will reach us by truck in a couple of hours. We'll be looking at a fucking military occupation here before too long."

"This might be the first time I've ever been happy to hear those words," she replied and rubbed her cheeks. "But I'm damn glad we have the cavalry coming."

It had been a long day for all of them, and while it was still far from settled, it was great to know they would have support in their endeavor.

"Wait, did I hear that right?" a deep, rumbling voice said from behind her. Jeffrey had been far more compliant than she'd come to expect from people in his position, but she assumed even he had a limit. He probably saw it as people attacking his business, and the only reason he had been accommodating thus far was because he saw it as a cancer that needed to be aggressively cut out for the whole body to survive.

But there were things he wasn't willing to do. Getting the military involved appeared to be that line.

"Did you hear what right, Mr. Gottfried?" Niki asked and tried to not sound sarcastic or annoyed with the man.

"You're getting the military involved? What's the point of that? What would they be able to do that our security team couldn't handle?"

"A whole lot," she pointed out. "For instance, they are better equipped to deal with the Zoo monsters should something go wrong. We'll go ballistic on this, and there's no reason to not go all out. We don't want to risk any kind of outbreak from the lab."

The man didn't seem even vaguely appeased by her explanation. "If we bring the military into this, don't you think we could bring specialists in? You know, the kind who know how to deal with Zoo creatures."

"These are the best we can get on short notice," she assured him. "And they won't deal with anything. Their role is to set up a perimeter and make sure nothing from inside gets out. That's the first order of business in here, do you understand that?"

Despite his assurances that he enjoyed her speaking to him honestly—the whole breath of fresh air sentiment he'd expressed on meeting her—she could see he wasn't used to people speaking directly to him like that. When he was in a worse mood, it drew a more aggressive response.

She didn't give a shit, though. It wasn't her job to play babysitter to rich assholes who wouldn't know their head from their asses if they were given an anatomy textbook and nothing else to do but read it. She turned to Dr. Terrance, who also wanted a word with her.

Absently, she rubbed her temples but it did very little to assuage the pain that built slowly in her head. Long days like these made her appreciate those she spent away from it that much more.

"You!" he shouted and limped closer to where she stood. "You motherfucking bitch! You shot…you shot me and you think I'll simply let you walk away from this? You'd better get used to owing money because you've made me a rich man."

Niki took a deep breath and turned to Jeffrey. "On a scale of one to ten, how fired from his position would you say Dr. Terrance is, Mr. Gottfried?"

The CEO looked confused for a few seconds but shook his head. "Well, on a scale of one to ten, I'd say ten. You're fired, Dr. Terrance, and given the kind of shit you tried to pull, you're lucky that's the only consequence of your actions from the company."

She understood that the man needed to find a scapegoat for his situation but wondered if she needed to make it a little clearer for him. Helicopters could be heard approaching in the distance, but they were still too far away to count as help. She didn't like the fact that she needed to play politics but it was necessary, apparently.

In response to the researcher's belligerent glare, she shook her head. "I told you that you would have to answer my questions, Doctor. You didn't do it quickly enough and you intended to try to abscond. In all honesty, you should consider yourself lucky that I only left you with a flesh wound to remember me by."

"You're a fucking psycho bitch, you know that?"

Niki turned back to face the man fully, walked toward him, and fought to not lose her temper again. "Yes. And remember that because I'm the psycho bitch with a gun. Actually, I'm the psycho bitch with a gun who saved your ass down in your lab. You—and everyone else—were minutes away from being savaged by one of the creatures that escaped despite all the security you put in place. Remember that and my name for the next time you screw up and need someone to shoot you in the leg before they haul your ass out of the goddamn fire."

Terrance took an instinctive step back and almost fell when he put his weight on his wounded leg. He grunted in pain and grasped a nearby chair to keep himself on his feet.

"Get him a fucking ambulance," she instructed and shook her head before she turned her attention to Jeffrey.

"Should I be concerned?" the CEO asked as someone guided the scientist away to have his leg looked at again.

"What about?" Niki countered, still not in the mood to deal with him.

"Well, he did make a threat. He said he intended to sue you."

"I'm surprised you care about the state of my legal situation," she commented with a smirk.

"As nice as that would be, I am more concerned about whether G & G will be liable as a result of his injury, as well as that of the rest of my employees. The dangers they have been subjected to—"

"Were an unfortunate oversight." She finished his sentence for him. "The kind that comes from trusting the work of a Harvard trained professional like Terrance and not seeing his willingness to conduct such experiments despite the dangers."

The man narrowed his eyes and it was clear he didn't understand that she was trying to say.

Niki sighed deeply and rubbed her temples yet again to get the pain to at least diminish, which would make it easier to think. "You have to understand that he wasn't your employee. Not at that time, anyway, and I have the power to fix any problems that might result from his time working under the banner of G & G. And, as all the research as well as my personal report will show, he was the problem that needed to be fixed."

"I'm not sure I understand," Jeffrey mumbled under his breath.

Fucking hell, this one was thick. She tried not to sigh again since that would make it sound like she was being sarcastic or condescending with him. This would already be difficult enough without him becoming hostile with her over perceived slights.

"You'll have to forgive us for the fact that we hacked into your company's databases," she explained, speaking slowly and making sure to add emphatic pauses here or there to drive the point home. "The fact that the red flags were raised was enough to have a warrant issued, but we couldn't risk the details being released through a leak in the Justice Department. Therefore, we needed to break into the lab's servers."

He nodded and a hint of recognition began to appear in his eyes.

More prodding would be needed, she realized.

"We were only able to work through this legally because you were the one who called us in. You did so when you discovered discrepancies in the lab's budget and recognized the signs. You authorized the DOD to enter your facility and allowed us to discover what might ultimately cost American lives—lives you saved by acting preemptively."

Finally, the penny dropped in his mind. He nodded a few times and turned to look at Terrance before he focused on her again. She had offered him the out he needed. "Ah....yes, I did call you in, didn't I? I was alerted by a few irregularities regarding the lab, and I immediately alerted the DOD since you people were the ones who provided us with the contract and would clear the situation up as quickly as possible, yes?"

Niki nodded slowly, relieved that the dumbass had

finally engaged his brain. "I couldn't have said it better myself."

"We can't say how much we appreciate the alacrity of the DOD's response to our alert. Your efficiency in dealing with the rogue scientist will certainly be noted and commended to your superiors."

She smiled and patted the man on the shoulder. "You don't have to do that. We were only doing our jobs."

"No, no, I insist. Your quickness and efficiency likely saved the lives of many of my employees."

They were both playing politics and it wasn't long before Jeffrey moved away to no doubt work on the narrative that would set Terrance up as the patsy in this situation. She wouldn't give him any ammunition to say otherwise and hopefully, this would be all that was needed to stop him from trying this kind of bullshit again.

The helicopters reached the landing zone that had been set up for them and Niki made her way to where the teams had begun to disembark. They were all armored—not with the kind of armor she was used to with Taylor and those like him but good enough, she supposed—and well-armed. Assault rifles and grenade launchers meant they were all ready to deal with the possible threat inside.

One of them stood out from the others and so drew her attention. The woman wasn't dressed in any of the armor and was only armed with a pistol holstered on her hip. She wore the distinctions of a higher-ranking military member, but Niki couldn't distinguish exactly what rank.

She noted the agent approaching the helicopters almost immediately and jogged forward to greet her.

"Agent Niki Banks?" she asked and extended her hand.

"That's me." She shook quickly. "And you are?"

"Lieutenant Colonel Hannah Carson. I've been assigned to deal with this situation and my briefing was short and to the point. I was told there is a potential threat inside this lab that would require immediate action from my team, is that correct?"

Niki nodded. "That would be the gist of it. You'll have the full cooperation of the lab's security team, so they will brief you and your people with the details of what to expect in there. However, containment should be the number-one priority for your team, as you don't want anything inside that lab to escape. The creatures are still secured for the moment but have been known to be... crafty in finding a way out."

"I understand. The first-response team who came with me in the helicopters has been tasked with reinforcing the perimeter and assessing the situation. We will only begin with the process of clearing the lab level by level once we have the whole facility secured."

"I won't tell you how to do your job or anything, but no one will judge if you guys simply level the entire lab once you've killed all the monsters inside. Even the owner would be fairly relieved to see it all go up in dust and collect the insurance money. Assuming he has it insured, of course."

The lieutenant colonel smirked and actually laughed. "You know, I think I might actually like you, Agent Banks. I don't generally run well with intelligence folks but you might be the exception to the rule."

"I appreciate being the exception to your rule," she commented. "I'll go ahead and leave this in your capable hands. To be honest, I've had enough of having to hold the hands of rich brats and tell them everything will be all right. My team will fill you in on everything you need to know and stay out of your way. This is one hundred percent your show."

Carson shook her hand again. "Have fun finding more places for us to clean out for you."

CHAPTER NINE

He'd had a good day despite his somewhat shaky start. The work had helped to clear Taylor's head and put him into the mindset he'd needed to be in to keep the work going. Vickie was right. They were merely cogs in the machine that Vegas had become, a piece of the tax machine that governed the whole city.

And not a particularly large piece either, their good numbers notwithstanding. It was good that they had something to keep them together.

The workout had been rewarding too. Even with the interruptions, he felt the comfortable burn and heat that would last for hours after he had finished. Not only that, but he felt more himself every day. The muscles that had atrophied during his time in a hospital bed had begun to return to normal.

Unfortunately, after the shower, he had decided to check his email and so saw the invoice that had been sent with the costs of their use of one of Marino's planes.

Merely looking at the number in the final total was

enough to put a bad taste in his mouth. He didn't like having to work with the man. They were still dealing with the effects of his attempts to force them into line and there would undoubtedly be more in the future. He simply didn't trust the mob boss to not make another attempt once he had consolidated his position in the city's underworld.

He picked his phone up and headed to the shop where he could still hear people moving around. Bobby and Tanya were supposed to have closed it almost an hour before, but they were still working. More importantly, Vickie had stuck around to show the ropes to the newest addition to their team.

At least, he amended, the possible newest addition to their team. The hacker had probably talked the girl into joining their group. It would have been an easy sell after Elisa had been rescued from Africa where she'd almost been sold to local dictators along with the suits she'd stashed away in. He did remember the woman going out with Vickie.

"Elisa," Taylor announced and caught their attention as he walked into the shop. "It's nice to see you again, although it's much sooner than I thought we'd be seeing you. How've you been?"

"I can't complain," the woman answered and swiveled her chair to face him. "I quit my job as a reporter for the Crypto-Inquirer, so you guys don't need to worry that I'll spread the word of how you robbed a local casino and earned a nice six-figure payday from it. On the downside, though, I now need a job. Vickie was kind enough to tell me you guys currently have an opening in the position she used to hold."

"She told you that, did she?" he mumbled and settled into a nearby chair. "Well, I'm glad we don't have to worry that you'll stab us in the back. I'm still not sure if we should put you on the payroll, though."

"You're in a sour mood." Vickie pointed out the obvious. "And you weren't that bad when I left you in the gym. What's up?"

"I saw the bill from Marino for using his plane to head to Africa and back. It's a little over three hundred and fifty thousand dollars. The guy wasn't kidding when he said he would make all his money back. At this rate, we might end up owing the bastard, and that is a position I don't want to be in. I hope we don't have to call on his services again."

"Yep, that'll explain the bad mood," the hacker said and took a deep breath. "Anyway, I've shown Elisa the ropes and she has some skill."

"I did study business and econ while in college," the woman stated. "And I minored in sales and marketing and I know a thing or two about selling a product. Plus, I worked in a telephone sales company to pay my way through college."

Taylor nodded and rubbed his beard gently. "I think we could probably find a use for you, especially since Vickie will vacate her post. You do understand that you'll have to deal with mercs and the like who work in the Zoo—people you probably aren't used to dealing with. They won't exactly be the politically correct type and they won't give a shit if you're not a fan. In fact, I'm fairly sure that'll simply amuse them more."

He could see Vickie grinning from where she was still seated in her office chair but he decided not to engage her.

She knew better than most the temperament of the people the newcomer would have to deal with and had probably already covered it.

Elisa tilted her head. "So, you're saying they're much like you, right?"

Taylor thought about it for a moment. "Sure, I guess that's one way to put it. I'm sure Vickie has already told you that the way you'll make the most money is by making yourself memorable. If you get them to want to talk to you, they will therefore be more willing to spend. You'll earn a commission of ten percent for every upsell you make, on top of a base salary. This is an entry-level position, of course, but you're still in a position to make a decent amount of money. Well, what people in entry-level positions would consider a decent amount of money, anyway."

Vickie rolled her chair a little closer again. "This sounds like you're trying to scare her away from the job, Taylor."

"Nope. It's the same pitch I gave you, give or take. I don't want to paint any unrealistic pictures of the work. We're not the kind of company that can pretend it's any different."

"It's fair enough," Elisa replied and folded her arms in front of her chest. "I knew I wouldn't be able to work as a reporter for the Inquirer, not when I knew the precise details of what we were reporting on. There's a kind of shock that comes with...you know. Seeing it firsthand took all the enjoyment out of it."

He leaned back in his chair and studied her for a moment. "I'm fairly sure you could have found another reporting job out there. What made you interested in coming here to work? Again, I don't want to make it seem like you're not welcome to work with us. I merely think we need to understand your decision-making process, given that it's what brought you here in the first place."

She took a deep breath. "I guess that's a fair question. I was very interested in reporting and for the longest time, that was all I wanted to do with my life. But the shock that took me out of the Inquirer also kind of took the passion for the work too. I decided I wouldn't be a reporter anymore when we were flying back from Africa. Vickie and I talked about her wanting to break away from her role, which would leave it open for someone new to come in. We had the idea that I could take her place. It did start to make sense."

Taylor looked at Vickie, who continued to pay attention to what they were discussing. He wasn't sure he liked the fact that she played the role of recruiter for their little company. Despite the fact that he'd technically only hired Bobby, he preferred to have first and last word on the people who were employed. It had been easier to accept the loss of control when both Vickie and Tanya had come via Nicki, but when the hacker pushed her people on him, he knew she expected him to go for it despite any misgivings he might or might not have. While he still had the final say, resistance could generate all kinds of complications he'd much rather avoid.

There was a simple and elegant solution, of course. It would make him look generous and genius while still making sure someone else did all the work.

"Fair enough, I'm sold," he stated and saw a hint of surprise in both women's faces as he relaxed into his seat. "We've needed some fresh blood on our team but there's not much we can do to train you for the role. You either have the skills or you don't. I'm no expert in upselling so Vickie will have to supervise you and make sure you get into the swing of things."

The hacker's lips parted in indignation for a moment. "Oh, you motherfucker."

He had some self-control and managed to not grin when the two women thought through what he had said. It was the option that made the most business sense.

Elisa looked at Vickie. "So, she'll train me."

Taylor shrugged. "Vickie will still be in charge of the department, but with you able to take over most of the work, she'll be able to focus her efforts on what appeals to her most. If she wants to work with you, she'll do that. If not, I'm sure she'll find something else to do—right, Vickie?"

The hacker glared at him but eventually shook her head. "Yeah, I'll find some way to stay busy."

"Speaking of busy, were you able to get anything on that trace I asked for?" He picked a mug of coffee up from the table, sniffed the stale and cold liquid, and put it down.

"What are you talking about?" Elisa asked and glanced at the other woman for answers.

Vickie turned to her computer and pulled up a couple of files for them to look at. "The people who stole our shipment—the suits you were in—were alerted as to where and when it would arrive. It was very likely someone here in the US who has their finger on the pulse of whatever is shipped out there and happens to know when something will be well-protected or not."

"Well?" he asked and leaned closer. He could see the

files displayed on her screen but that didn't mean he could fully understand them. "It's time to use the brand-new cyber operative services of McFadden's Mercenaries."

"I thought we were going with McFadden's Mercs," Bobby called from the other side of the shop.

"Well, yeah, sure, but it's still a crap name."

"You have a ton of those," Vickie pointed out.

"Blame that on whoever thought it was a good idea to call their child Fadden."

"Because?"

"Scottish tradition had men adding their name with the Mc prefix for their children's surnames. Hence, McFadden would be the son of a guy called Fadden."

"Right," she muttered. "Okay, I didn't have much to work with since even though very little communication comes through sub-Saharan Africa, there's still enough to make any comms going through difficult to find. Still, I did manage to do some digging, and with the timeline of the shipment in mind, the amount of warning time required, and the relatively isolated location, I was able to break into the cell towers in the region. If you think our security is bad, theirs was a walk in and take what you want, so I could obtain at least the remnants of the kind of phone conversation we're looking for. From that, I was able to narrow the location of the other side of the conversation to Louisiana."

Taylor scowled and tugged his ginger beard gently. "Good work, Vickie. Keep it up. I assume they used some kind of VPN to mask their location, right?"

"You have been listening. It's adorable and even a little

gratifying. But yes, they put work into masking their location, but it shouldn't take me too long to dig them up."

He turned to Elisa. "You know, if there's one thing you should learn before coming to work with us, it's never to underestimate what Vickie can find. Seriously, if she had a mind to, she could absolutely demolish my reputation. Everyone's done some supremely weird shit in their time, and this one can track it all. It doesn't help that when I was growing up, kids liked to film themselves doing stupid shit and never considered the consequences of having that on the Internet until years later."

She couldn't help a laugh. "Now I'm a little curious about what kind of crap you got yourself into when you were a kid, especially if it'll damage that precious reputation of yours. And I'm sure Vickie is equally as interested."

"Nah, not really," the hacker replied. "From what I know about Tay-Tay, it'll probably only be him trying out for *The Voice* while singing a Disney song or something equally uninteresting. While it might be funny to watch at least once, it wouldn't be worth the fact that it'll destroy my mental image of my boss forever and ever."

"You could not be further off the mark," Taylor grumbled. "I was always more into K-Pop."

Her eyes widened and she looked at him like she had something to say, but she caught the amused smirk on his lips just in time. "You're fucking with me. You're totally fucking with me. You know, Tay-Tay, one of these days, I actually will go digging and I'll find everything. Then, we'll have a drinking game with your shame as the goal."

"And won't that be a fun day," he replied. "In the meantime, though, I think we can find something to keep your mind occupied. Something like giving our new recruit a good idea of what the ropes are supposed to look like."

Vickie shook her head. "You always have the best jobs for me, Tay-Tay."

"You're the one who sprung this on me without so much as a warning, Vickie. I'm merely making the best of the situation."

Taylor stood and gave her shoulders a squeeze. Despite the faux-hostility of their exchange, they both knew they were working together on this.

"Okay, newbie, here be the ropes," Vickie called. "We have people who call in when they need to place orders and other times, we're the ones who make the calls. They aren't usually cold calls since we deal with repeat customers and so we simply make sure we have all the details of their orders in place. We can make cold calls too and connect with possible clients who have been referred to us, but they usually know we'll call."

"That's the part of the job that's covered by your base salary," Taylor explained.

The hacker nodded. "Sure, and it's far and away the easiest money you'll make. They want what we sell and they're more than happy to pay our prices. The fun part is when they want to have a conversation. I don't know what's happening in there—maybe someone sprays testosterone all over the fucking jungle—but they like having someone talk back at them. I've used that as a distraction to make sure they're not paying attention when I get them to sign off on new expenditures. Well, no, that's not quite right. They know, but when you talk to them, they don't care. It's something of a tightrope, but it's been forgiving, at least in my experience."

Taylor smirked, shook his head, and moved to the door. "I'll leave you guys to it. Try not to have too much fun, Vickie."

CHAPTER TEN

There weren't many things that Jennie would have preferred to do on a weekday night.

It wasn't a tough decision when it came down to it. She had been invited to a work dinner, and there were a couple of other connections people wanted her to make. But if there was one rule that she had picked up during her time working in the private sector, it was to spend as little of her own time on work as possible.

She spent eight hours a day every weekday and much of her weekends monitoring and developing projects for the partners at her firm to pass off as their own. Of course, she made more than enough money in the private sector, and in many cases, more than she knew what to do with.

But it wasn't about the money. People acted like it was but she wouldn't play that game. Making a living was one thing, but there was more to life than what she was paid for. Biology was one of her passions but computer engineering had been her pastime, her hobby since she was five.

Of course, she hadn't been the only one who took up the hobby. She would never admit it, but Vickie had surpassed her in many areas, although she would always tell herself it was only because the tyke had that much more time to practice. And, of course, a willingness to go the illegal route whereas she needed to stick to the straight and narrow if she wanted to keep her job.

But those were merely excuses and not very good ones either.

Still, if there was one element of her software engineering she was proud of, it was Desk. The project had come in as a request from her sister while working for the FBI and there had been some strings attached, but it had ultimately given her firm considerable good press as well as an in with the government.

More importantly, it helped Niki keep the country safe or some shit like that. Her sister had always been more of an idealist than she had. It hadn't always been the case, of course, but the last time Jennie let ideals guide her actions, she had ended up in the middle of the Zoo, had been forced to pick a gun up for the first time in her life, and watched people die by the dozens before she was dragged out by Taylor McFadden.

That was the end of her attempts to follow her heart over her head. She had put hours into therapy to overcome what had happened that day. It was never a good sign that the life-or-death experience you escaped had a name with the word "battle" in it.

The Battle of Armageddon Gulch or something like that, although it was appropriate on some level. The experience was something she wouldn't easily leave behind.

Of course, all that had gone into her design for Desk the AI. Personality was one of the most important parts of AI creation and it was always best to base that personality on herself. Going with someone else had always ended up with software problems—life-threatening software problems.

But now that she looked at it all, the programming told her there was maybe a little too many of certain issues she hadn't worked out herself. While she could get therapy for her problems, they didn't have any for AIs yet.

"No, they do," Jennie corrected herself. "It's merely that all you have is me to help you. The blind leading the blind is the correct term, I think."

"A biblical reference," Desk replied through the computer speakers. "It's not quite apt in this scenario, as I would say you know a great deal about what you're doing."

She had questioned the aspect of leaving the AI functional and operational while she checked and updated her software, and it made sense in her mind in the way that surgeons always tried to keep their patients conscious while conducting brain surgery. It was to make sure that everything still worked while they did what they had to do. She'd read somewhere that sometimes, they had people play the violin during the surgery.

"Really?" Jennie finally answered and checked where the reference came from in the software. "I was talking about the Mumford and Sons song, but I guess that probably referenced the Bible too."

"That is correct, of course."

Niki would have a field day with that one. Where had biblical references come up in Desk's software?

"You know what I'm tinkering with, right, Desk?" she asked. "I'm still not sure where your obsession with Taylor comes from. I'm fairly certain there's nothing in what I wrote to give you that."

"My personality is based on yours. Therefore, when your obsession became apparent, it started to pattern into my subroutines. There is no mystery to it."

"Yeah, you keep saying that but I keep running into problems. You're not supposed to grow attachments to people, you're supposed to help them. Be detached. You know, like AIs should be."

"What is the standard for AI behavior in that respect?"

Jennie opened her mouth and recalled that there was still significant debate as to what should and should not go into AI development. Most of those involved in the process still hadn't determined a standardized way to make it work.

In essence, there was no specific definition as to what AIs "should" be unless she considered their film counterparts. The real problem was that developers needed to implant idiosyncrasies in their AI's personality and keep it from being too human since that tended to upset the people who bought it.

In this case, though, she hadn't thought it would matter. Niki didn't buy into the AI-phobic bullshit. Why would she care?

"My personality is based on yours and given that my software is in a continual state of self-development, any alterations I am allowed to implement are made based on the personality programming you have instituted," Desk explained. "Your obsession with Taylor was registered as well as your protectiveness of humans who you have designated as family."

Jennie leaned back in her seat and tilted her head. She couldn't believe she was having this conversation with a damn AI. Ironically, if she split hairs, she was having this conversation with herself in software form. The thought was something alarming that rattled around in her head for a few long minutes.

"So…are you telling me that you see my family—Niki, Vickie, etc—as your family and are trying to protect them in the same way I would?"

She saw a spike in the personality section of the software before Desk answered. "I've thought about it and I've determined that you designed me to protect your designated family. That was the intention behind all the work you put into my creation. It took almost two hundred working hours to put me together, and there's nothing that tells me you did it for the recognition. You knew your sister might be in a dangerous position and you wanted someone like you to keep a watch on her, despite everything she's told you about being able to take care of herself. I would imagine she thinks she's the one who needs to watch over you."

"She always was the tougher of the two of us. Physically, anyway, and when boys were handsy or bullying happened, she was always the one who threw her fists up and put all those Muay-Thai lessons to good use. Niki put more than a few idiots on the ground whenever she needed to. I think that instinct continued when we grew up. She was the only one of the family to tell me she thought it was a bad idea for me to go to the Zoo."

"Therefore, you feel protective of her since she was protective of you. Is it so strange, then, that I would feel the same need to protect the people you want to protect?"

"I don't think I've ever felt protective of Taylor in my life."

"Agreed. Your views on Mr. McFadden are a good deal less protective and much less familial. I would have described it as a crush, but that relationship has altered over the past few months. I am unsure how to define it from this point forward."

Jennie rubbed her temples in the same way her sister did when she had a headache. The AI almost gave her the full psychiatrist treatment, and she didn't know what to think of that. Was Desk really that much better of a psychoanalyst than the people she had paid exorbitant amounts of money to?

Probably not. Then again, she wouldn't have to pay her anything for the analysis.

Regrettably, the headache showed no sign that it would go away, and Jennie didn't see anything she could do to improve on the work she'd already done. It wasn't like Desk was dangerous. She was merely a little odd—which was normal for an AI at this juncture.

"I'll shut you down for the night, Desk," Jennie stated as she began to close the protocols she'd brought up. "I can give the DOD the requisite clean bill of health and there's nothing more to do here. Don't go trying to take over the world now."

"Would you take over the world in your spare time, Jennie?"

She narrowed her eyes. "I guess that's a good point.

Have a great night."

They really should have had this situation resolved by now.

Then again, Niki reminded herself, all the security was still necessary. The Pentagon remained a location that was a prime target for infiltration, which meant that as long as she worked in the area, she could expect there to be dozens of invasive checks. She couldn't fault them for wanting to make sure she wasn't smuggling anything that would either endanger the people inside or be used to take information out.

There were too many reasons for them to simply give up the practice, and if she had learned one thing during her time with the DOD, it was that people put security over convenience.

And somehow, shit hit the fan anyway.

"Are you done?" she asked once they had completed the third search through her bags. "Or do you guys want to get the cavity search done too?"

"That won't be necessary, ma'am," the security guard mumbled with barely masked hostility.

She finally passed the last ring of defense for the Pentagon and pressed forward with Jansen and Maxwell close behind. Despite the fact that they had worked with the DOD far longer than she had, they were still submitted to all the same checks she'd had to endure, although they seemed less reluctant than she had.

Maybe she would get used to being searched every time she set foot in the building.

Niki knew her way through the halls by this point, or at least well enough to find her way to the office of the man she had been called in to report to. Not many people were present to get in her way at this hour, and she maintained a brisk pace. She wanted to get this done and over with in enough time to find somewhere to crash for the night.

The secretary looked like she was wrapping her day up when she saw the three stride down the hall toward Speare's office. She smiled politely.

"They're waiting for you inside," she said and gestured toward the door.

"They?" Jansen asked in a low tone as they were guided in and Maxwell shrugged.

Sure enough, Speare wasn't the only one who waited for them. A tall, dark-skinned man with short-cropped black hair was with him. He was dressed in civvies, but the way he stood made Niki place him immediately as a commissioned officer. Everything about him exuded military in the way that even the most casual clothes couldn't disguise. He looked like he would be uncomfortable in anything but full military regalia.

Speare, on the other hand, was relaxed and seated behind his desk. He appeared to have been interrupted mid-sentence when the door was opened.

"Your visitors, Mr. Speare," the secretary mentioned by way of introduction. "Do you need me for anything else?"

"No, you have a good night, Sally. Close the door and I'll see you tomorrow," he replied. He made no effort to stand from his seat and gestured Niki, Jansen, and Maxwell inside before the secretary closed the door behind them.

"Nice to see you all again so soon," he commented and

made no effort to introduce the man who had been in his office when they arrived. "Agent Banks, thanks for coming in on such short notice. As I'm sure you're aware, we're here to discuss the details of the missions you've undertaken so far and Mr. Stern has joined us for that. You can have a look in those files over there."

Niki picked up the files in question from the desk. Sure enough, mission reports from her, Maxwell, and Jansen described the missions she had engaged in thus far for the man, but there was more to it as well.

"It would seem that many of the people you deal with aren't a fan of your style," Speare noted and his expression had become a little more serious than before. "A fair number of unkind words were used to describe your interactions. Abrasive, uncaring, and vitriolic are the most flattering you'll find in there, and if I read your most recent mission report correctly, you shot one of the lead scientists in Virginia."

"When he was about to escape questioning," Jansen added. "I feel that needs to be mentioned."

She nodded slowly and scanned the complaints that had been filed with the DOD over her operational style. The word 'bitch' seemed to be a firm favorite.

"Are people still allowed to throw the word hysterical around these days?" she asked. "I thought they would know better, given that these assholes probably go to five or six harassment seminars a month. They have to know they can't simply throw that word out whenever someone without something tiny swinging between their legs contradicts their dumbassery and still expect to be taken seriously."

Speare rubbed his chin gently before he exchanged a glance with the military man. "Is that all you have to say about the statements? No further comments?"

Niki closed the file and placed it on the desk. "Nope."

She felt like there was a tense moment between the two men on the other side of the office before both grinned. Speare laughed as he pulled the file closer and tossed it into a steel garbage can.

"Good. Me neither. These assholes have become a little too comfortable for my tastes. They need to be reminded that they work for us, not the other fucking way around. With that said, I am of the opinion that you bringing a hacker in was a little outside the norm. We prefer to keep our operatives in-house when it comes to classified information. Don't get me wrong. I am aware that the AI you requested isn't available as yet and I like your improvisational attitude, but maybe bring these people on board with us so we can have a better idea of what they're up to. Also, keep in mind that we can keep a lid on them easier when they operate in-country should you decide to go on another field trip outside the country."

Niki nodded. "Understood."

"Now, on to more pressing concerns." He took another file from his desk and leafed through it. "I've been notified of the fact that you've been out to dinner with one of your preferred freelancers. McFadden is a good operative, I won't lie, but there have been indications of a possible romantic involvement with the man. Is that correct?"

She bristled. While she was aware of the security that was part of her working with the DOD, she had absolutely no intention to allow them to dictate what she could or could not do on her own time.

Then again, these people were about as paranoid as they could be and it was the reason why they had brought her on in the first place.

Still, she wouldn't be one of those people who gave her whole life up simply because she wanted to keep her job.

"Your information is incorrect," she stated and tried to keep her voice as neutral and professional as possible. "There is no romantic link between McFadden and myself. With that said, I will not rule a future link out. The man may be a Cro-Magnon, red-headed Jason Momoa wannabe, but he certainly has many hidden talents."

That caught Speare's attention and he looked dubiously at her for a moment. "I don't want to know."

"I cannot claim to know what those talents might be," Niki continued and kept her voice firm. "Even so, I will not surrender my right to make that choice."

"Making demands, are we?"

She shook her head. "Merely marking off where the responsibilities to my role with the DOD end, and that is with my personal life. If I'm stuck under twenty stories of alien monsters before we see light and I decide I need release, I won't be too choosy about where it comes from. Even if he's the last one, I'll ride that like a stick-horse. I might even yell 'yeehaw' all night long."

She could almost hear eyebrows raise behind her. It was her intention to shock, of course, since that would be the quickest way to get her point across to the man.

After a long and slightly tense pause—during which Speare likely waited to make sure she was finished—he chuckled. "Well, I don't know if I would put it that way, but since I'm not on the firing line myself, I'm less concerned about where you get that release of yours and more with getting the poor unfortunate souls to sign a release to make sure they know about the risks involved."

While having the topic raised rankled somewhat, it did feel oddly satisfying to air the feelings she had mulled over for the past few weeks about Taylor. With Speare, Stern, and her team present probably wasn't the best time to do that, but it was nice to know where she currently stood with it all. Playing the cat-and-mouse bullshit simply wasn't her style.

She had to concede that the man had also raised a fair point, but she didn't have to make a noise about it. "Is there anything else?"

"Mr. Stern has a couple more possible missions for you in that briefcase of his. Mr. Stern?"

It sounded like a fake name if she ever heard one but it didn't matter. The man picked up the briefcase that had rested on the ground beside his right leg and handed it to her.

"Look through those with Jansen and Maxwell and choose whichever you feel are the more dire situations that require immediate attention. I look forward to our next briefing, Agent Banks." He stood and strode out of the room with a simple nod at her boss, his bearing even more indicative of a military history when he moved.

"Great," she muttered, took the briefcase, and handed it to Jansen without so much as a second glance. "You have a great evening."

"One more thing, Agent Banks."

"Yessir?"

"You were hired because we saw the potential in you— the hard-nosed bitch who had the ability to make the hard decisions and get shit done no matter what."

"But?" Something in his tone suggested there was one and he responded to the small challenge with an odd smile that revealed an unusual hint of grimness.

"But don't kid yourself. It takes courage and a certain kind of crazy to step onto the dark side every single day but it's also seductive. I've been there, Banks, and I know how it feels to have the power to do what you want when you want. It's fucking awesome but it's also addictive. Soon, you need and want what it offers and it becomes easier to go there and more difficult to find your way back."

He drew a breath and regarded her with narrowed eyes. For once, she had no smart retort. Instinct told her he hadn't intended to raise this, which made it seem all the more important.

"I've been stuck on the dark side, Banks—stuck in the place where it began to feed on me and strip away every-thing I was or believed in. I was lucky. I had someone who cared enough to drag me back kicking and screaming. Do what you must but don't let it own you. Don't give in to the seduction and always make sure you can fight your way out every time. And for fuck's sake, find someone who will haul your ass over the line again if you can't make it on your own. I don't want to have to can your goddamn ass because you've gone rogue or serial killer on me."

He turned to the papers on his desk and his stiff posture indicated that the conversation was over. Thankfully, her bodyguards were already at the door and for once, neither of them ventured a comment. She needed time to process what Speare had said, and not only because he'd surprised the crap out of her. His warning resonated alongside the voice in her head she'd tried to ignore over the last few weeks.

The inspection on leaving the Pentagon was far less rigorous but it was still time-consuming, and Niki pulled her phone out the moment they were cleared and while Maxwell pulled the car around to pick them up. She wanted to have a chat with Vickie before she settled in for the night.

The line dialed for a few seconds before someone answered.

"McFadden's Mechs, how may I direct your call?"

The voice was feminine but it certainly wasn't her cousin.

"Hi, this is Niki Banks," she stated curtly. "Who the hell is this? And where's Vickie?"

"This is Elisa, and I'll get Vickie on the line for you. One second…"

"Wait," she snapped. "Not the same Elisa who Taylor and squad went all out to rescue from her own stupidity?"

A pause on the other end of the line tugged at her patience. "That's oversimplifying it, but sure."

Niki narrowed her eyes. What the hell was she doing in the office? The last she'd heard, the woman was returning to Chicago.

"Should I transfer you to Vickie now?" the woman asked and broke the pregnant silence.

"You do that."

CHAPTER ELEVEN

Pizza for dinner. They were going all out.

Taylor wasn't in the mood to cook for himself and as the whole team appeared to be making a late day of it, he thought it was only fair that he buy them all something to eat. After his workout, he had been hankering for something round and covered in cheese anyway.

With that said, he wasn't a fan of having people present for this long. It wasn't that he didn't want his team around him but rather that there were times when he needed to be alone.

But that was what came when you were the one in charge. Heavy hung the crown and all that.

Vickie and Elisa worked together and both had begun to take the calls from their clients. Finally, it looked like the hacker needed a break and she wandered to where Taylor was seated in the break room.

"You don't look happy," he noted and pointed out the obvious. "Is everything not going as well with the newcomer to our little group as you might have hoped?"

She scowled at him, picked up one of the slices of pizza, and put it on a plate before she sat next to him. "Yeah, you're fucking hilarious. For your information, she's doing a fantastic job. So...in your face."

"My face? You're the one who put your faith in her being able to do a good job. You should be ecstatic that she's doing well, right? And in my case...well, I'll always be in favor of something going well for our little endeavor, so what exactly do you want to rub in my face? Our collective success?"

She scowled and shook her head. "You...wouldn't understand."

"If what you feel is jealousy, I'm sure you can stow it. You're still a vital member of our team and no one can do what you can do best. You know that, right?"

"I'm not jealous. I...okay, maybe a little. I showed her how to operate with the guys in the Zoo and made myself a nifty little profit of five hundred dollars. No biggie, only everyday stuff. Then she gets all flirty and uses those voice skills of hers, and she nets a cool three grand. On her first call."

Taylor's eyebrows raised. "Oh...okay. I can understand a little jealousy. Seriously, three thousand dollars?"

"She has some skills."

"Well, the guys are only interested in what can give them something to tell the other creeps. Having a new voice to talk about with whatever skills she might have is probably what it's all about. You can chalk it down to the novelty of it. Once they get used to her, profits will taper off and be closer to what you're used to."

Vickie studied him with an odd look in her eyes. "It sounds like you're hoping for fewer profits."

"Nah, but I know how skilled you are at manipulating the dumbasses over there. And I thought you might appreciate the knowledge that just because Elisa got a bigger commission than you did, it's not because she's any better at it than you are."

"Not only more than mine. My biggest commission so far has been two grand if we don't count rush orders and she beat it on her first day."

"And you're the one who saved her life and graduated to a new position to operate our missions, and allowed Elisa to take the job you had outgrown. Remember, you're the one who identified her talents, which makes any of her successes yours as well. By, like, definition."

Vickie smirked. "Yeah, I guess you're right. I could say all the good stuff happening to this company of yours can be put squarely on my shoulders."

"And that'll be proven by the fact that you'll get a massive bonus come the end of the quarter. Of course, we did talk about putting that bonus in a trust fund that would be released to you once you graduated college, right?"

"Oh yeah, we did talk about that, didn't we?"

"A kind of incentive to get you to finish your college education, you know?"

"But you, Bobby, and Tanya will get your bonuses without any kind of extra work involved. How is that fair?"

"Well, we've all graduated higher education. But in this case, you'll get your bonus first, so that should settle your complaints about fairness."

The hacker scowled at him for a few seconds but finally

relaxed. "I guess that's okay. Sure, having the money would be nice but then I need to pay taxes on it too. And it's not like I have anything I want to spend it on right now. Maybe I'll buy real estate or something when I eventually graduate, but I'm fine as is for the moment."

Taylor smiled. "For myself, I'd probably reinvest my share into the strip mall, open more sections, and draw more businesses in. Maybe I could even get some kind of grocery store open here since everything is set up for it. Either way, it's moot as I said I'd add my share to yours but yeah, you're better off investing the money instead of leaving it languishing in a bank account. Tax problems alone are bound to make life difficult."

Vickie grinned. "It's kind of easy to forget that you know what you're talking about. It's like with all the big muscles you have going for you, assuming you're only a big hunk of muscle with little to no brains to work them feels like the right thing to do."

He nodded slowly. "Yeah, I blame pop culture these days. Who says the jock can't be smart? It's the twenty-first century. People can be strong enough to beat your ass with one hand and do calculus with the other. In fact, one of the most athletic people I've ever met was a doctor. It's fucking crazy, but a doctor working in the Zoo these days needs to be fit."

"I'm fairly sure you have to be a little crazy to go into that jungle willingly in the first place."

"True that."

She looked up and directed his attention to the desk where Elisa worked. The woman was obviously in conversation with a client on the other line, but she waved Vickie over frantically. Thankfully, there would be no follow-up on Taylor basically calling himself crazy. Then again, it wasn't anything they didn't know already.

The hacker dropped onto her chair and used the momentum to roll it toward the desk. She picked up the landline from where Elisa still held onto it.

The young woman's amused expression disappeared almost immediately, which triggered Taylor's concern. There wasn't much in the world that could worry the girl, and whatever had her on her toes had him on his too.

"Wha...no, I didn't say that," Vickie said and looked flustered. "We... No, we didn't, and I resent... You need to stop interrupting me."

There was only one person in the world who could put her off-stride like that. His eyebrows lowered. Sure enough, the girl's worries were warranted. He knew he should probably cut in and help her, but he really, really, didn't want to. This was her cousin, after all, and who was he to interfere with their family?

Taylor sighed when she became more and more flustered, even to the point where she began to stutter. He could practically hear Niki's anger through the phone, and he moved a little closer.

He didn't want to get involved, but there was no harm in listening to what they were talking about in case Vickie needed support after the veritable barrage of verbiage, right?

His mind made up, he chose one of the other extension units that Vickie had set up throughout the building—in case she needed it—and picked the phone up carefully from its cradle. He didn't even dare to breathe before he pressed the receiver to his ear.

"I don't know why you're reacting like this," Vickie said. " I know you have that little infatuation you're nursing, but that's no reason to throw a hissy fit for no apparent reason."

"I told you that in confidence," Niki replied.

"And who the fuck do you think is listening in on this? The NSA?" the hacker countered. "Besides, you told me because you wanted me to be in on the fight with you. To help you. And that's what I'm doing. Helping you."

Taylor felt a twinge of guilt over listening in. It wasn't enough to make him hang up but it was still there.

"And I'm not throwing a hissy fit," the agent continued. "It's only… I'm surprised what's her face is still with you guys."

"Girl, please. You were all but pulling at your hair and throwing shit. Accept it and move on. Besides, the fact is that she isn't still with us—she came back because I suggested it. She said she would have trouble being a reporter from that point forward after everything that happened, and I wanted to give myself a role more suited to my skills with the group. It worked out best for everyone. So chill the fuck out."

Niki paused for a few seconds, and Taylor thought he could hear her taking deep breaths to calm down.

"Okay, I'm chilled the fuck out."

"Good." Vickie snorted. "Now get your head out of your ass and…"

Her voice trailed off when she heard something beeping. It was his phone, telling him he had a message. The jig was up and he would have to find a way to explain the fact that he had eavesdropped on a private conversation quickly, or Niki would yell at him next.

"Hi," he said hastily. "This is McFadden from McFadden's Mercenaries. Who's this?"

"Taylor?" Niki growled something unintelligible.

"Oh, Niki, nice to hear from you again. You know, I wanted to have a word with you. You know, whenever was convenient for you."

"How long have you been listening in, Taylor?" she asked and sounded much quieter and angrier than she had during her conversation with Vickie.

"About long enough to know that you've been dressing my girl Vickie down for something that's not her fault. She has a business to help me run, so why don't you lay off her, okay? Or, at least, on the topic of what she does to help keep this business afloat. If you want something to get on her case about, you can have a chat around the fact that she wants to start training with the suits we have coming in. She wants to learn how to defend herself."

"You what?" Niki roared.

"You know, Taylor," Vickie grumbled. "I was working up to the right time to tell her. Thinking through the details so I could plan it perfectly. Going for subtlety and tact. I can only guess you've never heard of either before."

"Nah, I thought it was something you should get out of the way as quickly as possible. For one thing, if you start and you didn't tell Niki about it, she'll tear me about three or four new ones. If you hold yourself back for it, you'll blame her, get bitter over her protectiveness, and that won't be good for anyone. Get it out in the open, make it all work, everyone's in the loop, and we have everything out of the way."

Neither woman said anything for a few seconds.

Vickie spoke first. "Well…yeah, I guess that makes sense. Anyway, the long and the short of it is that I wanted to be a larger part of the operations. Given that we couldn't know what it entails, I thought it would be a good idea to learn how to defend myself if need be. Learning how to use the suits is a part of that. I'm looking out for myself while looking out for these dumbasses."

"See, that makes sense—right, Niki?" Taylor asked.

The agent remained silent for a few long moments. "Yeah, I guess it makes sense."

"There we go. There's nothing more to it. Vickie wanted a promotion and considering how much work she put into helping me, Bobby, and Tanya get out of Africa alive and well, I thought she deserved that much. I also feel she needs the ability to defend herself given that she might be put in a situation where she would need to do so—and has been in the past. It was a good idea and in that vein, we needed someone to take her former position since she would be too busy to do all the work herself. She'll train Elisa and make sure it's all still working the way she would want it to. Is that what you need to know, Niki?"

She must have realized that he had listened in on the conversation and didn't know what to do with that information. He hadn't meant to sound quite so hostile but maybe he felt a little protective of Vickie too.

"Sorry," he said finally. "I didn't mean to sound like that."

"No, it's fine," Niki replied quickly. "And what you said

made perfect sense. I guess I'm only... Things are crazy around here, so I might have..."

Her voice trailed off, and Taylor didn't want there to be any awkward silence on the line. "Yeah, I get that."

"Also, McFadden's Mercenaries? You honestly can't think of anything better than that, can you?"

"No, I cannot. But the more I keep saying it, the more I realize it's kind of catchy, you know? Easy to remember and shit. Besides, it's good to have a consistent marketing brand. You know, constant consistency."

"And what if you're not around for that name to be there anymore? What if you're in the hospital? Or the morgue. How consistent is that name then?"

He nodded. "I guess I haven't thought it all the way through."

"No shit, cowboy, you didn't. Now..."

The statement trailed into nothing and he tilted his head and waited for her to finish her thought process.

"Well, not that it matters what I think, but I can agree that Vickie's making a good, adult decision and has put thought into it. Far be it from me to tell her what she can or can't do, and I appreciate that she's placed her personal security as a priority."

"There you go. My work here is done," he muttered. "You girls play nice now."

He put the receiver down and knew they would continue to talk. They needed to figure some shit out without him around anyway.

And he did too, honestly. Like why the hell he was so attracted to a nutcase like Niki Banks.

CHAPTER TWELVE

It surprised Vickie that Taylor had listened in on the conversation. At any other time, she would have put him through a wringer about interfering with her personal life—and Niki's too, in this case—but that didn't feel right. She knew he would merely talk to her about how much she had intruded on his personal life, and listening in on a phone call because he was curious didn't make the cut in this situation.

While she wouldn't let him get away with it, she had more important things to worry about at the moment.

She turned her attention to the phone pressed to her ear.

"Are you sure he's off the line?" Niki asked.

"You heard him hang up," she grumbled in reply. "Anyway, it doesn't matter. The guy probably knows about anything we might be talking about anyway."

"Right. Still, though, you might have told me he was listening in."

"Are you saying that because you think I knew he had

tapped into our line? Seriously? I am proud of him for peering into personal lives that have nothing to do with him since I could have taught him to do that myself but still, the low-tech and old-school tactic of listening in on a landline phone call was something even I didn't think he was capable of."

"Whatever." Her cousin didn't sound happy about it but it wasn't like the woman could do much to change the situation.

Still, she didn't like her to be in a bad mood. "Well...I have to say I would have thought you would have fought a little harder to stop me from training with the suits and shit. You've always seemed to be against it in the past."

Niki couldn't help a laugh. "Have you even paid attention to what I've been up to lately? Seriously, my job involves dangerous shit. And it's not always fun. I had to shoot a scientist today."

"Good heavens no, not the scientists!" Vickie shouted and her voice dripped with sarcasm. Elisa paused in her conversation and glanced at her, and she waved her back to work. "But seriously, though. Holy shit, Niki, what the fuck are you doing shooting scientists? I thought they were supposed to be the good guys."

"Not this one."

"Did you kill him?"

"Nah, it was only a flesh wound. The guy was about to run away once we discovered what he was doing and Tweedledumbass wasn't in position at the door. I had to remind the researcher that he's not fast enough. The worst he'll have to deal with is a minor limp and he'll maybe need a cane while he's recovering. I'm not saying he'll be fine, though. He'll definitely have something to remember me by."

"I don't know if anyone's told you this yet, but you're kind of a psycho, cousin."

"I've been reminded of that regularly, especially by the people I happen to shoot. Right now, I need to find somewhere to bunk for the night. Stay safe, Vickie."

"You too. And try not to shoot any of the hotel staff."

"As long as they're not trying to develop any kind of monster that will inevitably find its way out and kill innocent people, they should be safe."

"I don't know. You can't ever be sure what these room-service chefs are up to in those kitchens, especially late at night when they don't have much else to do."

Niki laughed. "Fair enough. Talk to you later."

It hadn't been the worst first day she'd ever had, she decided as she headed in for her second day at her new job. Elisa did remember the first time she had walked into one of the local Chicago news stations as an intern, excited to finally get some experience in the field she had hoped to work in for many years to come.

She had ended up having to play nanny to one of the biggest divas there. The woman was the anchor for their cornerstone news section, and she'd spent most of the day hunting a particular brand of potato chip that was low in sodium as the woman refused to work if she didn't have her favorite snack.

Elisa had always wondered if it was only because she

didn't like having new people around her and therefore demanded she be gone for most of her first day. It was debatable, though, because it had happened consistently for the first two weeks of her internship until she was transferred to another section. That had been a vast improvement and was the department where they actually did reporting instead of handling unstable women who were only kept on board because they had a loyal fan base.

Working at the suit shop was an altogether different experience. Vickie had told her she would have to dive into the deep end and would be required to sink or swim. After her first experience, she thought she'd done a good job of swimming. She'd even made a decent chunk of money while she had been at it, with Vickie mostly giving her pointers and letting her get on with it.

Apparently, the people who worked in the Zoo were happy to have some kind of distraction from the death that loomed over them, and the other woman had taken advantage. The hacker had been good at sounding like the kind of person who would hold their attention and gave them all the sass she was known for. Vickie had explained that it mostly came down to them having stories to tell their buddies, which would get them free drinks at the local bars.

Elisa hadn't realized there were bars in the Zoo, but once it had been mentioned, it seemed so obvious. American soldiers in bases around the world were given downtime when they could leave their bases and head out to get wasted, but that wasn't an option there. Besides, morale had to be a fragile thing, which meant that somewhere for all the military personnel to fraternize between missions was probably a good idea.

Still, the concept that they were willing to part with cash in the interest of giving themselves an experience with someone outside the Zoo had sounded odd and almost impossible to her, at least until she had one of them on the line. The guy was a client and immediately friendly, likely because he'd been friends with Taylor and Bobby, as well as Vickie.

It had simply come naturally to her. Instead of Vickie's sass and overall aggressive nature, she had gone for something a little more subtle. The useful tactic was one she had learned through conducting a variety of interviews with people who wouldn't have talked to her if she had tried the blunt approach when asking questions.

She hadn't quite flirted but had been generally friendly, inquisitive, and a little sultry, and worked her Hispanic-Italian accent in to make sure he remained interested. Some people might call it dirty. All she knew was that she gave them what they wanted.

The day ended and Taylor sent them all home. She had managed to find a room in a local hotel while she looked for an apartment. Vickie had told her that their boss would possibly offer the use of some of the rooms in the strip mall if she needed somewhere to stay, and if her house hunt didn't go well, she would take him up on it. It was a last resort, though, as the location didn't look much like her style. It wasn't that her standards were ridiculously high, but they were certainly higher than that.

Elisa pulled her rental car into the empty parking lot

around the strip mall and couldn't help a small wince as she circled to the back entrance of the shop.

Desperation might change her views, but she was far, far away from that point.

She knew Taylor lived there and it felt on par with his character, all things considered. It added to the sense of mystery around the man and of course, this was his building. He had sunk a ton of money into it, and if he chose to live here himself, that was his call.

Bobby and Tanya arrived and settled in to get their work done while she geared herself for another day at her desk. It had been explained that part of the job was also logistics to keep the whole business running, all the deliveries to and from the Zoo on schedule, as well as making sure they had all the pieces and parts they needed to be able to complete repairs without unnecessary delays.

It was the kind of work she had done in the past, of course, and she knew a thing or two about it. Very few calls came in during the morning. Clients usually called in the afternoon or evening. Early in the afternoon was when they finished with their workday and turned their attention to reports and arranging the deliveries. Later in the evening was early in the morning for the people in the Zoo, who picked up the work that hadn't been done the day before.

Still, it was the kind of mindless activity she could see herself doing with a show or something playing in the background once she was used to the ins and outs of it. Almost before she knew it, someone tapped her shoulder.

Tanya motioned for her to remove her headset. "It's

lunchtime. Make sure to set the phones to take messages and join us."

They had ordered food in, something they did often to support a few of the local restaurants with their business, and today's delivery provided a wide selection of Thai food. Elisa had never been the biggest fan of Asian cuisine but she had a very practical policy when it came to keeping herself fed. If she wasn't paying, she wasn't complaining.

"Will Taylor and Vickie join us for work today?" she asked and looked at her colleagues.

Tanya's mouth was full, and she simply gestured to Bobby, who was still piling food onto his plate.

The large mechanic needed a few seconds to realize she had asked a question and focused on her. "Oh... Vickie has school today. She's a little flakey when it comes to attending but Taylor has managed to get her to go whenever she can make the time."

"So...he makes sure she goes to class instead of working here?"

He shrugged. "I think it was something Niki insisted on. Still, Vickie is awesome and needs a little extra focus, and Taylor has been good at pushing that forward in her."

"Huh." She grunted, leaned back in her seat, and toyed with the food on her plate for a few seconds. "And Taylor?"

Bobby shrugged. "I'm not his keeper. As long as we're on schedule, the guy will probably be out there getting more work or finding a way to improve the premises. If I know him at all, I know he's not hanging around some-where getting tanned and drunk while we're working. And if he is, he probably earned some time off."

Elisa looked at Tanya, who didn't have anything to add

to that. Of course, Taylor was the boss and you didn't keep track of what your employer was up to. But from what she'd seen, he was more than an employer to them—or, at least, to Bobby. They had been in the Zoo together and earned each other's trust enough during their time in that hellhole that it resulted in them working together when they came home.

She tilted her head in thought and used the time to eat a few forkfuls of noodles before she formulated her question. That was the real issue, of course, and over the years, she had learned to frame her questions to make sure she would get as much information as possible. She wouldn't push too hard, though. After all, she wasn't a reporter anymore.

"You and Taylor were in the Zoo, right?" she asked finally and directed the question at Bobby. "I think I heard something like that from the two of you."

Her companions exchanged a quick look but she could understand their apprehension given how they had met. She had been a reporter and for all they knew, this could be an attempt to put a story together for herself. Their assumption would be that she wouldn't care what they thought about what she was writing or even what the consequences would be if she revealed everything they told her in a detrimental light.

It was an unfortunate view on news reporting and one that many reporters had worked hard to earn, given that they had done precisely what everyone feared they would. They always pushed for the good story instead of worrying about the safety of the people they wrote about.

Elisa had always tried to avoid that kind of dishonest

dealing, but she could understand why people were wary about what they said in front of reporters.

Still, she hoped the idea that she was no longer a reporter would be enough to let them know she could be trusted. Until they realized that, she wouldn't badger them about it if they didn't want to talk.

Finally, Bobby pushed past his apprehension and nodded slowly. "Taylor was in the Zoo much more than I was. I spent more time in the shops, fixing and repairing the suits and vehicles they took out there. I did actually go in there once, and that was enough to convince me that I wasn't cut out to do it on a regular basis."

She nodded thoughtfully. "It makes you wonder what one might need to be cut out for that particular job."

Bungees shrugged. "You do have to be a little wrong in the head. Anyone with an appropriately developed survival instinct would never choose to go out there regularly. Courage, I guess, needs to be a part of it as well. Being an adrenaline junkie is also required."

All that made sense, but she chose not to push further. She remembered that the surge of adrenaline hadn't been a particularly bad feeling, but when she had time to relax and push past the initial sensation, all she was left with was a sense of emptiness. It didn't feel right and it wasn't something she wanted to repeat.

While it had left its mark, her experience had been a quick skirmish and nothing even remotely like being in the Zoo.

That reminded her of all the people who were sent into the jungle and didn't have the choice. They were required to adapt or die and in that situation, many of them died. Of those who didn't, a fair number of them came out like Taylor.

"How about you?" Elisa asked Tanya, who had mostly finished what was on her plate. "Were you in the Zoo at any time?"

The woman rubbed her cheeks gently and shook her head. "I've never been, thankfully. I had a little experience with hunting here in the US when we dealt with creatures appearing. At that point, no one but Niki believed that what was happening was due to the Saharan Crisis, so she brought in almost anyone who was willing to take the risk. I was one of those but I dropped out once it became clear that the money was better spent on actual professionals."

Elisa narrowed her eyes. "Niki..."

"Banks," Bobby finished.

"Oh, the scary black ops woman," she recalled.

"Right," Tanya said. "And, since the two of you haven't met, she's a spitting image of you."

"Huh. That's... I don't know if I should take that as a compliment or not."

He grinned. "I don't know. She's not terrible looking, so I'd say yes."

Tanya nudged him in the ribs, and they shared a laugh before they refocused on their meals.

They looked up when the sound of the gate opening caught everyone's attention. Elisa clearly remembered the four-by-four Taylor drove, especially since it had been the car he had been driving when they first met. While she wasn't sure why the vehicle had stuck in her mind, it seemed appropriate. She had feared for her life at that point and odd things would be remembered. That was merely a part of life.

Her new boss climbed out and somehow made the vehicle look small. He waved and walked to where they were seated.

"What are we having for lunch?" he asked as he entered the break room.

"Tanya and I played rock paper scissors to pick the food," Bobby grumbled.

"She won?"

"Yep. So we got food from the Thai place that opened down the street."

"How is it?"

"Not bad. It's not Italian food but it has its draws. Do you want some?"

He shook his head. "I already had something to eat, but thanks."

"Have you finally tried the Il Fornaio lunch menu?"

Elisa couldn't help a smile as she watched the exchange between the two men.

Taylor scowled. "Have some patience. I'll get to it. But no, I paid Jackson's a visit. I met up with Alex and her new boyfriend. He's a nice guy and funny."

"A little jealous?"

He grinned. "You wish."

"Who's Alex?" she whispered to Tanya.

"I'm...not sure. If memory serves me correctly, she's the bartender at one of our haunts," the woman answered.

It seemed obvious from the conversation that this Alex and Taylor had been an item, although it was unlikely to have been anything serious. He seemed like the kind of guy who would find love in the arms of whoever he was with, and while that could have its moments, it was also not a situation that offered permanence.

"What are you up to today?" Bobby asked as he finished his meal and carried his plate to where he could wash it.

"I spent most of the morning having a chat with our suppliers to see if they'd be willing to reduce prices to help offset our increased costs for delivery," Taylor replied.

"And?"

"They said they'd let me know. It'll probably be a no, though, unless we start making more orders—for which we need more clients, which will increase our shipping costs, and so on and so forth."

The mechanic glanced to where Tanya and Elisa were still seated. "I don't know. Maybe our new additions will help bring more clients in."

He nodded and poured himself a cup of coffee. "That is a possibility."

CHAPTER THIRTEEN

Niki obviously knew there were many hotels in DC. She hadn't expected there to be quite as many on her phone, but as it turned out, most of the large hotel chains wanted in on the sheer numbers of people who would visit the city for business or tourism.

They came for the politics or the history, and visiting the various government buildings was still a massive attraction to the minds of ordinary Americans as well as the odd special-interest group from outside the country. She, quite frankly, didn't see the appeal. While the history was interesting, it was better studied from afar—maybe from a comfortable living room when you had nothing better to do.

She couldn't envisage spending thousands of dollars to visit DC.

Still, the very fact that there were so many meant there was a fair selection for them to choose from, even on the list DOD employees were allowed to use. She finally decided on a three-star establishment that was a little closer to the Pentagon as she wanted to settle in for the night as quickly as possible. The files she had been given weighed a fair amount so there would be considerable work for them to do the next day.

Besides, after the conversation with Vickie and Taylor, she felt too exhausted to go bargain-hunting through the city. It wasn't like she had to pick up the bill and thanks to Speare, she wouldn't have to explain budgetary concerns to any pencil-pushers.

That, she decided, was one of the perks of her job. After a quick meal from the room service menu, she fell asleep once she'd set an alarm to wake her at eight in the morning.

She was usually up at seven, but after the day she'd had, she felt a little jet-lagged and an extra hour would be a godsend.

It was a decent enough night of sleep, and Niki partook of the free breakfast the hotel offered before she used the in-hotel gym. Feeling a little more mentally energized, she returned to her room for a shower and change of clothes before she dug into the stack of papers that had been left for her to sift through. Maxwell and Jansen would have gone through their documents in the same way she did, but given that she was the one in charge of the whole operation, a day to focus purely on the paperwork was necessary.

It was as close to a day off as they would ever get. Niki hadn't thought to ask Speare about what kind of time off they could expect. She assumed it was one hell of an oversight on her part, but the truth was that she wouldn't count on much time off. Maybe she could squeeze in a couple of vacation days here or there, but who would take over the task force while she was off sipping mai tais in the Bahamas?

Taylor? Not likely.

For her to have any time off, it had to be when she had someone in place she trusted to keep the work going while she was away.

She didn't realize how quickly the hours passed as she poured over the paperwork provided. There were dozens of intelligence notes on fifteen different locations where the goop was being used. She had forgotten that much of it was used for cosmetic purposes and was peddled as a bonafide youth cream the rich and the popular used to slow the ravages of time on their skin.

"I have to wonder if any of those assholes will turn into a monster one of these days," she muttered under her breath. Most of the locations had already been warned against testing the goop on animals. This reduced the number that would be able to produce for the market with FDA approval, which kept it from reaching the vast majority of the population. Of course, that didn't stop a handful of Hollywood celebrities peddling the products under their names while making sure anyone who bought it did so with all the legal paperwork signed to prevent them from holding the sellers responsible.

People were desperate to stay young and were willing to do almost anything, including risking the use of an unknown and potentially dangerous substance to hold the customary signs of aging at bay or make them less obvious.

She could understand that, she acknowledged. There were few things more natural than to fight back against

Father Time, but there should be limits. People were supposed to know the difference between keeping themselves young and risking their lives to make themselves look young.

Niki paused, looked out of the window, and realized that the sun had already begun to set. The city lights were coming on and her stomach growled noisily to remind her that she needed to eat something before she returned to work. She had no intention to push through the night since her whole body ached simply from having been hunched over the hotel room desk all day.

"Skipping lunch is never a good idea," she muttered as she stretched slowly in her seat. "Note to self. Stop working all fucking day without a break."

She shook her head and pushed to her feet, with more stretching required. A few joints popped around her knees and shoulders but that was to be expected at her age. Her mind leaned toward picking up the room service menu for another meal in her room and spending the rest of the evening watching TV. Before she'd fully made the decision, her phone rang.

Reflexively, she scowled as her stomach grumbled again. Speare was probably calling to ask why they were still in the city when they had emergencies to mitigate and respond to, and she knew what her answer would be. They needed downtime to study the material they'd been given not twenty-four hours before, especially since they had also completed a mission a day earlier.

"The assholes need to chill the fuck out," she snapped and picked the phone up. "What?"

"Well, that's a nice way to greet your subordinates,"

Jansen replied. "Is this a bad time?"

Niki took a deep breath. "Nah, it's fine. I thought it would be Speare calling and I wanted to put him on the back foot immediately in case he planned to get on our ass for still hanging out in DC."

"That does sound like him, but no. Maxwell and I finished our work for the day and we thought we might head to a nice little Italian place we've been to before. We thought you might want to come out with us since I'll go ahead and assume you've been stuck in your room all day ?"

It was a good assumption. "Uh...yeah, okay. Are you guys sure you want me along? As my greeting showed, I'm not exactly the most sociable of animals, especially after a long day of making sure idiots aren't making mistakes that kill people."

"We've done the same thing as I'm sure you're aware, and you know how they say that misery loves company? They're right about that."

He made a good point. "Fine. Give me...I don't know, fifteen minutes to get ready, and we'll meet in the lobby."

"Are you sure all you need is fifteen minutes? I don't want to perpetuate any stereotypes, but—"

"You'll power through it anyway."

"Well, if you have to shower and get clothes and makeup together, you might need a little longer."

"Jansen, I'm the master—or mistress—of the quick prep. I'd be ready in five minutes, but I don't like rushing when I'm in my off-hours. I'll see you down there in fifteen minutes."

Niki prided herself in being on time and in fourteen

minutes, she was already in the elevator and on the way to the lobby. She wasn't sure what kind of dress code the restaurant had, and she'd settled on something that would fit into most establishments she knew of. Jeans were paired with a white button-down shirt and a dark blazer to make it all look a little more formal, just in case.

She'd had a feeling that Maxwell and Jansen would be late, but she checked her watch when they arrived at the lobby. Her expression smug, she made sure they could see her check her watch again when they approached.

"Twenty-five minutes," she announced as loudly as she could. "You gave me shit about being late and I'm here waiting for eleven minutes for you two to spruce yourselves up for a night on the town."

"In fairness," Jansen stated, immediately defensive, "I didn't give you shit about your ability to get ready quickly. I merely thought you would need a little more time given that you worked at a desk all day and might need a little time to relax before heading out."

"Bullshit," she responded and gestured for them to follow her to the entrance of the hotel. "Relaxation doesn't need time. Winding down needs time, but if we're all going out together, I won't be winding down much, will I?"

The two exchanged a glance and shrugged together.

"I guess not," Maxwell conceded.

"Okay, you guys know where this nice little Italian place is, so you lead the way," Niki asserted. The men laughed as they stepped onto the sidewalk and hailed a cab. They did have a car in the underground parking lot but there was no point in driving through town and trying to find somewhere to park for three hours.

Or, at least, that was what she had heard about Washington. She hadn't spent much time in the area and certainly not enough to go out for a dinner that had nothing to do with work.

It was, as promised, a pleasant venue. Considerable work had gone into making it look authentic, with paintings of what she assumed was the Italian countryside and music that was reminiscent of Sinatra in the fifties playing softly in the speakers spread out through the building.

They had a reservation and the hostess guided them to a larger table, where they were asked if they wanted drinks before the menus were brought for them. All three ordered a beer the bar had on tap.

While the hostess moved away to collect their drinks and menus, Niki looked across the table at the two men she was seated with.

"Look...I know I was a bitch earlier, but I appreciate you guys inviting me out. All my plans revolved around ordering the chicken parm from the room service menu and watching something vaguely superhero-based on the room TV, so this is a massive improvement."

"In fairness, the chicken parm was damn good," Jansen told her.

"I don't know. I had the steak frites but I'll take your word for it. Even so, you need to work hard to fuck chicken parm up."

The waitress returned with their beers and gave them time to decide what they would order.

"So," Niki muttered as she picked her menu up. "What did you guys think about the ring of usual suspects Speare put together for us?"

Maxwell chuckled. "These guys are the epitome of putting profits over lives these days. I don't care how huge you are in the industry, if you peddle Zoo goop as a way to make yourself look younger, you deserve to see your whole goddammed business go up in flames."

"The only problem is that too many innocent people go up in flames with them," Jansen pointed out.

"That's not what I mean," his teammate countered. "You see these guys and they piss themselves over having to wreck a lab they spent who the fuck knows how many millions building. But in all that, they never once consider the fact that their actions are what caused them to lose it all in the first place."

"These people are trained from their first day in business school not to plan for the long-term," Niki reminded them. "They're not terrible people, per se, but they don't think in terms of lives saved. They've thought about dollars and cents for as long as they can remember, and this goop shit is merely another thing they can profit from. Most of them are desperate to get in front of whatever is being launched, and they don't care about how they get there. Of course, that only lasts until the point where something goes wrong and they're all kinds of anxious to throw the blame onto any scapegoat they can find."

"Then they are kicked around the corporate ladder, moved to another project, and do the same thing." Jansen concluded her thought. "I've seen the same names attached to a number of different projects we need to investigate, and it'll always be the same story of apologize, drop out of public view, and come back and do the same damn thing."

Maxwell chuckled softly. "It's weird. We don't usually

do this. Speare generally chooses the projects and Banks decides how we handle them."

"Why wouldn't all three of us work this whole thing out?" Niki asked. "Three brains are better than one, after all, and if we'll all be in this, we might as well be in it together. At least this way, we'll all work on the same page toward the same goal. Hell, you two will be able to protect me better if you're in the loop, and I'm all for that shit."

She dug in her purse and withdrew a couple of the files she had brought. "These are the ones that caught my eye while I looked through them. You guys don't mind doing a little extra work over dinner, right? You know, since we're talking about it anyway. Not that I expect us to get anything done. We'll probably get sloshed and hope that none of the images inside ruin our appetites."

"Count me in," Maxwell grumbled and took one of the files. The waitress returned to take their order and suggested the veal pasta dish that was the chef's specialty.

Niki's intuition told her it would be one of those nights, but she didn't mind. They were all working together and getting drunk while mocking the mistakes that should have been incredibly obvious by this point. People continued to make them, however, which was the reason why they were there.

And she had to admit there was an upside to this kind of work while drinking. Maybe she would start doing this a little more often.

"We need more data," Jansen complained and his voice began to slur somewhat as he inspected the third bottle of red wine that had been delivered to their table. "We're working off too many assumptions. I mean...okay, they're good intelligence operatives and shit but in the end, they make assumptions and we can't operate effectively based on that alone."

She nodded slowly but needed a few seconds to keep pace with what the man was saying. "What we need is a hacker—a dedicated hacker, you know? Someone who can break into these places and provide us with the info we need. Think about it. The first thing you learn at Quantico is that many of the people who supposedly hack into something are usually running con jobs? They retrieve basic info like the name of a supervisor or something and call someone to say they're a supervisor and they need access to certain areas. Most people don't even bother to check. We need con artists in our crew. Like...get the whole cast of fucking Ocean's Eleven out here and set them to work for the good guys saving lives and shit."

At this point, she had no idea what she was saying, but the other two looked like they made sense of it.

"Do you have someone in mind?" Maxwell asked. The man showed fewer physical signs of being wasted, which was to be expected given that he was much larger than his two partners.

"I do," Niki muttered, pulled her phone out of her pocket, and dialed a number she had committed to memory. It didn't matter that she had already put it into her phone's contact list. Memory was always better than having to rely on a phone's memory card.

"Yeah?" Vickie asked when she answered after three or four rings.

"That's a very nice way to answer a call from your cousin," she grumbled.

The girl hesitated before she spoke. "Are you drunk?"

"Yes, but that's not the point. The point is that I want to bring you in on a job. I can give you work now that you're not taking calls from those dumbasses in the Zoo."

"Are you trying to hire me?"

"Do you want the job or not?"

"Probably not."

"Ugh, fine," Niki muttered. "I'll run it through McFadden first. It serves me right for trying to work you out of that idiot ginger's clutches. Maybe this whole desire to drive mechs will go away if you're not anywhere near him and all that asinine testosterone."

The hacker laughed aloud. "All right, that's a plan. But make sure to get yourself a good night's sleep before you make that call. I don't feel like cleaning your messes up again."

"Yeah, whatever. Leave it. I was born this way."

She hung up and noticed the confused faces of her partners.

"So we don't have a hacker?" Jansen queried and took a fortifying sip from his wine glass.

"No, we do—and in fact, if I play my cards right, we'll have two. But I have to take more roundabout measures to get her on our side," she replied. She didn't want to have to make the call, but if getting Taylor onboard would get Vickie onboard to help them, it would be worth it. And yes, it might be a drunken eureka moment, but when Desk was finally cleared for duty, she'd have the two best hackers in the business.

CHAPTER FOURTEEN

His eyes were open before the alarm went off.

Taylor didn't enjoy the feeling of being jolted out of a deep sleep with the help of a loud alarm—no one did—but there was something supremely disappointing about waking up on his own with the realization that he didn't have enough time to roll over and catch a few more Z's before the abrasive noise dragged him out again.

There was always the option of simply turning the alarm off and waking up whenever he damn well pleased, but that was a slippery slope. It would inevitably lead to a lack of discipline in his life, and it wasn't something he was willing to risk at the moment.

As a result, all he could do was stare at his damn phone until it vibrated and rang a tune he'd never heard of but now hated for the sole reason that it was his alarm. He knew he would end up hating any song he chose for that purpose, so it was better to have one he didn't know rather than sour those he knew and liked.

He retrieved the phone and turned the alarm off before he dragged himself out of the cot. His focus had been to do the necessary renovations and get his business productive, but maybe he would have to get his hands on a real bed sometime soon. The cot wasn't a terrible place to sleep, but it also wasn't the best way to get a good night's rest.

Finally, his gaze settled on the screen of the device still in his hand. There were a couple of notifications he hadn't paid attention to in a while, but three missed calls were something to keep his eye on. Someone had put a fair amount of effort into trying to make contact with him.

Well, enough to call him three times and leave messages.

The number was familiar, and he knew whose voice he would hear when he dialed into his voicemail box.

"Look, McFadden," Niki said on the recording. "I don't know what you're doing right now that won't let you answer your phone and honestly, I don't care. Or I think I don't care. Of course, I wouldn't call you if I didn't care, and I definitely wouldn't leave you a voice message. Wait —shit..."

She sounded drunk, slurred a couple of words he couldn't fully hear, and hung up, which led him to the second of the voicemails.

"I won't apologize for calling," she continued as if she'd never ended her previous message. "I can call whoever I like, whenever I like. I'm a strong, independent woman who can make any calls she chooses, thank you very much. That's all I have to say. I won't apologize. Oh, and answer your damn phone."

It apparently wasn't all she had to say, and he pressed to listen to the next message.

"Like I said, I don't care what you're doing at this point. We didn't agree to start dating or anything, so I don't know what you want. We're definitely not exclusive at this point, although I'm sure you have no idea what the word means. Still, if...no, I don't want any more wine. Anyway, Taylor, call me when you get this. Assuming you're not dead. In which case call me anyway."

She laughed—which was an unusual sound from her— before she hung up for the last time.

"Declining the wine sounds like the wise choice," Taylor muttered. He'd seen Niki sloshed before but never to the point of making calls from wherever the hell she was. It wasn't a terrible look on her. It at least showed that she knew how to relax and could turn that on or off at will. He wouldn't tell her how to live her life.

But he did want to make sure she was okay. He knew that whenever he went on benders like that, he tended to wake up in unfamiliar places with a pounding headache and his mouth tasting like literal shit. She would probably need someone to talk to—if she didn't already have someone.

He pressed redial on the number that had called him and waited to be connected to her phone.

"Hello?" The voice almost didn't even sound like her. It was thick and raspy, almost a Niki-like croak.

"Well, don't you sound like a hundred bucks." He laughed. "How does your head feel? Should I raise my voice to make sure you can hear me properly?"

He did raise the volume until he could hear her groaning. She had probably pulled the phone away from her ear, and he waited for a few seconds before he spoke again.

"You spent the night out with friends, I see," he continued. "It's not the kind of thing I would have seen you doing, but there's so much about you I don't know about. For instance, I didn't know you thought we should talk about being exclusive. When did that come up?"

"What?" Niki muttered again. "Oh...fuck, what did I do last night?"

"You went in a little deep on the vino last night and left me not one, not two, but three separate voicemails. I'll go ahead and guess that these people you went drinking with weren't close friends, because close friends don't let their friends drink and dial drunk."

"Fuck you. How about that?"

"That sounds more like the Niki Banks I know."

"And why the hell didn't you pick your phone up last night? It wasn't that late. Was it?"

"I'm not sure, but I did have an early night," Taylor explained. "I've hit the gym a little harder than usual and badly needed a recovery day. It comes and goes ever since that helicopter's rear-entry-without-permission."

Niki paused for a few seconds before she laughed. "Did you say the helicopter butt-fucked you without permission?"

"There was no consent. We live in a modern world and helicopters need to get with the program like the rest of us."

She chuckled for a few more seconds before she groaned. Presumably, even laughing was enough to make her hangover headache worse.

"It didn't even give me the benefit of a reach-around either," he continued. "Which, at that stage of the game, is plain rude."

"Come on, stop it." She growled in both amusement and annoyance. "It hurts to laugh. But how are you doing? Are you still on the road to recovery?"

"I'd say I'm at about eighty-percent of my potential—which, coming from the guy who had trouble walking a couple of months ago, I'll take it. How about you?"

"My head feels like a killerpillar danced all over it, my mouth tastes like I coughed up a hairball of someone else's hair, and everything hurts. Red wine always makes me like this. I was out with Maxwell and Jansen, looking at potential cases over dinner and drinks. It ended up as far more drinks than dinner. I'm not sure what happened after that. I think I called Vickie, then you... Oh, right. I tried to talk her into joining us because we needed IT help to dig a little deeper into the cases that landed on our collective plate. She said no so I said I would go over her head and talk to you. Things kind of escalated after that."

"I thought I heard you turning wine down in your message. Did that not stand?"

"No, I think Maxwell suggested a toast. That guy could probably drink the collective population of Ireland under the table."

Taylor grinned. "Well, I'm glad you're making friends with your coworkers. But you mentioned wanting me to bring Vickie in. I obviously don't tell her what to do most of the time, but I'll see if I can't talk her into it. Now that Elisa has taken over most of her duties at the office, she would be open to take on outside contracts and probably make a percentage of what I do while working for you."

"I assume you'll add her share to your future invoices."

"You know it. She needs to make up for her loss in revenue somehow now that Elisa will take all the commissions, right?"

Niki chuckled. "I anticipate still having Desk—probably in overwatch but also as backup—but there's enough work to go round. I guess you guys have it all worked out on your side if you say she'd be available."

"It's Vickie who has everything worked out. All I can do is follow as close as possible and try to file the paperwork, as well as keep people from killing her."

She tried to laugh again but all she could do was groan. "Fucking hell."

"You know, the best cure for a hangover is a greasy stack of cold pizza to settle the stomach, Gatorade for the electrolytes, and a couple of aspirins to get rid of that headache. It works every time for me."

An odd sound made him think she was struggling not to retch. "And I'm sure it would help me if I were somehow the highest point in Vegas."

Taylor laughed. "I'm not sure how my height would help with a hangover cure."

"It's because your larger body is better at processing larger amounts of alcohol than mine is, so those half-assed cures might work for you but not for me."

"Try something nutritious and full of proteins if you're not into cold pizza," he suggested. "The kind that help the liver to detoxify your body and rehydrate you after a long night of drinking. How tall you are doesn't matter."

Niki was silent for a few long seconds. He could hear her breathing into the phone. Maybe she was trying not to puke. He'd been there himself a few times and could sympathize, but it sounded more like she was hyping herself up for something.

"Why do you have an extra suit in your collection?" she asked finally.

"What do you mean?"

"You know—the one that's somehow set to my specs and calibrated perfectly for what I need."

"Oh, that extra suit."

"Come on, Taylor."

"Well, it should have fit. I made it for you. I'm glad you liked it."

"No shit. The fucking question is why."

"Because the FBI gave you shit to work with—the kind of shit that'll malfunction and get you and others killed. Friends don't let friends fight cryptid monsters in shit suits that aren't suited for them if you'll excuse the pun."

"I won't. It was terrible." Niki paused for a few seconds and once again, he couldn't tell if she was thinking or keeping herself from throwing up. "Okay, Taylor, I have a bad feeling I'll regret this, but we need to get through it. I'll need three new suits from scratch and training in their use —at your going rates, of course. I assume this won't be a problem. If you can repair them, you can build them, and it'll be a good start to another income stream for you. We'll get back to Vegas tomorrow. And, of course, I still need Vickie's help with our task force."

"Oh yeah, you did mention you needed her help. You didn't mention the details of what you needed her for."

"No, I did not. And no, I won't either. But it'll be good to get her away from all the testosterone in that fucking place."

"You do know we have more estrogen than testosterone around here, right?"

"Please, don't get me started on your hiring practices. I don't need to know about what's going on in your head when you pull people into your little business."

"Come on. You pushed one onto me and pressured me into it. The second was a part of your team who needed another kind of work, and the third... Well, shit, it's your fault I have her on the team too."

"Oh yeah? How do you figure that, John Wayne?"

"What's up with all the cowboy references lately?"

"Never you mind, Nick Neanderthal. Answer the question."

"Ugh. Go back to the Wild West quotes."

"Stop deflecting, Taylor."

"It wasn't direct, but you were the one who forced Vickie into my hands. She, in turn, forced Elisa into my hands. I'm not saying you're responsible, but you're on the hook for it anyway. That shit was out of my control."

"I thought the business was yours. That the company was yours."

"It was a pincer movement. Besides, I might have started it but we're all a part of it. What the hell kind of boss would I be if I didn't acknowledge the needs of the people who work with me? We're a small business and in the end, we're in it together."

"She admitted that she appreciated your help, didn't she?"

Taylor bit his bottom lip for a second and nodded, even though he knew she couldn't see the gesture. "Yeah. Yes, she did."

"I thought so. Fine, I'm willing to put myself on the line for thirty-three percent of the blame for the Elisa situation. The other third goes to Vickie, of course, but you need to take the remaining third."

He took a deep breath. "It's harsh but fair, I guess. Do you need anything else from me? Is there anything else you want me to take the blame for?"

"There aren't enough hours in the day for me to detail all the bullshit you should take the blame for. But as of right now, that should be everything. Oh, and clear your schedule for tomorrow. We'll get there at four in the afternoon, but I expect there to be work done already, especially at the rates you've been charging."

"You know our rates are much lower than those in the general market, right? That's the whole selling point that lets us stay in business."

"They're still fucking exorbitant. Anyway, I'll see you tomorrow. Four in the afternoon. You don't have to come and pick us up, of course, but you still need to be ready for us when we get there. Got it?"

Taylor sighed. "Yeah, I got it. See you then."

She hung up, probably to get herself something to help with the hangover. He wouldn't tell her to do anything different. He decided to pick his battles, and there was no way for him to help with Niki's hangover. If the truth be told, people's bodies were always different and there was no single cure for the hangover. The fact that many of the so-called cures were purely placebos was also something to take into account.

He shrugged, rolled his shoulders slowly, and checked his watch. He had time to put a quick workout in. Bobby would have to open the shop if he was a little late.

CHAPTER FIFTEEN

"Stop biting your fingernails."

Vickie snapped her head up and broke her stare at the screen in front of her. She was biting her nails, an odd habit and one she didn't often indulge in—and never intended to. It was usually only when she was lost in thought and it didn't matter that she was doing it.

But it mattered to Tanya, for some reason. The woman stood and peered over her shoulder as she pulled the hacker's fingers away from her mouth.

"Why?" she asked, genuinely curious.

"It'll screw your nails up and it'll take all the skills of the best manicurists in the world to get them right again. Believe me when I say you don't want to have to handle that shit."

Tanya didn't look like the kind of woman who put too much work into her appearance. Then again, the better-looking women tended to put that much work in because they didn't want it to look like they were doing all that. The natural look was difficult. Niki was one of those who achieved it effortlessly. Vickie could see the work Elisa put in, but that was expected from the job she'd left behind. Tanya didn't look like she'd even applied makeup, but she still looked gorgeous.

Maybe that was what Bobby saw in her. No, he wasn't the kind of guy who went for looks—or not only looks. Personality was what drew him in. She could never pull that off and had put effort into not looking like the kind of girl people were attracted to. Her short hair, the darker makeup, and the tats all worked toward that end.

She didn't want to tell Tanya to fuck off but she wasn't sure how to tell her that biting her nails was something that helped her focus sometimes. It was that or something to smoke, or maybe something to eat. she didn't know why chewing on something helped her focus, but it did and she never bothered to question it.

Maybe having beef jerky to chew on would help her but sometimes, she couldn't exactly give herself a schedule of when the right time to focus was.

"What?"

Oh, shit, Tanya was still there. What could she say?

Vickie opened and closed her mouth a few times and tried out a couple of ideas in her head before she settled on one. "I...paint my own nails."

She wasn't sure why she said that but it sounded right. If she would inevitably ruin something, let it be her work, right?

"Well, it's a matter of health," Tanya pointed out. "You don't want to have weak, ruined nails later on in your life, you know?"

The hacker scowled. "Right. Okay, fine, I won't bite my nails."

"Plus, it's a gross habit that annoys the hell out of me."

"Right. I guess that makes sense. Sorry, I didn't mean to gross you out."

Vickie looked at where Elisa was working. She didn't want to give anyone any problems with working with her. While she wasn't much of a team player, when she needed to be she could accept that compromise was required.

"What has you stressed out?" Tanya asked and placed a hand on her shoulder. "People tend to only chew on their nails when they're tense. Okay, not that you're a regular, normal person, but still."

She wondered what it would feel like to be offended by that statement. The concept was entirely alien. She wasn't a normal person and that was exactly the way she wanted it.

But she wouldn't tell Tanya what had her on edge. Having Elisa and Niki in the same place would probably result in fireworks. Both were cut from a similar cloth and were bound to rub each other the wrong way.

"No, nothing's the matter. I'm only trying to keep my mind on business," Vickie lied and turned her attention to the screen again.

The other woman nodded and moved away. There were bound to be questions about what she was doing now that Elisa had taken over what had been her job. Taylor mentioned that she would still work in the shop as well as keep up with her studies, but most of her paycheck would come in the form of a portion of what he earned while working his operations with Niki. It was a smooth transition and one that rewarded her for pursuing work that suited her better than dealing with assholes from the Zoo.

No, they weren't assholes, not really. They weren't necessarily nice people either, but they were somewhere in between.

She would have to come up with a word for that.

"Seriously? Nothing's the matter?" Tanya insisted.

Vickie scowled at her. "Fine. Whatever." She gestured with her head to draw Tanya to the break room and away from where Elisa could hear them from her desk. "I'm a little worried about Niki and Elisa being in the same room together. Given that they're both...you know, crazy and will be at each other's throats within an hour of Niki getting here. I'm not sure what I should do about it. It's not like I can quarantine Elisa for the time Niki's here, and I should rather assume they can act like adults around each other, right?"

The other woman looked surreptitiously to where Elisa was engaged in a phone call. "Sure, in a perfect world but not the one we're in. I'm not sure if quarantine will help, but we can probably circle them and keep them separated somewhat until they get used to each other's presence."

"So, kind of like getting cats used to other cats?"

"That's more or less the system I would use, yes." Tanya grinned and looked far less worried than Vickie felt and like she looked forward to the challenge of keeping Elisa and Niki from each other's throats. "Like, from what I remember of Niki's interaction with Elisa, I can see why the reporter might have issues with Niki's cavalier attitude toward her narrow escape from both the mob and the mercs, but I'm not sure why Niki doesn't like Elisa being around."

"It's a little complicated but the basics of it, I would say, is that Niki sees something of herself in Elisa. Something like that. It's not a flattering image for either one of them."

The woman nodded thoughtfully. "I guess that makes sense. Still, getting them to know each other better should help them adjust to having the other around. Because the chances are that we won't be able to keep them away from each other every time this happens."

"Right, but for now, what do you suggest we do?"

Tanya mulled over the problem for a few seconds before she snapped her fingers. "Okay, I have an idea. Elisa will have to go out and physically visit our suppliers sooner or later, given that it's their product as well as our service that she'll be selling. With that in mind, maybe I could go ahead and do that today—say an hour before Niki is due to arrive."

"Taylor and Bobby will want to know about it since you'd have to schedule it with them," Vickie protested.

"In that case, I'll tell Bobby at literally the last minute, and he can give Taylor the heads up in turn once we've already gone. Neither will have any say in it and will have no time to consider the reasons. They'll simply react to our actions and be none the wiser regarding our ulterior motives. On the other hand, though, you will have to be able to lie to Niki if she decides to ask Taylor about it."

"Shit. Well, I can handle that part. I'm fairly sure I can, anyway."

"It's not like we're talking life or death here."

Vickie shrugged. "You never know. Niki has a fiery temper and easy access to firearms."

"Well, that's your problem, I guess, given that I'll be far, far away from the fallout of any Niki-based explosions."

She opened her mouth, paused, and closed it again. Had Tanya outsmarted her?

"Fuck," she muttered finally. "Outplayed, I guess. And by a sister, no less."

The woman grinned and patted her on the cheek. "The thing you have to remember about me is that I am one hundred percent a bad bitch. Having said that, Niki is a badder bitch, so if you think I'll sit and take it from her, you'll have to think again. She's your cousin and is likely to take any news of an uncomfortable nature better from you, right?"

"You'd think that," the hacker muttered and tried to be agreeable. Tanya wasn't wrong. Niki was one of the baddest bitches she'd ever met and despite everything, she couldn't blame her teammate for not wanting to be caught in the middle of a situation she was only trying to help fix.

She was right. Tanya did have a mind for this kind of thing, and Vickie made a mental note that she be included in the decision-making from time to time. Hopefully, she and Bobby wouldn't do much pillow-talking, though, since anything he knew ended up with Taylor before too long.

Her companion was about to add to her statement when something suddenly caught her attention. She pulled her vibrating phone from her pocket and pressed to answer.

"Hello?" Her look of confusion bordered on annoyance that quickly disappeared. "Oh, my God, Jax. It's so nice to hear from you. Give me a second. I need to get somewhere with better reception."

"Jax?" Vickie whispered and raised an eyebrow.

Tanya covered the microphone. "My son."

"You named your son Jax?"

"You know, after that biker TV show? I forget the name of it but that was the name of the main character."

"Oh, right, the cute blonde one. I remember."

"Right. Anyway, I'll be in the gym. I'll give you a heads-up when everything goes down."

"Sure." She waved at the woman, happy that she had a chance to have a conversation with her son. The knowledge that she had a kid was buried in the back of her head somewhere, but Vickie had almost forgotten about it. Weird. She would need to up her game of knowing everything about everyone around her. If she didn't, maybe no one would believe in her abilities anymore.

She rolled her shoulders, pulled herself out of her seat, and took a deep breath before she returned to where Elisa was seated. The woman had finished her call and was adding the new information into the software Vickie had developed for their orders. It hadn't been that difficult. During her first stint in college, her professor had let them develop these kinds of programs since they were all the rage for new and upcoming companies or even those that were already established and needed to upgrade.

Of course, she had quit the moment she realized he was taking their work and selling it under his name. It wasn't technically illegal since all the work of the students technically belonged to the faculty, but it was still a slimy, slimy thing to do. She dropped out and spread the word of what the man was doing to the rest of his students. Apparently, stealing from them wasn't the only slimy thing he was into, and it wasn't long before people began to come forward.

It was a mess and enough to get her family off her back about dropping out of college. For a while, anyway.

"What was that about?" Elisa asked and continued to type into the computer while she looked at her companion. The woman was good at that, Vickie realized. It revealed coordination and muscle memory, likely from hours spent typing stories that she needed to work at but that didn't require all her attention.

Their new recruit definitely had skills, she had to admit.

"I...well, Tanya reminded me that you would need to go and visit our suppliers. You are selling their product, after all, and making a killing off it too."

"Yeah. Things may have slowed after the first day, but it's still fairly good."

"Yeah." Vickie violently crushed a surge of jealousy that showed its face again. She wondered if it happened to run in the family. "She said she'll take you out to have a look at their facilities. That will give you a better feel of what you're peddling to those poor unfortunate assholes you've mesmerized with that flirty voice of yours."

"My voice isn't...that flirty. Believe me, I can make it much worse. They like it when you're soft but with a trace of firm to let them know you mean business."

"You know that—"

"Yeah, they probably making as much money off free drinks as we do from their business. Taylor briefed me. It's not the most flattering aspect of the job, honestly, but in the end, we're all working for the same thing. If I can help them fit in better while making money for myself, I don't see how it's a bad thing."

Vickie nodded. It was the same thing she'd told herself when she started with this as well.

"That makes sense. So, Tanya wanted to get you out there sometime this afternoon, so make sure you don't have any big calls waiting for you."

Elisa narrowed her eyes. "Wait...this afternoon... Isn't that when your black ops cousin is coming? Isn't that what Taylor said would happen?"

She pursed her lips. "Huh. I guess you're right. It's interesting how that worked out for you, right?"

It took the woman a few seconds to understand what she meant but finally, a knowing smile slid across her face. "Well, now...I guess it wouldn't be the worst thing in the world if I wasn't here but out on business when she arrived. I'm well aware of the fact that she doesn't like me. I'm not sure why, but I don't want to risk the chance that she might decide I should have gone all the way to the Zoo. Call me crazy, but I don't believe for one minute that she doesn't have the ability to send me there if she wants to."

"She...wouldn't."

Vickie didn't truly believe herself when she said that.

"Right," Elisa muttered. "Well, the good news is I don't have any big calls waiting for me today. Hell, I've already dealt with most of the orders I needed to confirm, and I had a couple of cold calls lined up. Most of the merc teams I was supposed to contact aren't available at the moment, so I'll probably pick them up tomorrow."

The hacker nodded. That was more or less how the job

went, and it was far easier when one wasn't focused on studies or keeping the team alive.

Maybe now that she had less to do on the actual job front, she would be able to focus her efforts a little more. Someone had said she should always whole-ass one thing, not half-ass two things.

She couldn't remember who it was, though.

CHAPTER SIXTEEN

Getting used to this kind of thing seemed like a very bad idea.

Niki had seen task forces have everything thrown at them when the political powers-that-be wanted something done as quickly as possible. Sometimes, those running the task forces let that extra money go to their heads and were left almost crippled when the rug was pulled out from under them. She didn't want to be one of them.

Still, having a dedicated plane to get her to and from different locations was definitely a perk, and one she intended to make full use of until it was inevitably and probably unceremoniously yanked away from her. Jansen and Maxwell both seemed fairly comfortable working on it, so maybe they had a better view of how much she could expect from Speare.

Despite all that, it simply felt trashy to even ask. She would get the job done regardless of the perks that came with it. The only real argument was whether she would be as quick on the draw with the benefits as she would without them. It was therefore her job to make sure they knew that not only were the additional benefits well-used, but they were required if they wanted her to be as effective as she could be.

The plane began to descend and triggered the odd lifting feeling in her stomach. It was weird how being airborne was enough to make her think of Taylor and the man's deathly fear of flying. She tried not to give him too much trouble over it, especially since he had been willing to jump on a plane and fly halfway around the world to save someone's life. He had control of the phobia but it was still there.

The minutes ticked past before the entire plane shuddered when it made contact with the ground. Her body stiffened a little before they slowed to a crawl and began to taxi around the airfield to one of the hangars where the plane would be secured until they needed it again.

The fasten seatbelt sign deactivated, and Niki was the first on her feet. She needed fresh air, the kind that the jet's air-conditioning system couldn't provide.

It was mid-afternoon in Vegas, so the fresh air she could expect was the heavy kind of dry heat that smacked you in the face when you emerged from an air-conditioned environment.

The door opened slowly and she stepped out first. The hangover was long gone and although she still felt a little delicate around her head and in her stomach, she did feel much better. She simply wasn't built to spend her nights drinking anymore. It was a little depressing to think about but it was one of those things she needed to make her peace with.

As she descended the steps from the plane, she could see someone already waiting for them inside the hangar. Her two bodyguards, who followed her quickly, reached for their weapons at the sight of the four-by-four parked in plain view, but she waved them off.

"You do realize we're supposed to protect you here, right?" Maxwell reminded her with his hand still on his weapon.

Niki glared at him. "Yeah. Well, I guess you guys can...I don't know, check the rest of the hangar. If you thought Taylor was a threat to my life, you wouldn't have let me hire him, now would you?"

She gestured again for them to back off and this time, they both relaxed. They should have recognized him, honestly, because they'd seen enough pictures of the man. Both had done their research regarding the team she called in to deal with actual cryptids.

"Jesus," Jansen muttered. "I thought the suit added all that bulk. I honestly didn't think he was that big."

Ah. In that case, she couldn't blame them. She had spent enough time around the man to grow used to his sheer size, despite her making up new nicknames for him whenever she could. With a build like his, he could have elected to play football in any number of positions that called for someone big, powerful, and incredibly athletic.

There was nothing like having someone else meet him for the first time to make her remember the fact that he was a freak of nature.

"Well, the suit does add bulk to the frame, I guess." Still, he looked like he had regained much of the weight lost during his stay at the hospital after getting ass-fucked by a downed helicopter, to quote the man himself. It had been a while since she had seen him at full capacity but this was much closer to it than he had been a couple of weeks before.

He leaned against his vehicle, his arms folded in front of his chest, and waited for them to approach. As they moved beyond the aircraft, he pushed himself away from the four-by-four and removed his sunglasses, tucked them into the chest pocket of his red Hawaiian shirt, and walked forward to meet them.

"Welcome back to Sin City," he said cheerfully. "How long have you guys been gone, anyway? Did you get any work done around the country before you came here to regroup and maybe get a little gambling in before we head out to kill more monsters out there?"

Niki smirked. "Sure, whatever. What are you guys up to while we're out and about, saving the world and looking good doing it?"

"Only running a business. Being the backbone of the American economy."

She slapped him firmly in the chest. "So, did you come out here to pick us up? Because you do know we have our own vehicles out here."

"I'm here to make sure you guys get to the strip mall without incident. Given that you'll give us all this business, I thought it would be fair of me to come down here and greet you in person."

"So you're buttering us up, is that it?"

"Don't take it too hard. We'll work together just fine. If you guys want to pick up those vehicles of yours, we can get going to the shop. I can show you the work we've put into those orders you made."

"Do you have the suits ready?"

"Not really. It takes more than two days to assemble them, but we're well on the way. Bobby and Vickie have put in the hours to get them at least functional so you can try them yourselves."

"So they're functional but not ready?"

"There's a difference between being able to walk around in them and having them combat-ready, yeah," Taylor snapped in response.

Niki nodded and turned to where Jansen and Maxwell completed the procedure to secure the hangar. "You guys grab the SUV and follow. I think I'll ride with Taylor to make sure the money we're spending on McFadden's Mech's isn't a waste."

Both men nodded and jogged to the black SUV in the back of the space as Taylor gestured for her to get into the four-by-four. He climbed into the driver's seat and started the vehicle. The other two followed them out and onto the airstrip, and he led them to the road. They were ten or so miles away from the actual city of Vegas, which gave them time to talk.

Niki wasn't sure what she wanted to talk about, although the silence wasn't exactly uncomfortable. Music played over the speakers and reflected Taylor's enjoyment of heavy metal, although not the thrasher music he usually listened to.

There was that, at least. He looked comfortable enough, kept his gaze on the road, and nodded his head to the music while he mouthed some of the lyrics and maintained a decent speed.

"So," Niki finally said when she settled on a topic she wanted to discuss with him, "you said Vickie and Bobby were working on the suits. What happened to Tanya? And isn't Elisa supposed to help you guys too?"

Her attempt to obscure the real topic she wanted to hear about didn't work out too well. She would never have called herself the most subtle of characters, but she had at least tried to cover her true interest.

Taylor didn't look like he was fooled and gave her a firm look to make sure she knew what she had done before he refocused on the road.

"Tanya mentioned that Elisa needed to go out and have field time at our suppliers' locations. Given that our new employee probably should know a thing or two about what she sells to the good folks out in the Zoo, it was a good idea."

"And you signed off on it, then?"

She wasn't sure if she would like any answer he might have had to offer. If he sent Elisa away, he would have done so for Niki's benefit, and she didn't like anyone holding her hand. If he hadn't signed off on it... Well, he would have wanted to keep the woman around.

"Actually, Bobby was the one who told me about it almost a half-hour after they'd already left," he grumbled. "So while it's a good idea and something we intended to do anyway, the timing is a little suspect. It looks like someone didn't want to be there when you arrived."

"I wonder why," she muttered.

"It might have something to do your threatening

to send her to the Zoo when you first spoke. She still calls you 'that black ops woman' from time to time. You should be happy to have made such an impression on her."

Niki flipped him off, which annoyingly, only earned a grin from him in response. "That's not really my point."

"Then what was your point?"

She considered telling him. Then again, she wasn't sure what about Elisa got on her nerves so much in the first place, so explaining it to someone like Taylor seemed like a terrible idea overall. He would simply mock her for it.

It was, she decided, best to not elaborate. Sometimes, it was best to let sleeping dogs lie.

"Nothing. Never mind."

He eyed her for a few long seconds, and she was afraid that he would insist on learning about what had her unsettled like this. In the end, he turned his attention to the road again.

It wasn't that long a drive before they finally pulled into the shop, but it felt like ages to Niki. He seemed to have gone back to focusing on the road while he nodded to the music, but she felt uncomfortable being this close to him. The fact that she couldn't help herself from trying to catch a glimpse of him through her peripheral vision only made it worse.

Thankfully, once they were inside, it was all business as Bobby and Vickie pulled the three suits out for their new clients to inspect. She recognized the one she had used before, but the other two looked new. Like, straight out of the box new.

"As I said, we have the three suits that were ordered ready and functional but not all of them are exactly combat-ready," Taylor stated once they were all gathered in the shop. "By my standards, for a suit to be properly combat-ready, it needs to be specialized for the pilot who will ride it. I've brought this one up to spec and it's already been used in a combat situation, but we'll have to get the other two ready for the two of you to use."

Niki recalled using the suit. It was easier to work than those she had originally trained with and much better than the one that she had gone into combat with the first time.

Still, it was something to get used to and if Jansen and Maxwell had never piloted one, they would discover that it wasn't quite as instinctual as many people thought it was.

"So, we'll need to have a look at your piloting styles," Taylor continued. "You'll be decked out and walk around in the parking lot, perform basic actions, and get used to the way the suit moves. Bobby will keep track of everything, and he'll also have all the kill switches if you end up doing something that could injure yourself or damage the suit, in that order. We'll do the calibrations in real-time, so if there's anything you're uncomfortable with or would prefer to have, contact Bobby through the comms that will be active. Do you have any questions?"

Jansen raised his hand.

"We're not in a fucking school here. If you have something to say, go ahead and say it," he told him.

The man's hand lowered immediately. "Sorry. I merely wondered when you had the time to put Niki through the paces of determining what her specs for the suits are."

Taylor shrugged. "Not that it matters, but I based it off what I saw of her in the field. When we first started working together, we headed out into the wild to deal with some cryptids. I had my suit and she had a piece of shit the FBI had issued her with. We found a horde of the monsters working from the trees and they attacked us from above. She held her own fairly well, gunned down a number of them, and forced the rest into a kill zone I'd set up for them. Her suit had rockets in it, but she didn't bother to use them for the main fight. Once those that attacked were dead, she found the nest with a clutch of eggs. We debated leaving them for the biologists to have a look at but elected to not risk it and blew them the fuck up. That's the story of how I already knew the calibrations Niki needed for her suit."

Maxwell chuckled. "Yeah, that sounds about right. I seem to remember her doing the same thing but more metaphorically, and it thoroughly tore a couple of CEOs a new one."

"Less metaphorical for that scientist, though," Jansen reminded him. "As I recall, she blew him two new ones. It was a through and through, after all."

Niki smirked but Speare's final words to her robbed the memory of any amusement she might have felt. In a moment of clarity, she realized her bodyguards were essentially followers. They had never experienced what her boss had called the dark side and it was easy for them to revert to casual humor. It left her feeling a little uneasy—something she would have to explore in her own time—and she couldn't help wondering how far their protection duties extended. If they didn't understand the dark side, would they even know when she needed help to get back?

The question left her feeling oddly vulnerable, and she grasped at the now seemingly insignificant memory to pull her out of her spiral of questions. She remembered her first fight with Taylor in a distinctly different way than he did. More importantly, she recalled the fact that she had absolutely no idea that her suit had rockets until he pointed it out after the fighting was over.

Even so, she wouldn't correct him. If that was how he remembered it happening, who was she to say he was wrong? He was the expert, after all.

CHAPTER SEVENTEEN

"Fucking hell," Taylor mumbled and rubbed his temples. "Bobby, see if you can't turn the sensitivity on the arm controls down. Maybe that'll keep Jansen from hitting himself constantly."

"It's...dammit. I have sweat on my face and it's instinct to wipe it off," the man complained as he marched the suit carefully to the part of the parking lot that had been designated as the starting area.

"You have to get past those instincts," Bobby told him through the comms while he reduced the sensitivity on the arms. It wasn't permanent but it would work for the moment.

"It burns like all hell when the sweat gets into the eyes, though," Maxwell pointed out.

"You might want to look into getting a sweatband," Taylor suggested. "There were a couple of guys who swore by using some kind of Vaseline or petroleum jelly to keep the sweat out."

"Vaseline is petroleum jelly," Niki interjected.

"It's one of the name brands, sure, but you don't need to pay for the name," he countered. "There were a couple of guys who used the grease from their suits above the eyes to keep the sweat out too."

"I get the feeling these things get funky-smelling after a while," Maxwell commented. "Kind of like a football helmet if you didn't clean it often enough."

"Well, you best keep your suit clean then," he snapped. "Now, let's run it again."

The two lined up again and this time, pushed forward a little faster. Taylor had immediately seen that Maxwell, the more athletic of the two, had at least some experience with powered exo-suits or perhaps had more of a natural feel for the suits. Jansen was in decent enough shape, but it took a little something more to work his effectively.

He wouldn't say he didn't enjoy putting the two men through their paces but would have preferred Niki to have been in there with them. She needed more practice and seeing her level of skill would give the other two an idea of what they needed to do to advance their abilities.

But she had elected not to join her two comrades. Either she didn't want to be in a suit any more than they did and had the authority to avoid it, or she thought she had enough training.

Or maybe she wanted a different kind of training. Absorbing what he had to show the other two men about working a suit was instructional in its own right.

Then again, that felt like he was playing with his ego. There was nothing he could teach that hadn't been drilled into her by the FBI instructor she had trained with. The guy was probably a better teacher than he was too.

Jansen now did a little better. The elevated power system enabled the suit to do more work. Normally, power consumption would have been an issue but the nuclear power cores were made to last for decades, maybe more, and the housing meant it would take a literal nuclear explosion to get into them.

Or something in the Zoo, he mused. Whatever powered the goop in there would be able to find a way through the insulation of the power cores. That reminded him of the sheer number of suits that had failed inside and what the goop could do with that amount of power.

It was a sobering thought and one he had only allowed himself to think about when he was deep in his cups. Terrorists getting their hands on it was the stuff of nightmares, but he had seen actual nightmares that didn't have nuclear power at their disposal.

"Taylor, are you still with me?"

Bobby needed his attention, and Taylor snapped out of what had been reluctantly pulled into. He had no intention of thinking about that anymore. All the specialists out there had to have thought about that too, and they knew more about the possible consequences than he did.

"Yeah, I'm still here," he responded quickly and looked at the mechanic. "What's up?"

"I assumed you would yell at these bozos over their poor performance or something."

He looked at where Maxwell and Jansen made their way to the starting line again. The sun had begun to set and he could tell that he was starting to lose them. They had been excited and interested in the beginning, had cracked jokes, and taken his advice. But now, he could almost feel the annoyance with themselves starting to creep in and that would turn into resentment at him real fucking fast.

"I'm not a goddamn drill sergeant," Taylor muttered. "You guys have run around enough in those things for now. A day of working out in them won't get you too far."

"But I was starting to have fun," Maxwell muttered as they relaxed against the side of the building. He knew the feeling. Even with the hydraulics turned to one hundred percent, the weight of the suit was still on the pilot's shoulders. It was important to ease it a little when one was still adjusting to it. He recalled his first few hours in the Zoo and how he had leaned on a tree whenever the opportunity presented itself.

"Get those off," he said and moved forward to help them remove them. "Now, I know everyone's so happy about using these, but what none of the games and VR sims talk about is cleaning your suits once you get out. You guys are lucky. All you have is about an hour's worth of sweat to clean. My first time in one of those, I was in the Zoo for almost a week and I needed to clean a week's worth of literal blood, sweat, and tears out of my suit before I turned it in to that motherfucker, so you'd better believe he'll know what to look for if you do it wrong."

Both men laughed, and Niki chuckled too.

"Do you think this is funny?" he asked and tilted his head in a challenge.

She stopped laughing. "Well...yeah."

"Do you think you'll get out of this? I remember the state you left your FBI suit in when you took it off. You didn't even bother to try to clean it. Come on. I won't do it for you. You'll learn how to take it apart and keep it running too."

Her laughter faded but she did as he told her and walked to where Bobby waited to show them exactly what they needed to clean. It was a little gratifying that she attended to the task without offering him any backtalk but it was also a little disappointing. He had grown to enjoy the way she could counter almost everything he had to say with all the vigor of someone who actively hated him.

Was that a thing of the past now? Did she simply not hate him anymore?

No, that sounded ridiculous. She loved Vickie to bits and could still talk the ear off the hacker if she had a mind to. He didn't want that to change, however she felt about him. He still couldn't believe she was even remotely interested in him. Maybe it was more of her learning and coming to terms with being around him.

Something like that.

"This is weird," Niki noted aloud as the trio took the pieces apart and began to clean them under Bobby's instruction. "But interestingly, it's not the dumbest thing I've ever done in my life."

"Careful there, Banks," Jansen warned her. "You sound like you're feeling right at home with this and are trying to find a way to mask it."

"Yeah, well, like it or not, you guys are my tribe now," she pointed out. "And that includes you, Tweedledee, and your brother, Tweedledumbass. It's about time I found out how to fit in better with you guys."

Taylor couldn't help a small smile. Tweedledee and Tweedledumbass did sound a little too creative for Niki to have come up with on her own. He would have to look up the origins of the nicknames.

"Next time we do work on these babies, we'll introduce the weapons." His voice cut smoothly into the chatter and instantly caught the attention of all present. "Oh yes. If you guys think it's difficult to go through the paces while you have to worry about not hitting yourself in the head, imagine what it'll be like when you have to worry about shooting yourself in the foot. Literally. Oh, and then we can talk about when and where it would be best for you to use the rockets that will be mounted on your shoulder."

Both Jansen and Maxwell looked a little confused as well as scared at the concept, but Niki immediately saw through his tough posturing.

"Quit being an asshole," she admonished and punched him in the shoulder. "You won't give these guys weapons before they know how to operate their suits properly. Besides the risks to themselves, their suits, and the population in general if something goes wrong—"

"Bobby will have the kill-switches if something were to go wrong anyway," he protested.

"Besides the risks," she insisted, "you wouldn't dare give them the opportunity to bring your whole shop down on our heads. You love this ugly-ass building way too much to risk it."

Taylor nodded slowly. "That's…uh, a good point. I don't trust you guys to not launch a rocket before we can stop you and knock my whole livelihood down, and I know the DOD won't pay for that shit even if I did bill them for it. Maybe we could take them out to the desert."

"Or we could keep training them to use the suits," Niki

countered. "It took me a solid week of practice when I trained with the FBI to get it right."

His eyebrows shot up and she had to know what was coming. He would bring up the story of her charging through a wall when she had been in training and probably make her regret that she had ever told him about that.

Even so, it felt like a shitty move on his part and while the laughs were certainly warranted, it wasn't his job to make her look bad in front of her team.

"Keep working on those suits," he said instead, patted one of the shoulder pauldrons, and walked away from the group. "I'm going to get my hands on some coffee."

He wandered toward the shop but heard footsteps catching up with him. Taylor turned to where Niki approached hurriedly.

"Do you need coffee too?" he asked and raised an eyebrow.

"No. I mean, yes, there's always time for coffee, but I wanted a quick talk with you."

He gestured for her to follow him, even though that was what she was doing anyway. "What's on your mind? Do you think we should hold their hands and make sure they know we love and support them regardless of how well they do in those suits? You know, I have half a mind to get you to go through the motions with them."

She laughed. "No, nothing like that. I'm a little worried why you're taking it so easy on me lately. First, you give me more credit for the fight in that forest when we first started, and then you missed an easy opportunity to tell them about how trash I was in those suits when I first started. What gives, McFadden?"

"Regarding the fight in the forest, I think I'm giving you about the right amount of credit. You fought well in there and you had my back too. I'd say that since I've been through more battles like that, I'd have better judgment as to what constitutes a good fighter. If you think you were anything but a solid combatant…well, adrenaline is known to play some crazy tricks on the mind."

"And the rockets? Those I didn't know I had until you pointed them out to me?"

Taylor paused and chewed his bottom lip. "Okay, fair enough, I may have misremembered that. Like I said, adrenaline does play crazy tricks on the mind."

"Right. Well, thanks, anyway."

He grinned as they reached the break room and he poured two cups of coffee from the machine and handed her one. "No one will think less of you because of me. I have your back, Banks."

"So, will we talk about how much Vickie will charge for her work in service of her country?"

"What's there to talk about? You already have my invoice for her services."

"And I'll go ahead and guess that you didn't talk to Vickie before vastly overcharging the DOD?"

Taylor shook his head. "She was the one who put those numbers in place based on her previous earnings as well as the amount of work she would have to do. I thought it was an incredibly fair pricing model."

"Yeah, you would, given that you're the one charging."

"And you're not the one paying."

"Well, technically, we're all the ones paying since it comes out of the taxes you and I pay every year."

"Yes, and given that what we're doing is keeping all the taxpayers safe at the expense of my team's safety, I don't know why you're complaining so much."

He turned as Vickie jogged toward them. While he wasn't sure how she knew they were talking about her, he was well beyond the point of questioning the woman's abilities.

"Is she complaining about my rates?" Vickie asked, her head tilted boldly.

"Yeah, you're fucking right I am," Niki snapped. "Your prices are fucking bullshit."

"Well, if you think you can find someone who's better suited for the work and who would be willing to work at reduced rates, I invite you to go ahead and risk the market out there."

Taylor looked at the agent. "She has a good point there."

Bobby and the other two entered the shop and used a forklift to carry the cleaned and ready suits, already in their crates and prepared for transportation. It was one of the first things he'd learned when training to fight in the suits.

"What happened to the friends and family discount?" Niki asked the hacker as the rest of the group appeared to assemble for the negotiation.

"That is the friends and family discount. Do you know how much I could make if I hired my services out to the highest bidder? Hell, do you know how much I made working the phones for Taylor and the company?" Vickie didn't look like she intended to back down, which meant he didn't need to step in for her.

"So, what? This is a monthly salary kind of situation?"

"Do you really expect to call in my services for more than once a month?"

"That could happen."

"Well, in that case, I'll be saving lives more than once a month and deserve to be compensated for it."

Another good point, he thought smugly but remained silent.

Before they could continue the discussion, his phone vibrated in his pocket. He pulled it out and checked the number—or lack thereof—before he raised his hand to stop them from continuing. "Since I assumed there would be a discussion involving this, I took the liberty to bring in a third party to act as a consultant." He pressed to accept the call and put it on speakerphone. "You're on with everyone."

"Consultant?" Niki demanded. "Where the fuck do you get off? Who is this?"

"Good evening, Niki," said the unsettling and calm voice they all had come to recognize.

Her shock wore off quickly. "Desk? Why the fuck are you consulting with Taylor on this?"

"As I am tasked with working with and for both parties in this debate, Taylor thought I was uniquely placed to provide an unbiased perspective on the discussion."

The agent didn't look happy but she clearly had no argument against the AI. Taylor wasn't sure what Desk meant when she said she was uniquely placed, but he wouldn't push against it. She was the one who contacted him and offered to help and had assured him that she would remain neutral in any disagreement between the two women.

Niki turned her attention to Taylor and pointed a finger at him. "You are a devious, conniving motherfucker, Taylor. I'm a little impressed. I didn't think you had something like this in you."

In fairness, he didn't, but he wasn't about to tell her that.

He couldn't understand why she had so much trouble with the pricing model. Vickie would be a vital part of the operation and the pricing to include her wasn't much of a bump compared to what he had charged when she was with the FBI.

Then again, she had complained that his prices were too high then too.

All that aside, he had very little to do with the discussion and left the three of them to negotiate and compromise between themselves.

Vickie seemed to have gained at least some courage when it came to dealing with her cousin, and with Desk's help, they did appear to drive toward something they were all happy with.

"Okay." Niki sighed and rubbed her temples. "Fine, I think I can sell the increase on the task force in bringing you in if you drop your price by fifteen percent. I will be able to contact your university to fund you a twenty-five percent scholarship, and that's for the duration of your time in college. If we consolidate that, you won't be able to renegotiate your pricing model until after you've graduated."

Taylor leaned closer to Jansen and kept his voice low so as to not interrupt the discussion. "So, she's always like this, right?"

The man nodded. "Yeah, basically. She's a little more aggressive with the CEOs and shit but it's probably in her nature to be a negotiator. Speaking of which, I wondered if I could get your advice on some of these operations we've been planning. We have had some input on what to look for from some Zoo-based specialists—"

"So you guys finally contacted Dr. Jacobs. About damn time if you ask me."

"Yes, well, we know what kind of projects to look for but we're still not sure what kind of situation calls for immediate action. You know, emergencies in which drastic measures are truly called for."

Taylor shrugged and the man glanced at his massive shoulders. "Honestly, I'm fine with you torching any lab that experiments with the stuff, and more so with any facility that experiments on live test subjects. Do you have anyone who works with that?"

"Not that we can tell since that's illegal, but we have quite a few ways for people to work around reporting that kind of thing—which is what we need Vickie and the AI for. But in the end, we should probably know about what kind of a timeline we'll be looking at."

"Timeline?" Taylor scratched his beard and thought about it for a second. "As far as I know, most of the monsters were already created as the creatures we were killing. But if they're testing on live animals, you can't expect a long timeline. The goop starts affecting DNA from the moment it interacts with biological material and probably shows stable physical changes in under a week. Of course, those aren't the ones you need to worry about."

"The increased intelligence is one of the more important factors."

"It's one of the later stages—that I've seen, anyway. Like in this situation here...where you see their advanced formative testing is progressing. Of course, Vickie or Desk getting confirmation isn't a bad idea but at that point, you should already be prepared for something to go terribly wrong within days, if not hours."

Jansen nodded, apparently well aware of what happened when something went wrong. Taylor would need to hear that full story.

Both were torn away from their conversation when the two women appeared to wrap up their discussion.

"Fine, I'll take it," Vickie stated finally and shook her cousin's hand. "But the pricing on the invoice won't change until I have it in writing from you and the university that my tuition is lowered by twenty-five percent."

"Agreed," Niki said and shook the hacker's hand firmly. Neither had let anything get too intense during their discussion. Taylor assumed Niki was well aware of the fact that she wouldn't make any of the payments from her pocket, so there was no point in being too harsh about it.

The agent walked to join Taylor and Jansen where they were working.

"I was going over the possibilities we could expect from our future operations," her bodyguard offered by way of explanation. "Given what we faced the last time, I thought it was best to have as much data as we could get our hands on."

She advanced on him, plucked the file he was showing Taylor from his hand, and turned it to show the front while her finger pointed to the bright red stamp there. "You know, I would make some kind of joke about how I'll have to kill you now that you know about these top-secret operations the DOD is running but fuck it. The chances are you'll be dead soon anyway."

"You keep hoping and praying for that to happen," he muttered as a small smirk played across his features.

The agent smiled venomously at him and slapped the folder against Jansen's chest. "I'll need Vickie. Your negotiator—who is a complete and total heartless bitch, by the way—already has the numbers. Send me an invoice every two weeks of work. I'll talk to Jansen and Maxwell later about the suits and I'll get back to you. We will want one each ready to go immediately and maybe we can look at having one more in reserve, just in case...well, you know."

"I do."

"Don't screw me, Taylor." She sounded resigned and tired but like she had begun to relax. "I'm working with a big budget, but don't think I'll simply throw money around. I will expect results from you."

"Don't worry, Niki. I would never...screw you." He made sure she heard the pause.

"You're fucking hilarious. Now, if you'll excuse us, we have to make arrangements for our stay in Vegas. I'll be in touch."

CHAPTER EIGHTEEN

"You know, it's funny," Elisa muttered softly and ran her fingers through her hair as she studied the parts and pieces that had been laid out for their inspection. "I should pick up on what we're looking at. I've been in one of those things and I even managed to survive a combat situation in it, but I still have no clue what we're looking at."

Tanya nodded. "It took me a while to know my ass from my head in one of these for my first few weeks. It took me many long hours working at the shop to get a better idea of what we were looking at. I'm still not sure about most of the stuff. Bobby's worked with it for years and so has Taylor. They both have degrees in mechanical engineering, so expecting to know as much about it as they do in only a few days is a little unrealistic."

The woman was right, of course. She had her degrees but they could not have been more distant from mechanical engineering. Still, she was a fast learner and while machines didn't quite talk to her the same way paperwork did, she would learn more about it if it killed her.

Although hopefully, it wouldn't.

"So, what do you think about this job so far?" her companion asked as one of the warehouse workers showed them out of the area where the parts and pieces were stored and into a visitor's center. "I'm not sure I was put through the paces like you were when I started here. Of course, I asked Taylor for the job and he was willing to bring me in at the ground level, where I worked and learned on the job. He let me crash at the strip mall until I found my apartment. You, on the other hand, were thrown into the deep end and had to deal with a couple of sharks along the way too."

Elisa laughed softly as they were offered coffee. She could tell that the people who ran the business were already working way past their closing hours, and the fact that they had obviously remained open to allow one of their smaller clients to have a look at their inventory was probably not the most exciting thing in their day.

She and Tanya were being shown the way out as slowly and as subtly as possible. The fact that the lights of the warehouse began to go out as the two women made their way to the exit validated her suspicions.

"Sharks is right," Elisa whispered as they stepped outside and walked to their car. "I didn't think Banks would be a problem once I was done trying to paint Taylor as a casino robber, but I think she hates me more now than she did before. I simply don't understand why."

"I've given up trying to understand what runs that family crazy the way it does. Vickie, Niki, and her sister

Jennie are all nuts. They're all smart enough to have developed into a supervillain family that could go up against dudes dressed as bats if they wanted to but elected to be morally sound instead. Jennie, as far as I can tell, was actually in the Zoo herself and had her ass dragged out of a metaphorical and yet terrifyingly literal fire by none other than Taylor McFadden. I think that was enough of a connection for them to stay in touch or something. I never really understood that particular dynamic. Anyway, you don't... Well, it's not a good idea to not worry about Niki, but if she ever comes after you, you'll be awake, facing her, and you'll be armed."

She narrowed her eyes as she stepped into the shotgun seat next to Tanya. "You know, amazingly, that doesn't make me feel better. Even if I was armed and ready for her, I still don't think I would ever stand a chance. I don't know if you've realized this, but I have never actually met her face to face and even I know she's scary. I'll go ahead and stay well, well away from her."

The woman nodded. "That's a good call. And it's really what we've done here, although..." She paused and looked at her phone before she started the car. "Vickie tells me that we're clear. Niki has left for the night and we should do the same. It's a little late for us to head to the office, but I guess we can go somewhere else. I don't want to say you might want to go out and get a drink, but..."

"You think we should go out and get a drink." Elisa picked up where Tanya's voice trailed off. "I do need a drink. I need many drinks. I need...any number of things, but a drink can be the start of it all. Do you have a place in mind?"

"I'm kind of new to Vegas myself," her companion said with a small shrug. "But I know a few places. Maybe we can find a couple of new ones if these don't pan out."

"It sounds like a night of fun to me."

Niki took a deep breath and looked around the room a few times before she focused her attention on the drink in front of her. The temptation to order a beer had been almost too much to resist, but she had stuck with a glass of cranberry juice for the moment.

Jansen and Maxwell had similarly stuck to the non-alcoholic drinks and had found a place to sit on the other side of the room, where they chatted like they were old friends catching up. She hadn't seen them without the suits, weapons, and the stiffness that came from their job. Hell, they probably were old friends but she had never thought to ask them about it. They had worked together long enough to have developed a relationship that extended beyond their work life.

She would have to talk to them someday and not only about their work. Maybe they didn't want to be her friend but accepting the fact that they had lives beyond what they did for a living would probably be necessary if she wanted them to keep working with her.

And she did. Jansen and Maxwell were both the kind of men she wanted to have on her team. They were loyal, talented, productive, and creative. Well, maybe Maxwell was less creative than his partner, but he more than made up for it with his other talents.

Another member of her team was also present, of course. He was hard to miss, even in the dark environment of the bar they were in. It wasn't exactly her kind of dive but it did seem like his.

The massive ginger made his way through the crowd and people stepped instinctively out of his way in the narrower places. He looked at home in the venue, and he carried a large mug of beer as he slid into the booth she was in and sat across from her.

"So," Taylor said and paused to take a long sip of his beer before he continued. "I've heard no word from you for three days. Not even a peep. And then a call to come to a trucker dive outside Vegas with no clue about what you're up to and what I should expect, and whether I should come armed or ready for a fight against cryptid bastards. The fact that you called me to a bar and not a lab in the middle of nowhere was a hint but still, a heads-up would have been nice."

"I'm sure it would have been," Niki replied as she traced her fingers over her glass and picked up a few beads of condensation along the way. "But I needed to keep a low profile on this. There are people who could have picked up some trace of a scent of where you were going and tried to create a problem."

"I'm not in touch with Marino anymore. You know that."

"I don't, actually. Your relationship with the mother-fucker has always been nebulous at best. Think about it. You currently have an employee who you saved from his grasp by telling him you would handle her. I don't know what you owe him. And more importantly, I don't know what he thinks you owe him. Therefore, the less I shared over an unsecured line, the better."

"I thought that was what you needed Vickie for. I thought it was why you had her sequestered for the past few days."

"Vickie's been busy, so again, this was the simpler solution. Now, do you want to shoot the shit here all night or do you want me to tell you why I needed your help out here tonight?"

Taylor gestured for her to continue as he took another sip.

Niki leaned closer and kept her voice as low as possible while still audible to the man across from her. "Like I said, Vickie's been busy and picked up on one of the goop distributors that had a shipment go missing. She kept working to find out where it went and tracked it to a local gang. They have someone working at the factory. This is where they tend to operate from and if Vickie's right—and I've stopped questioning her by now—they're looking to unload it tonight. Oh, speaking of which, she wants me to give you this."

She pushed a small device across the table to him and gestured to her ear. It was an odd sensation having Vickie in her ear like that, but it was better to be in constant contact with her than not.

"Good evening, Niki, Taylor, Tweedledee, and Tweedledumbass."

"We have names, you know," Jansen pointed out, still speaking like he was talking to Maxwell.

"Sure, but who has the time to remember them?" the hacker asked. "I sure as hell don't. Okay, Taylor, I've had the two set up cameras all over this place to give me a bird's eye view of proceedings. Can you imagine, the owner didn't even bother to install cameras? Given how many criminals frequent his establishment, I think I should turn the system over to him once I'm finished with it."

"I'm sure he'll appreciate it." From the hacker's viewpoint, Taylor looked like he was fighting a grin and Niki couldn't help but grin herself. It was nice to see the two of them bonding so well.

"You know, watching you guys like this, it feels like I'm following the world's slowest-moving spy thriller. Or maybe starring in it. If this were a movie, do you think I would have some kind of quirky thing about me? Like, would I be addicted to orange soda or be chewing something?"

"I'm really happy you're not chewing on something right now," Niki noted. "Nothing's more annoying than having that sound in your ear."

"I'd say having some dumbasses selling Zoo goop as...I guess, some kind of meth, is much more annoying."

The agent shook her head. "I stand by what I said."

"Of course you do," Vickie murmured.

"What was that?" Niki asked.

"I said you have bogeys incoming. The guys with the gang tats heading to the bar now."

Taylor didn't shift his gaze away from the beer in front of him. He was no spy but he knew better than to look immediately the moment the target of their investigation wandered in. His companion paused for a few seconds and listened to what was happening in the bar. It wasn't long before someone raised their voice and slammed what sounded like shot glasses on the countertop. The noise gave her an excuse to turn to investigate without giving away the fact that she had someone with eyes and ears all over the venue.

Four of them—all wearing tank tops to show off the long-sleeve tattoos they wore, had approached the bar. They had ordered a line of shots, went through them at a fairly impressive pace, and were already halfway finished. She took a deep breath as she faced Taylor again.

"Someone's celebrating," she whispered and took a sip of her cranberry juice. "Do you think they've already unloaded the merchandise?"

"Nope, probably not," Vickie responded. "I've tracked their movements all around town. They have the merchandise on them and checked it periodically. In fact, they pulled it out and looked at it before they came inside. If they plan to sell it, they'll do it here."

Taylor nudged her arm gently and drew Niki's attention to three men who stepped inside. They didn't have the same gang tattoos as the other four but the expensive, flashy suits were more than enough of an indicator of their illegal affiliations.

"Vickie, what can you tell me about the three guys who just came in?" the agent asked.

"Oh, they're definitely with our shot-drinkers," the hacker replied and now sounded like she was chewing on something. "The guy at the front with the three gold rings and the earrings is Hector Chavez. He's Venezuelan and he's here on a work visa... It looks like he works at an import company. I'm sure he only imports...what does Venezuela export?"

"Crude petroleum, for the most part," Niki replied. "Although I doubt he has anything to do with that. I'd guess something along the lines of recreational pharmaceuticals?"

"Give the woman a candy bar," Vickie replied. "Wait... hold on, who is he?"

"Who?"

"The guy on the left with the watch and the ring in his eyebrow. I have his facial information and he has a prison record, but I find no traces of his existence until about five years ago."

"Fake ID?" Taylor asked. "Who would come up with a fake ID to infiltrate a South American drug ring?"

"He's undercover," Niki asserted immediately. "He's a police officer. Can you look his face up in the Vegas PD database for undercover officers?"

"Yeah, I'm sure I can squeeze that in during lunch. It might take a while, though. They've wrapped that part of their system up really well."

"Okay, this is what you do. I'm done with waiting for Speare or whoever to get their asses moving on this. Get hold of Desk. If anyone can get in, she can."

"Desk? Why?" The hacker sounded affronted and all signs of chewing ceased.

"Because I said so, dammit."

"But—"

"No buts, Vickie. She can get in there—better yet, tell her to take you in there. It's time you learned to work with her anyway."

"Well, excuse me. If you had Desk tucked up your little sneaky sleeve, what the fuck did you need me for?"

The sullenness in Vickie's tone was evident behind the snark.

"Look, this isn't the time to get into this. When we're done here, get hold of her and get that information. I need to add this guy to our list of interesting people who might or might not have intel on black market goop. We can fight about your hurt feelings once we've dealt with what's in our faces right now. This is not the time for your hacker hissy fit, so suck it up, get hold of Desk when you need to, and do what you have to do."

"Fine. But we will discuss this."

"Yes, we will," Niki retorted. "And until then, remember who the boss is."

Taylor ignored the silence that followed from Vickie and looked at Niki. "What do you want to do?"

"We can't wait for the police to not realize this isn't meth," she mumbled, her voice pitched low. "Or worse, let this sale slide because they want bigger fish. That was what the FBI always did when I was around. We need to take this stuff off the market."

"Unless you're suggesting we buy it from them..." He looked around to make sure no one was eavesdropping before he continued. "They won't simply give that shit away. What did you have in mind?"

"I thought you could start a brawl with the guys and distract them, which would then allow me to pick it up without being the center of attention."

He took another long sip of his beer. "And you guys would have my back, right? I won't spend the night in prison over working for you."

"We'll have your back and should there be any problems

with the authorities, I'm fairly sure a quick flash of my DOD badge would ensure that you don't spend any time behind bars. We could probably use some classified information bullshit to keep anything off your permanent record too."

"Huh." He grunted and studied her suspiciously. "I didn't know the DOD had badges."

"I guess you never had any trouble with the military police?"

"Not really. There were a couple of them at the Zoo US base, but they were easy to identify since they wore those thick black armbands if they were ever in uniform."

That made sense, so she simply shrugged.

Taylor finished his beer quickly and stood before she could say anything else. He was committed and ready to get into a fight, she had to give him that.

"If I didn't know better, I'd say Taylor is aching to get into a fight," Vickie said, the prospect of action apparently a rapid cure for the sulks. "And yes, I know he can still hear me but I know he can't respond so I'll keep going. How do you think he'll—oh, here we go."

She really did sound like she watched a movie from her little station. Niki didn't want to tell her to stop enjoying herself but at the same time, it felt like she didn't realize the danger Taylor was putting himself in.

Then again, for a guy who faced off against alien monsters, humans weren't particularly terrifying.

"Are you boys celebrating something?" she heard him ask over the comms. "Do you need someone to buy your drinks for you too?"

"Fuck off, asshole," the leader of the group snapped and

shook his head. "This is a private party."

"Whoa, hold the fuck up. I'm only trying to be nice here. There's no need to get lost up all your collective assholes."

She didn't want to tell him what to do, but it was interesting to see that he had chosen the nice route into a fight.

Niki turned as one of the men placed a hand on Taylor's shoulder and tried to push him back, but the hulking ginger didn't budge. He looked at the man's hand.

"Get your hand off me," he stated, picked the hand up despite the man's resistance, and twisted it away.

The others were quick to respond and Niki could see that he had already played the rest of the fight out in his head. The man closest was the largest of the group, probably brought along as muscle. Taylor leaned toward him and she flinched when his head made impact with the gang member's nose. The crunch was audible from the other side of the room.

"Shit, we should probably get involved, right?" she asked. Jansen and Maxwell stood casually and wandered closer to see if they could do anything to help.

Taylor had already targeted the third gang member while he continued to twist the arm of the first one. The man screamed and tried to pull himself free, but his captor remained unrelenting. He blocked a haymaker and brought his knee up, aiming between the man's legs, but the gangster jumped away and attempted to throw another strike. Taylor was faster and yanked the one he still had a hold on forward to twist him into the path of his comrade's fist.

It was a powerful blow and the first man fell.

Only two men remained standing, and both had begun to question whether they were on the right side of the fight, especially as the rest of the bar patrons now started to react to the confrontation.

Niki could see the other three—the new arrivals in the painfully bright suits—react as well. Two of them advanced on Taylor as they slid their hands inside their coats for what she assumed were weapons. She readied herself to draw her sidearm, but one of the men backed away with a phone in hand.

She knew who he would call but she didn't want any police present.

Before he could use the device, she caught the man by the shoulder and spun him so he could see the badge inside her jacket.

"Get out of here," she warned in a whisper. "And whatever you do, don't call the cops."

He looked confused but after another glance at the badge, he nodded and retreated from the scene. She would have to deal with it later and slipped her card into the man's pocket before she turned away to see what was happening with the fight. Hopefully, he'd call her but if not, Desk and Vickie would trace him soon enough.

Taylor handled himself with impressive ease. He threw his arm back and caught the Venezuelan closest to him on the jaw with his elbow.

The second had already drawn his weapon, but Jansen intervened quickly, locked his hands around the man's wrist, and twisted the pistol loose. Maxwell stepped behind the other two who still debated whether the fight was worth their trouble, caught both by the sides of their heads, and pounded them together. Neither showed any kind of reaction before they collapsed.

The last man was flipped smoothly by Jansen and thumped into one of the bar stools before he sprawled unconscious without so much as a whimper. He and Maxwell hurried to zip tie the disabled men and check that none required urgent medical attention.

Taylor glanced at Niki, who was already searching the clothes of the fallen before she retrieved a couple of opaque vials from one of the men's pockets.

"Is this what we're looking for, Vickie?" she asked and held them up to the nearest camera.

"Yep, that's it," the hacker replied. "Nice work, although it's not quite what I would have gone with. Maybe pick-pocketing or you pretending to seduce one of the scum-bags would have been a little less attention-grabbing."

"Sure," the agent replied but froze when she heard the familiar sound of a shotgun being cocked behind her.

"Get the hell out of my bar," the bartender told them belligerently and seemed both willing and able to use the pump-action shotgun. It was his turn to freeze, however, when he turned to see three pistol barrels aimed at his head.

"Put it down," Taylor warned.

He nodded. "Sure. Whatever. Uh...take what you want."

"We're not here to rob you, man." Taylor retrieved his wallet and removed a few bills, which he placed on the bar top. "This should cover the damages. We'll take care of these guys. If anyone asks you what happened to them—"

"I wasn't here tonight." The bartender completed his sentence with a deadpan expression.

"Good man."

CHAPTER NINETEEN

The proprietor's assurance of his future silence left little more to be said.

Taylor helped Jansen and Maxwell carry the unconscious and injured gang members out to the SUVs. A few of them had already begun to come to although not sufficiently to pose a problem. Niki was on the phone, likely arranging for them to be transferred to where they could be interrogated as to who had provided them with the goop and what they intended to do with it.

The fact that she had the power to do that was still a little terrifying, and Taylor wondered if he would end up at some black site or another if she ever made that call.

He scowled and pushed the last of the men into the SUV. Their recovery was slow and they would have one hell of a headache once they regained full consciousness. Those who remained unconscious would probably need medical attention when they came to—if they came to.

The agent finished her phone call and turned to where Taylor, Jansen, and Maxwell stood near the SUV.

"Well, I had a nice little chat with Speare," she told them. "He wasn't happy that the goop is apparently available on the black market these days, so he'll take these guys himself to see where they get their supply from."

"Won't that be heaps of fun for them?" Taylor muttered and regarded them with a smirk. "So, will we escort them to this black site?"

"No such luck," Niki grumbled. "We have another mission ahead of us."

He narrowed his eyes. "We as in…"

"Yeah, you and your team. Bobby's probably still in the office, right?"

"If he isn't, he could probably rush over there quickly. Where should I tell him to bring our suits?"

"To the airstrip—the one you met us at. We'll go there now."

"What about the idiots in the back?" he asked.

"Speare already has someone waiting for us there so we'll turn them over. It would seem this is something of an emergency."

"Should I go with you guys?" Vickie asked into their earbuds.

"No, I think you can still work with us from where you are now," Niki replied quickly. "Besides, you'll be safer there than where we're going. We can set repeaters up on location if you need them."

"I think I will need them."

"Besides, we won't go that far. Washington state, not city, so if we need you on-site—"

"I think I'm good here. I'm a brave bitch but I'm not that brave. I still need to start my training with the suits and until that happens, I'll be more than happy to hang out here, thanks. Assuming you guys don't need me to save your lives or something, of course, in which case... Maybe don't put all your eggs in that particular basket."

Taylor chuckled, pulled his phone out, and dialed Bobby's number.

It rang only three times before the call was answered. "Hey, Taylor. Do you need something? We were about to close shop here."

"You might want to hold off on that."

A beat passed before the mechanic spoke again. "We have a job?"

"Do we ever. And apparently, it's some kind of emergency. How soon do you think you can get the suits loaded on Liz and drive her to the airstrip?"

"The...airstrip."

"Right. The one Niki likes to work out of. How soon can you and Tanya get out there?"

An extended pause followed and Taylor assumed Bobby was having a hasty discussion with Tanya before he returned. "We can probably get there in an hour...maybe, depending on traffic."

"Well, sooner would be better, Bobby. Thanks for taking this on such short notice."

"I assume you're on short notice too. And...well, I'm paid much more for these jobs than I would be for working in the shop. As it turns out, I'm working my way toward some fairly big expenses in the near future. I'll see you there."

"See you then."

Taylor hung up. The man's mention of upcoming

expenditures did call for follow-up, but that would have to come later as Niki was already motioning for them to mount up. Maxwell would travel with her and keep an eye on the prisoners, which meant Taylor would give Jansen a ride. He gestured for the man to join him as they mounted up.

"You certainly know how to get into a barroom brawl, I'll tell you something," the bodyguard noted as they accelerated after Niki, who drove like a bat out of hell. "How did you know that being nice would get them in a fighting mood?"

"Like you said, I know how to get into a fight. They're not pros and are probably using from their own supply. They were hyped up and full of adrenaline and showed all the signs of paranoia. Someone being nice to them in that state triggers a response they usually manifest when police interrogate them and play good cop, bad cop. They get aggressive. If you insist, they get violent. It's simple, honestly."

Jansen nodded. "I was in intelligence for a while, but you don't understand the kind of shit that comes with interacting with people unless you…you know, interact with people. It's not the kind of thing you think about."

"Honestly, I didn't think about it either. It was mostly instinct and now that it's passed and the adrenaline is gone from my system, I can rationalize the shit my brain worked on at the time. It's not something I usually talk about but hey, being stuck in a car with someone who wants to hear it does help a little."

The man smirked, leaned back in his seat, and stretched gently. "Well, you've learned to trust your instincts, and I assume that comes with being able to rationalize and understand your own behavior. I wouldn't have expected you to do that but it makes sense."

Taylor shrugged. There wasn't much explaining to be done for a person like him. He did like to rationalize his own behavior.

Jansen had no further questions, and when Niki picked up the pace, he was glad all he had to focus on was the driving.

A handful of other SUVs waited for them at the hangar, as well as a group of men in suits who looked very aggressively like they tried to bring the idea of the Men in Black to life.

And given what they were there for, it did seem quite appropriate.

Niki had already exited her vehicle and now hauled their prisoners out. All appeared to be at least somewhat conscious, although a few still looked a little woozy from the experience. Taylor fortunately didn't have to be involved, especially since he was responsible for the condition of at least half of them.

Thankfully, the people Speare had sent were not interested in hanging around for a chat. The prisoners were transferred to the new SUVs and within minutes, the whole group accelerated out of the hangar.

"Talkative bunch, aren't they?" Taylor quipped. A message from Bobby said that he, Tanya, and the suits were ten minutes away, which gave the pilot and crew enough time to get the plane prepped and ready for departure. They looked like they had already been working on it since before the group arrived.

"People who make a living out of making people disappear and forcing them to divulge their deepest darkest secrets aren't the type to stick around for a cup of tea and a chat," Niki pointed out. "Where's the rest of your team?"

"They're ten minutes out. We should leave on schedule. It gives us about the right amount of time for us to talk about what we'll face out there."

She took a deep breath. "I think that would be better done with the whole team present. I'd hate to have to explain this shit twice."

"You don't know yet either, do you?"

"Well, I'm still getting all the details. It's an ongoing situation and we'll only get everything in hand once we're in the air."

She made a good point, and he folded his arms in front of his chest and leaned against the four-by-four. He kept his gaze on the road leading up to the hangar until he could see the elevated beams as Liz brought them up close. One of the airport workers was already bringing a small forklift closer, ready to carry the crates to the plane.

Bobby and Tanya disembarked quickly, and Niki gestured sharply for them to board the plane.

"What's going on?" the mechanic asked. "Will the cars be safe here?"

"Security here is about as good as you'll find in any of the casinos," Niki assured him.

"Yeah. You do remember that we robbed a casino, right?" Tanya reminded her.

"Well, unless you know of another team wandering around stealing shit in mech suits, I don't think we have anything to worry about. I'll lay out the mission plan on the plane. Come on!"

They all boarded and it wasn't long until Taylor found himself clutching the arms of his seat as the plane picked up speed down the runway until it began to gain altitude as well.

The fact that Niki didn't make any comments about his fear of flying was a little worrying. There weren't many things that kept her from taking her shots at him.

Once they reached cruising altitude and the seatbelt signs went off, the agent pushed to her feet, retrieved her laptop, and connected it to the TV, likely preparing a presentation for them.

"I'm sorry about the urgency of the mission but a situation is developing near Kennewick and we needed all hands on deck for this one. Vickie will join us from afar, and we'll need people to head in there to handle it. Three hours ago, an alert came from a laboratory seventy miles outside of the city."

"Let me guess, a containment breach?" Tanya queried.

"Bingo. They sent a couple of reports in on what might have broken out, but the facility has since gone dark. The military is already being mobilized to establish a perimeter. Apparently, they've already had a couple of sightings and a fair amount of shooting but no confirmed kills. The military in the area isn't equipped to deal with an infestation, which is why you need to head in there and clear it. Understood?"

This was more his speed. Straightforward cutting monsters down was preferable to playing with humans who didn't know that working with goop was a dangerous idea.

It wasn't a long flight, fortunately. In a little under two hours, the plane tilted into its descent and completed the landing without incident a few minutes later. Taylor only realized he was wound up tight once the aircraft came to a halt and he forced himself to relax.

They were far, far away from the end of the night, though, so the relaxation was merely the preparation for combat kind.

"It'll be late," Taylor told the team as the suits were unloaded. "And dark. Hunting in these kinds of conditions will be dangerous. Thankfully, the suits are equipped for that. If you turn on the night vision and motion sensor suite in the HUD, you'll be furnished with a full view of your surroundings within a hundred meters. You won't be able to see much beyond that, but the chances are you wouldn't anyway. Let's get rolling."

The three teammates pulled their suits on quickly as their transport rolled in to take them to the area.

Niki wouldn't join them, it seemed, although more transports had begun to arrive, likely to escort her, Jansen, Maxwell, and their suits to the same place. His team was obviously needed as a first response unit.

After almost a half-hour, the driver drew the vehicle to a halt. Groups of armed men were busy setting up defensive positions around them.

"This is the edge of the perimeter we set up," the driver shouted as they disembarked. "You can see the lab a little farther ahead. We've tried to press forward, but every advance has had casualties from…uh, unknown assailants.

We were advised to hold our positions, secure the perimeter, and await further orders. I guess you guys are it. So far, there haven't been any attempts to breach our line, but I guess it's only a matter of time."

"It's probably best that we go in alone, Sergeant. We'll be in touch."

Taylor settled into his suit and turned the vision on to help him have a better view of their surroundings. Movement was difficult to pin down since there were also normal animals in the forest around the area. He motioned for the group to advance, pulled the assault rifle from his shoulder, and readied both the weapon and himself.

Bobby and Tanya were probably going through the same thing, but they expected him to take the lead.

As he moved forward cautiously, he acknowledged inwardly that the situation didn't make sense. Something, he thought warily, didn't sound right.

Unfortunately, he couldn't identify it and decided he wouldn't let it steal his focus.

"Up top," Bobby warned. He shifted his aim to where he could see movement. Small creatures above caught his eye but they looked like squirrels.

"Nothing."

"Not there," Bobby responded and highlighted a position with his HUD. "There!"

Taylor swiveled, chose his target, and pulled the trigger without so much as waiting until he had locked on. His teammate knew what to look for, and he knew to trust him.

A three-round burst cut into the trees above them and

something dropped from the leafy canopy. Even in the adverse conditions, he knew it was not a branch.

They advanced on it, and Taylor identified all the markers that confirmed that the creature was not one that occurred naturally. The carapace covering the skull was all he needed to see.

"Leave a marker here for someone to pick it up," he instructed and left Tanya to put a small GPS device beside the body so Niki could locate it.

"Are all these monsters that creepy?" Vickie asked through their comms.

Taylor thought about it for a few seconds and shook his head. "No. Not all of them."

CHAPTER TWENTY

"I think that's the last of them," Tanya said and looked around. "Do you guys have anything on your sensors?"

Taylor shook his head. "Nothing. Not so far, at least. I think we can send word to the rest of the perimeter that it's safe to pull in closer. I don't think they'll have the time later."

"You don't think this is the last of them." Bobby said it as a statement rather than a question like he had his doubts.

"No, not the last of them. But from the looks of things, I'd say we're dealing with the last of those that managed to escape the lab. The rest were probably sealed in."

"Probably?"

He took a deep breath. "We have to start somewhere."

His HUD pinged to alert them that Niki had connected with the comm channel.

"Are we clear to advance?" she asked.

"As far as we can tell, the path to the lab is clear. How have things worked out for you?"

"The usual. I had the research director come in and talk about how they needed to save all their company secrets. Shit like that."

"I'm sure you told him very delicately to shove his company secrets into an area that is humid and lacks any easy access to sunshine?"

"Yeah, I told him to shove it up his ass. Once that was out of the way, he was kind of helpful. The security system inside the lab is unique, developed to counter the fact that they were dealing with creatures being tested with Zoo goop."

Taylor sighed. "Yeah, right. Where have we heard that before?"

"In this case, it's good. The facility was sealed almost immediately. The breakout was intense but it seems the whole lab is sectioned off and can be sealed in case of emergency. Apparently, in the last communications from inside, they received confirmation that the staff were able to isolate themselves from the monsters. It means we can still save them."

He looked at the building. If it was sealed and there were people inside, tough decisions needed to be made.

"Niki, you know I want to save as many people as we can, but you have to understand that we won't simply open it without careful assessment. If there's a risk that the creatures will escape and make this whole nightmare even worse, those people will not be a priority."

There was a moment of silence between them, and he knew she was thinking about what he had said. She had to know he was right about this.

"Sure," she said finally, her tone stiff and sharp. "But we'll still try to save them. The priority might be to keep that shit contained but we will also attempt to get the people inside out. Understood?"

He nodded. "That's what we're here for. Our preferred course of action is to go in and rescue people. I know that. But if we can't get those people out safely without the risk of letting the monsters out, you'll have to keep the lab sealed and bomb the fuck out of it. Do you understand?"

"You won't pull this shit again, Taylor," she snapped. "We won't have this conversation again either because you will not do your whole self-sacrificing bullshit."

"It's not about sacrifice, Niki. It's about priorities—lives saved. Tell me you understand that."

Niki didn't answer for a few long seconds. "I understand. The greater good."

"Exactly. Now get the people to move in and tell them to be careful. There might be more creatures lurking that we didn't take care of."

Bobby and Tanya watched him closely as he closed the comms with the agent.

"So, we go in there," Bobby stated gruffly.

"Yep."

"With an unknown number of monsters and critters in there waiting for us and no assurance that we'll be evacuated even if we did reach the people inside and get them out?"

Taylor nodded slowly.

"What are we waiting for?" Tanya asked carelessly.

He knew what he heard in her voice, however. She tried

to play it off as being flippant but she sounded terrified. Or maybe that was what he needed to tell himself because it made his next decision easier.

"Not you," he said firmly. "We need someone here in case there are more creatures out and about. Bobby and I will be able to make it work once we're inside."

The mechanic looked at him with an easily recognizable expression of gratitude. Tanya was silent for a few seconds but she finally nodded.

"If you let Bobby get hurt, I'll fucking kill you, Taylor," she stated.

"I'll hand you the gun. Now, let's go."

The two men advanced on the lab in silence. Taylor found the lock that was meant to seal the building and pulled it. After a few seconds during which he expected the main doors to open, he realized that only a small entrance on the side had been unlocked.

"It'll seal us in when we close it," he realized and let Bobby enter first. "Once we're inside, it'll be the decision of the people out here to let us out again."

"Yeah, I get that. And…thanks. I know that couldn't have been an easy decision to make but I appreciate you keeping her out of this. I have a feeling this situation will be more than what we've seen before."

"I have the same feeling. And you can thank me by not getting hurt. I'd hate to have to hand Tanya the gun she'll shoot me with. That feels like the kind of thing people would mock me over in whatever the hell kind of afterlife I've earned myself."

Bobby grinned. "Good point. And yeah, I intended to

try to keep myself from injury for personal reasons, but now that I know your status with those in the afterlife is at risk, I'll be sure to be extra careful."

"Yeah, you do that. Let's go."

Taylor didn't know what he'd expected from the facility. By virtue of their nefarious activities, he always somehow imagined that each one would be borderline decrepit and on the verge of falling to pieces. While some were better than others, they had reached this one early enough to have avoided the inevitable damage in the ground-level areas. All the lights were on and the floors were still a pristine white, exactly what he had come to expect from a lab. Even the glass walls were still intact.

The only signs that anything had happened were a couple of red flashing lights and small pools of liquid splattered across the walls and the floor. Tracks through them moved into the building.

"I guess all the people didn't get to safety," Taylor muttered.

"Fucking containment breaches. Why is it always a containment breach? Do these people not know what they're dealing with?" Bobby sounded affronted

"They don't, that's true enough, but they put in a ton of security based on the assumption that they were merely dealing with crazed monsters. They don't realize that the animals are a symptom. It's the…goop or whatever the hell the real name for it is. There's something about it—like it's intelligent and it wants to get out."

"That's a comforting thought."

He couldn't help but agree with the sarcasm in the

statement, not the words themselves. "Vickie, do you want us to plug anything in? We'll need a good idea of where we're headed if we're going to locate any possible survivors. They're hopefully still alive and still safely confined."

"Thanks, but the repeaters Niki is currently putting in give me more than enough access to the area. She also told me you guys need to try to rescue potential survivors who are still in the facility. Seriously, the first mission I run with you guys and it ends up being a fucking escort mission."

Bobby laughed aloud and Taylor looked at him.

"What? What's a fucking escort mission?"

"Oh." The mechanic grunted and his laughter ceased instantly. "I've spent a fair amount of time with Vickie, so that made some sense to me, at least."

"It means a mission where you need to escort people, also known as the worst missions in gaming history," Vickie explained. "Jesus H. Fucking Christ, Taylor—"

"Which is the guy's full name, by the way," he interjected.

"You need to pay attention when I ramble about shit, Taylor. I wouldn't have to explain anything to you if you paid attention. Seriously, this would save so much time as I wouldn't have to explain my massive wealth of pop culture knowledge to you."

"Okay, but if there's any stopping point between here and you getting us those blueprints…"

Vickie sighed. "Ugh, fine, but don't come running to me when you encounter someone who expects you to know something about the world around you and you're left standing with your jaw slack and nothing else to show for your presence there. I'm uploading the blueprints now. I'll check the rest of the facility too since they do have scanners in place, so I'll be able to highlight the locations where the survivors might still be hiding."

If Vickie was honest with herself, when she'd thought about doing this kind of work—helping Taylor, Bobby, and Tanya to kill monsters and shit—she hadn't seen it going like this.

In retrospect, she hadn't known what kind of expectations to have but she was sure it wasn't supposed to be like this. The ideal ran along the lines of her tapping her computer while her brilliantly-designed software worked its magic. With it, she could help them out of tight situations, open doors that were firmly locked, and maybe even kill a couple of monsters from the safety of her desk. Perhaps she could find a way to drain a room of oxygen or something like that. The story of the lab and the creature that died but didn't had captured her imagination.

Now, however, she studied blueprints, followed the directions, and hoped the oddly malfunctioning scanners were able to identify life signs of people who had been caught in a death trap of their own devising.

"Okay, the facility was built with a long list of directions in case anything went wrong," Vickie explained while Taylor and Bobby moved through the building. "You know, if you have to build a lab with warning signs encoded into it, you might not want to build it in the first place. Go out and build a hospital instead."

"Vickie!"

"Dammit, hakuna your tatas. Right. The building was built with the possibility that something might break out in mind. All the people working there were supposed to undergo drills and were taught to bolt into secured areas of the building. These are sealed off, easy to access, and built like vaults. I'll send you the locations now."

It wouldn't be easy to access them, of course. The one at the top of the facility was empty and hadn't been activated. A handful of others were, but it was difficult to tell which of them had people inside.

"Each of the safe rooms has to be triggered from the inside to be sealed. I'm sending you the locations of the rooms that were sealed but you should be warned that the people who triggered them might not have survived."

"How do you mean?" Taylor asked.

Vickie took a deep breath. There was something unsettling about watching the creatures at work and seeing them charging into the safe rooms that hadn't been sealed was difficult to watch. She couldn't see what was happening inside, but her imagination filled in all the blanks.

"Some of them were sealed inside with the monsters," she explained and fought to stop herself from throwing up. "So if you open any of the doors, you might find an entirely different kind of survivor."

Taylor froze and paused for a couple of seconds as he

thought about what she had said. Vickie wondered if this kind of stuff even fazed him anymore.

"Noted," he replied finally. "Where's the first location?"

"You have to go down fifteen levels. That's fifteen levels of twenty-five, by the way. It makes you wonder why these labs are always underground."

"That is self-explanatory," a crisp voice interjected. "Obviously, it's to bury the evidence of their illegal experiments and a pathetic attempt to secure the creatures to avoid the truth coming to light in the most gruesome way possible."

"Desk?" Taylor shook his head and seemed a little confused by her unexpected intervention. "What the hell are you doing here?"

"I'm between gigs, as it were, so I thought I'd begin my overwatch duties unofficially while I wait for the wheels of bureaucracy to turn."

"Over—what?" Vickie responded indignantly.

"Overwatch," the AI repeated. "Which means it's my job to make sure you do your job."

"Which is exactly what I'm doing—or would be if you hadn't butted in where you weren't invited."

"And not only do it but do it well," Desk continued as if she hadn't spoken. "I would only intervene if it were necessary and in this case, it is. Vickie, when you support your team on a mission, one thing is critical."

"Oh, yeah? And what would that be, O Great Overwatch Oracle?"

"Focus. Your mental distraction could get them killed."

A short silence followed during which her thoughts churned through the validity and the implications of the blunt statement. Her first instinct was to launch a tirade of protests, but it occurred to her that she'd never been in a real-life monster moment. She could see how easy it would be for a single teensy moment of distraction to make her miss a crucial detail her team couldn't see.

Not that she'd admit it, of course, and she'd definitely have words with both Niki and the snooty AI bitch who thought she was infallible. But for now, she'd shove all the anger and indignation aside, ignore the meddlesome AI, and…yes, focus.

"Right, fifteen levels down. You'll have to take the stairs since the elevators are out and…well, I don't know if you want to climb down the shafts. Can you guys even do that in those suits?"

"It doesn't matter. We'll take the stairs."

"Okay. You'll find the way to the secure room through the blueprints but let me know if you need any directions."

"Roger that. Moving out."

She rocked back in her seat and rubbed her eyes gently. No, this was not what she'd had in mind when she told Taylor she wanted to help him work these cases. Of course, it was a better use of her skills but she could concede that she would have to find a way to make this a little more her area of expertise. Maybe music would help her focus. She could always add something quirky like sprucing her work area up to make it fun without losing sight of the objectives.

Maybe having a dedicated work area was worth considering. She was pissed at both Niki and Desk for having apparently reached some kind of arrangement without consulting her and she'd vent when the time allowed.

Still, Desk had thrown a challenge out. She wasn't quite sure what or why, but she did know the AI had some kind of ulterior motive. Well, she'd make damned sure she met it head-on and surprise the crap out of her.

"Overwatch my ass, bitch."

CHAPTER TWENTY-ONE

Something about the creatures was immensely disturbing. Vickie couldn't put her finger on exactly what it was, though. They looked much like the mutants she had seen before. Hell, some of the games she'd played included beasts that were based on actual monsters from the Zoo.

Even those didn't creep her out the way those in the footage she watched did.

They prowled through the rooms of the facility. Some appeared to wander aimlessly without any clear purpose or direction. It was also difficult to determine how they had escaped until she noticed a handful progress through the corridors. Unlike the others, these seemed to be focused on something, although she couldn't tell what.

She narrowed her eyes and watched them closely when they approached the cells where other animals were held. They circled the area and nipped and probed at the cell walls until they found a weakness. She couldn't hear but it looked like they were communicating since the entire group converged on their location. They directed their combined efforts into prying the bars open and tore at the Plexiglas to create a hole large enough for the creatures inside to pass through.

It was their intelligence, coordination, and subtle power that triggered the rush of something cold through her spine. She wondered if Niki knew what she was getting into, being completely involved in situations like this all around the country. The agent had fallen headfirst into one hell of a niche that would probably get her killed.

Of course, her cousin was in nowhere near as dangerous a position as Taylor. Vickie wondered if he would have been happy to simply sit around, own a business, and work on mechs with Bobby. Probably not, she decided. He was most likely glad that Niki had arrived on his doorstep, quite literally, with the opportunity to continue to kill monsters.

He was a fun guy like that.

"Vickie, I need you to be my eyes on this," Taylor told her over the comms. For some reason, he spoke in a whisper despite the fact that his suit insulated sound from inside.

"That is what I've done thus far, right?"

"I need a little more than that, Vickie. We're working with something we've never had before, and I intend to take full advantage."

"Wait, you're talking about me?"

"Damn straight. There are electronic locks and seals on all these doors. Now that you have eyes on us, you can help to isolate us and watch our backs. In this situation, it's more important than ever before. If you can, close and seal the doors behind us and open the ones we need to get through. It will divide the damage we need to do into manageable portions."

Vickie paused and rubbed her chin gently. This was more like her perfect scenario in which she helped them, even from afar. Taylor had a mind for shit like this. Maybe that was why he had survived this long. And maybe, with him at her back, Niki would have a chance to survive her crazy monster-hunting career.

"Oh, I guess I could do that for you guys," she muttered and opened the door ahead of them to enable them to reach the stairs. "You know, if I can fit it between my other duties."

"You don't have any other duties," Taylor reminded her as he moved through the door and checked his surroundings before he gestured for Bobby to follow. "You made that very clear when you quit the other job I gave you and chose to be involved in this side of the... Hell, I don't want to call it the family business, but the number of your family members who work on this does make it seem appropriate."

She groaned. "Ugh, don't remind me. Having Niki and Jennie dealing with this is seriously a pill, even before we throw the bitch AI into the mix. I'm merely trying to find a way to make sure neither of them kills you. The way to the next safe room is clear, by the way, but you guys should know these creatures are making their way through the air ducts now. I don't have any eyes in there, and the sensors are troublesome. The engineers who put them together probably never thought they would need to detect alien monsters moving through them."

"A solid point," he agreed. "Bungees, keep your eyes on the vents and I'll keep my eyes on what's out here."

"Huh. It's nice of you to give me the bulk of the work," the mechanic grumbled.

"Well, if you want to take point on this, be my guest."

Bobby had no answer to that and the two men continued.

Vickie let her gaze drift to one of the other screens. More of the monsters were breaking out or being broken out. She grasped the arms of her office chair and watched them working together. They weren't even the same kind of animal, yet they played nice like they were a part of the same wolf pack, pulling together to help each other. They were communicating somehow, she was sure of it.

One of the creatures suddenly stopped moving. This one looked different than the others—thin, lean, and with six legs, a prehensile tail, and a narrow, long head. It stared directly into the camera like it could see her through the lens.

"Okay, you're super-creepy," she muttered. "Taylor, these monsters are jailbreaking their friends. You might have to deal with more of the fuckers. Keep yourselves safe."

"Yeah, yeah. Tanya's already coming for me with a gun if I let Bobby get hurt."

"And who's coming after you with a gun if you get hurt?" she asked.

"Well, hopefully, no one. I have a weird faith in humanity like that."

Bobby turned to look at his boss as they continued to move down the stairs.

"What?" Taylor asked and maintained a steady pace.

"I never understood how you can be so calm in these situations."

He chuckled. "You're fairly calm yourself, ice man."

"I'll take that as a compliment but I'm close to losing it here. I can pretend calm and I've been in combat before so I know how to keep myself chill in these situations. But there you are, walking around and making wisecracks while we're in the middle of a disaster area we have to somehow mitigate."

"I don't know." Taylor shrugged. "This kind of situation is about as commonplace to me as it could be to anyone. I'm well aware of the dangers but in the end, there's some-thing...kind of calming about being in a situation as black and white as this, you know?"

He could tell Bobby didn't know what he meant by that. Maybe he was simply a little fucked up in the head.

The lights remained steady, which meant the electricity was still on for them. The monsters tended to disable the electricity when they took over a facility, or maybe having them around was enough to make it degenerate. He wouldn't pretend to possess the kind of science required to know how or why, but it was a fact.

"We're moving toward the safe room," he alerted Vickie, although she knew that already. "Is there any chance you can open it when we get there?"

"Honestly, Taylor, this lack of faith has begun to get annoying. Try trusting me a little."

"Taylor!"

Bobby's tone of voice was all he needed to hear. He spun and the motion sensors in his suit blared when he twisted and located his target. It was long, slim, and difficult to lock onto. His teammate had already moved away to give them both the space to open fire.

The assault rifle kicked into life and Taylor pushed forward as the lean, black insect-like creature screeched and jumped back to avoid being shot. He advanced and drew his knife from its sheath as he attacked the creature. What looked like a stinger lashed toward his neck.

Taylor pushed forward and planted his foot on the creature's tail. He slashed his blade in a downward arc to sever it and immediately reversed to slice into its skull.

"There are more!" Bobby warned and adjusted his assault rifle to aim into the air vents.

Something skittered through the ducts and his partner opened fire without hesitation to punch holes into them and kill whatever was inside. Screeches followed the barrage and a few seconds later, blood dripped from the damaged areas.

"Having critters in the air vents will be one whole new level of suck," Bobby muttered and gave his assault rifle a moment to reload. "Are you okay?"

Taylor looked at the blood spattered over his suit. "Yeah. It's not mine."

"The fact that it's dark-blue or maybe a little purple was a dead giveaway, yes," the mechanic replied. "Still."

"I'm fine. Let's find the people we're supposed to help here. Vickie, where are we on the doors?"

"Again with the lack of faith. I think I'll be a little offended next time."

A series of clicks from the walls around them confirmed that the security was being disabled, one level at a time. The door began to open.

"The good folks at Fort Knox should take notes," Taylor muttered and jogged to the opening.

"No, they shouldn't. Actually, I think these people took notes from Fort Knox. And believe me, the security there is leagues and leagues ahead of what I see here."

He shook his head. "I'll go ahead and not ask you how you know about that. The whole plausible deniability thing will work in my favor if we ever have someone breaking our doors down."

"Don't worry about it." Vickie laughed. "We work for the DOD now, remember."

"I'm fairly sure that hacking into Fort Knox is still illegal for DOD operatives."

She had nothing to say about that and the door unlocked fully. The two men moved forward cautiously. Taylor knew a couple of the safe rooms had been infiltrated before they were sealed so they needed to prepare themselves for the worst.

As it turned out, someone waited for them. A couple of younger men in white lab coats stood closest to the doors and held a few chairs up. He assumed they aimed to defend themselves with the only weapons they had available.

"What the fuck did you think was happening?" he asked as they lowered the chairs and stared almost in awe at the seven and a half foot tall suits in front of them. "Did you honestly think the monsters could access the software that sealed this room and let themselves in?"

The two young men exchanged a glance before the one

on the right spoke. "Honestly? Stranger things have happened."

He paused for a few seconds and finally nodded. "Okay, fair enough. I'm Taylor McFadden and this is Robert Zhang. We're here to get you out of this facility. How many of you are in there?"

"There's…" The man hesitated and looked at his coworker. "Us, and… Mercy….there are twenty of us in here."

"Do you have any weapons?" Bobby asked.

Neither man responded and simply glanced at the chairs they carried.

"Right, stupid question."

"We need to get you guys out of here now," Taylor interjected. "Get your people together and we'll find a way through to the top. Do you know if anyone else made it to the other safe rooms in the building?"

"Sorry. We came here as soon as the alarms blared. At first, we thought it was another drill but the doors never closed or locked during those. That was when we realized that—shit, what happened to everyone else?"

Taylor looked into the hall they'd come from and at the dripping blood of the creatures they had already killed. "I'd love to give you good news, but you're the first safe room we've found any people in. Still, it's best to be optimistic, right?"

"Right."

The two jogged to the back of the room where a group of people still huddled close, afraid of what they would have to face if they wanted to get out safely.

"Taylor," Bobby said and turned as he gestured for him

to do the same. He connected only through comms. "Vickie sent word back from the other sensors."

"There are no life signs in the other safe rooms, Taylor," she told him. "The rooms have a monitor that should alert rescuers as to where the people are. None...none of the others show any signs of human life."

He scowled and shook his head. "Dammit."

"There's something else. The other rooms showed initial signs that they were sealed with people in them. They have separate oxygen reserves and enough food and water to last thirty people two weeks, give or take. But about an hour after the doors were sealed, the life signs disappeared. I want to blame poor engineering and say there's something wrong with the software, but it's not the most likely scenario if you take all the different variables into account."

There was nothing else to say. He shifted in place a little before he glanced over his shoulder to what he now knew were the sole survivors of the lab.

"Vickie, tell Niki that we'll get the fuck out of here and will bring twenty survivors. She should be ready to open those doors when we get there, provided that we don't have a horde of goddammed monsters on our tail."

The hacker didn't respond immediately, but when she did, he could hear a worried edge in her voice. "Sure, I'll tell her. But you should know, Taylor, that the creatures broke out of the lower levels of the lab. If you guys plan to head to the upper levels, you might want to get on that immediately."

He clenched his jaw and steeled himself. "Roger that. Bobby, we're heading out now!"

CHAPTER TWENTY-TWO

The group gathered swiftly. They didn't want to remain in the lab any longer than they already had and given the condition the people in the other safe rooms were in, Taylor couldn't blame them.

Still, this wouldn't be as easy as simply walking them out. He wasn't about to assume that this would go smoothly for everyone involved.

"Bobby, quick talk." He alerted the man as they continued to move. "The chances are the critters will catch up with us. They're already moving through the air vents and now, Vickie is tracking them climbing the steps. Somehow, they're disabling the lockdown systems and climbing toward us."

"If this is a pep talk, you should know that you suck at it. You know, constructive criticism and all that."

"What I'm saying is that we need to have two points of defense. We'll deal with the creatures coming from below as well as potentially from above in the air vents."

"Are you saying we should have had Tanya down here with us?"

Taylor nodded. "Yeah, I wish they hadn't needed her topside. We could have used another pair of eyes here."

"Eyes are not the problem," the mechanic pointed out. "We have eyes and more than we'll need. What we might need are another suit and more guns."

"And yet, in saying that now with the power of hindsight, do you still think Tanya should have stayed behind?"

Bobby glared at him through his visor. "What's your point?"

"You do know that she probably has more experience in dealing with these monsters than you do, right? And without a suit of her own for the most part too, so it might be argued that I should have brought her here instead of you."

"I have more experience with the suit."

"Sure, but it's still something to keep in mind when you next assume that you're the tougher of you two."

"I never thought that. And you were the one who suggested she stay behind in the first place."

"I know, and I'm starting to rethink a few of my decisions since we came down here."

"Including the decision to come down here?"

"You know it."

Taylor gestured for the group to continue to move with them and switched to the suit's speakers instead of keeping the conversation between him and Bobby. "We have to move fast and hard. There will be no delays, no stopping to catch your breath, nothing. I'll take the rear of the group since that's probably where we can expect the most creatures, and Bungees will take the vanguard. Keep your eyes on the air vents and tell us if you see or hear anything moving in there. No questions. We move now!"

He expected them to make things difficult somehow. Scientists always had questions about what was happening around them. It came with the job description and yet, they were uniquely qualified to understand the dangers they faced as well. They had nothing to say and aside from the terrified looks on their faces, he might have thought they had been in this kind of situation before.

They must have at least imagined something like this happening. It was something they likely considered every time the drills they had mentioned were run.

Taylor indicated for them to move forward, adjusted his rifle, and turned his sensors to the rear as they began to climb the stairs toward the higher levels. They were fifteen levels down and needed to ascend all the way.

These people likely called an elevator when a climb was higher than three or four stories. That was the rule he generally worked with himself. Now, they would need to all but sprint up fifteen flights of stairs to the top.

He could probably do that himself or could have when he was at the peak of his physical ability. But these people weren't even close to optimal fitness and he could only hope they were some of the more athletic scientists in the world.

They weren't, unfortunately. Five levels up, he could already see red faces covered in sweat. They sucked in desperate breaths and struggled to keep up the initial pace. Fear and adrenaline pumped through their bodies and would help to push them beyond their limits, but they would only get them so far.

His sensors activated. Taylor shifted and identified the movement coming up behind them, three levels below. He switched to the comms systems. "Bobby, you need to get a fucking move on! We have company incoming, and I'm all out of tea and crumpets."

"Roger that. I'm off to get you more tea and crumpets," the man replied before he activated the speakers. "Okay, people, we have to pick up the pace now. We have something moving behind us."

A few panicked screams followed, but his calm voice and demeanor were exactly what was required to keep them moving in a reasonably orderly fashion, despite the panic rushing through their veins. Patiently, he pushed them to move a little faster than before.

Taylor didn't know if he could pull something like that off. He was used to dealing with the hardened characters who responded well to being shouted at. People who had been yelled at for months through boot camp until they were inured to that kind of shitty treatment generally obeyed instinctively.

Of course, civilians would simply freeze if they were yelled at in a panic situation. They didn't have the instincts that kicked them into action.

Maybe there was a reason why he'd brought Bobby along after all.

He shifted and set his suit to continue up the steps, even though he looked in the opposite direction. Consciously, he let his legs relax to allow the suit to do its thing while he fixed his gaze on the farthest line of sight. His first alert was a glimmer barely visible to the naked eye. He steeled himself to not open fire until he had a clear shot. Unlike humans and regular animals, the sound of gunfire wouldn't work as the kind of danger indicator he needed.

In fact, in the case of the cryptids, it would attract them. The only thing that would give them pause was the sight of their dead, and he wanted them to have a good idea of exactly what waited for them. The suit moved him upward and it wasn't until they reached the next level that he could see a head, followed by a shoulder and carapace, turn the corner and flash a glare and a hiss as it bared its many, needle-like teeth at him.

Taylor didn't hesitate and pulled the trigger as soon as he had a kill-shot lined up. The three-round burst punched through the creature's armor and plowed into the soft flesh beneath. It screeched in agony and fell quickly from view. More came from below and he didn't need his suit to hear their sudden surge in activity. The sound of gunfire echoing through the stairwell and the sounds and smells of one of their own being killed would send them all into a feeding frenzy.

He'd seen it dozens of times before—maybe even hundreds, although he'd lost count a long time before.

"Bobby, keep them moving!" Taylor roared and continued to climb up the steps behind the group as he selected another target and pulled the trigger again. The civilians screamed above him. The gunfire was loud and triggered a fight or flight response in all the scientists that drove them up the steps faster than before. A couple of them retched from the effort but they pushed on.

He forced himself to remain calm, chose his targets, and

made it difficult for the monsters to continue their upward drive. The stairwell was narrow enough that they could only approach a few at a time, and while the ammo remained, he would be able to keep them at bay.

The question was what would happen when the ammo ran out.

They were barely halfway to the top. He could only assume that the next few flights would be when the creatures surged upward.

He wouldn't be able to hold them off on his own for long and he couldn't call Bobby in to help. The man needed to keep his attention on anything that might attack them from above. All the while, the creatures probed at the defenses. It was like they tried to draw his fire and waited for his weapon to click empty.

It wasn't long until it did and he immediately saw that they had, in fact, anticipated that sound.

"Shit," he snapped and drew his sidearm as they surged up the steps. The mutants even tried to climb the walls while a few continued to fall, but the firepower was reduced. One of the creatures, a powerful-looking lynx-like creature the size of a mountain lion, scaled the walls beyond the other beasts and used its claws to dig into the structure and push off to dive on him from above.

He was ready for it and lashed out with his empty pistol to catch the creature across the jaw. His assault rifle had reloaded, and once his adversary sprawled awkwardly and tried to regain its footing, he fixed his sights to punch three holes into it. Blood splattered across the pristine white walls.

The mutants shrieked in a shrill cacophony of rage.

They made it difficult to hear what was happening at the top and since the vocalization of human panic was similar to the monsters, he had difficulty tracking them through sound.

Suddenly, gunfire erupted above. Bobby had found something to attack at the top, and it wasn't something that came from below. He could barely hear things moving through the air vents that wound up the stairwell. Once his pistol had reloaded, he turned the software on that would allow him to locate targets above automatically. The suit moved on its own again and he pulled the trigger when a target lit up on his HUD while the assault rifle kept the monsters at bay below him.

Taylor could almost feel the intensity of their attacks growing. The mutants had been whipped into a frenzy and attempted to rush up the steps despite the determined fusillade of lead. They were closer to the upper levels with only three more flights before they reached the top.

"Vickie, be ready to open the upper-level doors and close them as soon as we're through," Taylor shouted as his assault rifle ran dry again. True to form, the monsters sensed an advantage and bulldozed forward. He released the rifle and let it reload automatically on his arm as he drew his knife clear of the sheath and leaned into his attack. The blade sliced a wide gash into another feline-like creature that parted the fur and carved into the flesh below. He paused in his upward climb, pulled back, and hammered a kick into the wounded animal to catapult it into the group that approached.

His blood went cold as the still living cryptid was ripped to shreds by the others.

"That's fucking new," he muttered and retrieved his rifle again.

"The door's opening. I'm waiting for you guys!" Vickie alerted them over the comms and the door at the top clicked and released. The air vents were isolated between the stairwell and the entry level of the lab, which would give them a safe opportunity to escape the building if they could seal the door off as well.

"Come on!" Bobby called and gestured for the scientists to hurry through the door as he turned to help cover the rear. He eliminated a couple of beasts that still harassed his partner and the man was able to ascend the final stretch and reach the door.

Taylor took a grenade from his belt, removed the pin, and lobbed it down the stairwell before he scrambled through the door and slammed it shut. The explosion from the other side could be heard and felt as Vickie sealed the door again.

"Fucking cryptids," he muttered and made sure the door was completely sealed.

"Taylor…"

Bobby had a way to make his voice sound a warning with only the one word, and he turned quickly. The scientists were spread out and a few had already begun to cross toward the door when they saw the movement.

Five mutants stood motionless and stared at the group. They resembled wolves but were almost the size of bears and what looked like carapaces grew from their shoulders. They remained fixed and silent as if they waited for something.

Taylor raised his weapon and motioned for the civilians

to gather closer together as he eased forward. Bobby stepped in as rearguard to keep them moving.

He pivoted when metal screeched and tore beneath a determined assault within the vent behind him. Something that looked like an elongated claw hacked through the ducting and arced with uncanny accuracy to target the unprotected scientists. The mechanic stepped forward and the claw swung once more at the civilians before it finally changed direction and plunged into the shoulder pauldron of the man's armor.

"Shit!" Bobby roared. The force of the impact was enough to drive him back a few steps and he knocked the civilians over when he was launched into the wall.

That, apparently, was what the wolves had waited for. They raced around Taylor and immediately lunged toward the vulnerable mechanic.

CHAPTER TWENTY-THREE

For some reason, Taylor couldn't seem to react fast enough.

"Bobby!"

The roar of the wolves as they attacked the man drowned out his cry. The claw—or what looked more like a scorpion's stinger—pressed into Bobby's shoulder with more force than he had given the sinuous limb credit for, and the wolves were more than eager to dig in as their victim was forced back. His suit was malfunctioning, and the rifle wouldn't fire. He tried to reach his sidearm, but one of the wolves caught his hand and dragged it away from the weapon while the others continued their attempt to savage his armor.

Taylor pushed forward as the blood pumped through his body with an impossible flash of heat and he hurried to help his friend. Something clutched and pulled at his back. Maybe not all the wolves had attacked his teammate and had waited for an opening from him, which he had given without thought.

He didn't care and ignored everything but the drama playing out in front of him. As he pushed forward, he drew his sidearm and fired blindly behind him without bothering to use the software to help him aim. He wouldn't leave Bobby alone and as soon as he could, he raised his assault rifle and opened fire on full auto, careful not to hit the mechanic as he drove the wolves away. A few fell, bleeding from multiple wounds, while the others turned to attack the new threat.

They hadn't anticipated anything like him. He continued to shoot but turned the fire into the air vents where the other creature still hid while he holstered his empty pistol and drew his knife instead. Taylor only then realized that he was screaming with rage. The blade gutted one of the wolves and he spun and almost decapitated the second one. He drove the full weight of his suit into the next and crushed it against the wall with enough force to leave a dent in the concrete.

The two that remained darted away from his back as the stinger disengaged from Bobby's shoulder. It retracted to the creature that controlled it and which was clearly injured given the blood that dripped from the bullet holes in the air vents.

The wolves attempted to retreat as well and somehow followed the other mutant, but Taylor had no intention to allow them to escape. He continued to fire at them even as they pulled away and the assault rifle felled them before they had moved even a short distance. Finally, the weapon clicked empty.

"Fucking assholes." He made sure the creatures were dead and the one that had hidden in the vents was gone before he returned to Bobby. The scientists watched him, fearful and a little in awe of what they'd seen.

"Check your wounded," he snapped and brought them out of their stunned silence. They immediately turned to check on those who had been injured in the attack. Small slashes and bruises were in evidence here and there but nothing life-threatening, at least not at first glance. He knew well enough to anticipate poisoning in the smallest of wounds.

For now, though, Bobby was his priority.

"How are you feeling?" he asked and examined the main injury, where the stinger had driven into his shoulder with so much force that it had almost pushed him through the wall.

"I'm...fine. The suit tells me there aren't any breaches in the armor." His friend pushed himself up, and Taylor immediately noted that his right arm didn't move at all and hydraulic fluid dribbled from the hole. "I feel like I've been hit by a goddammed bus, though."

"That sounds about right," he agreed and hauled the man to his feet. "The suit's taken considerable damage. The chances are we'll see a shit-ton of bruising once we get you out of it. Vickie, we're safe for now. Niki is clear to open the door."

"Roger that," the hacker replied quickly. "Opening your comm lines to Niki too."

"Can you walk?" Taylor asked Bobby, who had some difficulty remaining steady. It was something he'd seen before as the suit redistributed the fluid across its hydraulic system to keep it balanced.

The mechanic didn't answer immediately but took a

moment to try to perform a few tests and simple repairs to keep the suit functional.

"Sure," the man answered finally. "Not quickly, obviously, but I can walk."

"It's probably for the best that we're near the exit," he said and gestured to the civilians to keep moving.

"Taylor, are you there?" Niki asked as she connected to the comm line. "Are you safe?"

"For the moment, yeah," Taylor answered immediately. "Bobby's taken damage to his suit and a couple of the survivors are wounded, but we're clear for now. I don't think that'll last, though, so if you guys can open the seals on the doors, sooner would be better than later."

"We're working on it now," she assured him.

He didn't want to think about what would happen if they were suddenly attacked by the creatures, which would force them to keep the doors sealed with himself, Bobby, and the scientists still inside. It would be the right decision but it would still suck.

Thankfully, the whole group approached the entrance without any sign that the creatures were in pursuit. Bobby moved slowly but kept pace with the civilians, who showed signs of exhaustion from their hurried climb up the steps. A few were limping and others still looked sick from the exertion.

"I swear to God," one of them grumbled, his face red, "I will never skip going to the gym again. There's one right outside my apartment and if I get out of here, I'll sign up as soon as possible."

Taylor nodded. It was probably a good idea anyway,

and the company would most likely offer everyone involved in this clusterfuck a massive severance package. That would be more than helpful for those who opted for gym memberships.

They came to a halt in front of the door they had entered through, and Taylor waited until he could hear the sound of the seals begin to deactivate. The seconds ticked past while he kept his gaze on the chamber around them. Even with safety so close, he had a weird feeling that something would charge out once the doors began to open.

Fortunately, his fears weren't realized. He held his assault rifle at the ready and monitored the rooms beyond as the scientists pushed through to safety as quickly as their tired legs could move them. Bobby exited next, and Taylor followed close behind. He kept his rifle aimed inside as he stepped out, the weapon primed and ready until the door swung shut and sealed again.

Even then, he didn't allow himself to relax. If Vickie was right, the creatures had found ways to break through seals in the lower levels of the lab, which meant there was no reason to think they couldn't break out of the lab itself if they put their minds to it.

The question was whether they would put their minds to it. He shook his head as he finally turned away from the building and moved to where Bobby and the civilian survivors were. A few first aid stations were set up, and the military presence made itself known. Dozens of men in full combat gear aimed their weapons at the building, and a handful of smaller stations were being set up for larger weapons to be settled in place. It looked like these people were only a tick away from blowing the whole damn place to kingdom come.

Taylor wondered if it wasn't best to let them do their work. Better still, pull everyone back and drop a couple of bombs to be sure.

Or maybe that was why he wasn't the guy in charge.

Niki jogged to where he stood and simply stared at the personnel setting their defenses up against a possible monster attack.

"I would ask how it went but one look at Bobby's suit tells me you guys ran into trouble," she asserted, her head tilted as she studied him. "Oh, and yours looks like it took a fair amount of damage on the back too. What the hell happened in there?"

He tried to twist to see what damage she was talking about. There were no warning signs on his HUD, which meant there weren't any serious breaches, but it was still best to have everything looked at immediately.

"We got sloppy," Taylor admitted. "We were close enough to the exit and I think I must have relaxed a little. A few of the fuckers were waiting for us once we got to the top level, and they worked with something in the vents. I'm not sure what it was, but it was strong and it had one hell of a long tail. It struck Bobby first, and the other creatures reacted like they had waited for it and attacked quickly too. We reacted but not quickly enough."

Niki nodded. "I guess the fact that you're willing to admit you were to blame for the situation is a decent enough thing to do."

He couldn't help but smirk. "I'm not a fan of trying to look on the bright side, but I'll take it."

"Come on. I'll see what can be done to get that suit checked."

They moved to where the civilians were being examined by the army paramedics. They seemed well-versed in what to do when dealing with someone who was injured by a cryptid, and the few who had been injured were quickly tested for any sign that they had been poisoned. Toxicology tests would also be run once they had obtained samples of blood and other fluids to make sure, but they would treat any symptoms that manifested immediately.

None of the scientists or the medics looked concerned, however, which was enough to tell him that they were at least not in any immediate danger.

Bobby seemed to be in a similar condition and Tanya helped pull his suit apart. She peeled it off piece by piece while the paramedics asked him how he felt.

The mechanic knew better than to play the tough guy when it came to his health.

"I think I twisted my ankle and my right knee is badly banged-up too," he said as Taylor approached. "It's a little painful to breathe, so maybe something in the ribs too and my shoulder...I can't move it."

Tanya looked worried and Taylor couldn't blame her. As the suit was gradually removed, the true extent of the injuries became clear. Dark masses of bruising appeared on the man's shoulder where he had been struck, and it was a similar story with the rest of his body. He could only imagine the wounds that would have been inflicted if he hadn't worn a suit of armor.

Without a doubt, he'd be looking at pieces of his friend rather than his bruised and battered body.

Tanya turned as he approached and her concern quickly turned to anger as she moved toward him. "Taylor, you motherfucker, I told you to keep him safe. I told you what would happen…"

Her voice trailed off as he drew his sidearm from its holster and offered it to her. "You told me you'd shoot me. I said I'd hand you the gun. I remember."

She looked surprised that he actually followed through and focused on the weapon that would have required two hands for her to use. Either way, if she wanted something a little less bulky, it wasn't like there was any lack of weapons around them for her to use.

"I didn't intend to shoot you," she mumbled and turned as Bobby started to laugh but groaned immediately.

"Fuck, it hurts to laugh," he complained.

"Can we get him painkillers?" Taylor asked. The paramedic nodded, although the man didn't look happy about being told how to do his job.

He finally slid the sidearm into its holster once it became clear that Tanya wouldn't take the opportunity to take a shot at him. Well, not at the moment, anyway. The offer would remain open for a week, at least, since she was probably holding back while there was still a mission to complete.

"Okay, so things hit a bump, but when do they not?" Niki asked and looked around the group. "Then again, you brought all the survivors out alive and mostly intact with no deaths. I'll go ahead and call this a qualified success."

"There are still critters in there for us to deal with," Taylor grumbled and tried to smooth out the dents that had appeared thanks to the attacks from behind. "I wouldn't develop a torn rotator cuff from patting myself too hard on the back yet."

"We brought all the people out," Niki countered. "As far as I'm concerned, we can go ahead and take a page from the Russians' books and carpet bomb this whole fucking area."

"Why would that be from the Russians' book?" Tanya asked.

Niki and Taylor quickly exchanged a glance before the agent offered a reply. "That's...um, classified, but I guess the context tells you enough. The Russians had the problem of a Zoo infestation. Carpet bombing the place with extreme prejudice did the trick for the most part, anyway."

The woman wasn't that curious and knew better than to ask any questions. Instead, she turned her attention to help Bobby, who was already enjoying the results of painkillers injected into his system.

Taylor had heard stories about what the Russians had been up to in the Zoo but like Tanya, he wasn't curious enough to ask any questions.

"Hey, guys?" Vickie called over their comms. "Unless you're able to call in that airstrike within the next couple of hours, you might want to rethink not going in there again."

"What are you talking about?" Niki asked.

"Well, remember how I talked about the monsters in there being able to break through the seals that kept them in the lower levels?" the hacker explained. "Well, I don't want to sound paranoid or anything, but it looks like they are probing the electronic systems in the building, including the sealing systems."

"Fuck," the agent snapped. "Taylor, are you up for another trip in there?"

"Sure," he replied. "But I'm sure as fuck not going in alone."

CHAPTER TWENTY-FOUR

She hated being the bearer of bad news but Taylor and Niki needed to be told about what was happening inside. They needed to be fully informed of the situation if they wanted to make the right decisions.

Still, having to tell them something she knew was painful to hear was enough to make her entire body clench. Her fingers hovered over the keyboard while her gaze remained fixed on the feed from the cameras that were still available to her.

The fact that she lost visual of the different areas one at a time was significant. Not only that, but the cameras also went down in every area where the monsters moved, and that could not be a coincidence. Something in there was much smarter than they had been willing to acknowledge.

Whether they merely disabled the electronics in the area or targeted the surveillance system itself was difficult to tell. Either way, Vickie wouldn't take any chances, not with the lives of her friends.

"Vickie, we'll need more information than that," Taylor stated over the comms.

"No shit, Sherlock. Here I was, hoping you guys would simply jump into a goddammed cryptid nest half-cocked," she snapped in response while she tried to keep what access she still had to the facility. "I'm kidding, in case that wasn't obvious to you motherfuckers. It looks like the one that gave Bobby a free flight is more intelligent than the others. In fact, I would almost say the other cryptids are following it, taking orders and shit."

"That sounds about right," Taylor responded. "It's something we've seen before, at least. Besides, when we were in there, it looked like it commanded a small pack of wolves to attack while it hid in a nearby air vent. I'm not sure how it works but I guess it does."

"Well, anyway, they've picked up on the electronics. They are destroying those that keep the lab running and more importantly, keep the doors locked. All the seals are based on electromagnetic locks, and if they can disconnect the seals from the generators in the building, they'll be able to get out."

"Do you have any idea how long it'll take them to do that?" Niki asked and sounded a little alarmed.

Vickie couldn't blame the woman. It was their job to keep the situation contained, after all.

"Not really, no. It looks like they're probing, checking, and trying to find a way out—the same way they were able to break the seal on the lower levels to climb up to Taylor and Bobby. So, if we want to be specific, it could be an hour from now, it could be in the next five minutes, and it could be never. I'll go ahead and assume we won't take the chance that they might break the building seal and get out, right?"

"Fucking hell," Niki cursed. "Not only will we have to go in there, but we have to hunt every last one of these bastards down and kill them all."

"Well, at least the ones that call the shots," the hacker corrected and leaned back in her seat. It creaked, a now-familiar sound, and she reminded herself to oil it. Oddly enough, the current situation was enough to keep her from dealing with the small nuisance as well as other problems —like keeping herself fed. "You know, like the one that attacked Bobby."

"Yeah," Taylor interjected. "I'll kill that motherfucker. Tear its head off and mount it on my wall."

"I'm sure that'll break about fifteen different zoning laws," Vickie pointed out. "But hey, it's your business, right?"

"Damn straight. But you're probably right. I should avoid mounting potentially dangerous creatures on my wall, even if they're dead. You never know what the goop will do next."

"There's a better name for the stuff than goop, right?" she asked.

"Well...probably, but it's likely to be a Latin name about a mile long and I'll be damned if I'll memorize that," he replied. "I think it's best to just keep calling it goop and avoid unnecessary complications."

"Right, can we get back to the problem at hand, please?" Niki asked, her tone annoyed. "Or do you guys want to keep talking about the problems with building codes in the Las Vegas area?"

"Well, it's certainly a topic for later," Taylor answered. "But we'll get back to it when we're not looking for a way to keep these motherfuckers contained. Do we have a way to do that?"

Vickie sighed and shook her head as she tried to think of a way. "Okay, the localized sensors give me some idea of where you'll find them, but there are many blind spots, most notably those pesky air vents. That added to the fact that a fair number of the cameras have gone down since they started their little purge is enough to make things interesting once you're in there."

"That's a problem," Niki noted and stated the obvious.

"Not really," he countered. "These monsters seemed eager to attack us once they were able to do so, so it would seem like we could draw them in simply by...well, being there. They'll want to kill us and will hopefully abandon all thoughts of escape until they've dealt with the intruders. Isn't that how they acted while we were in there?"

The hacker paused and turned to check the data she had collected while Taylor and Bobby had been inside. Sure enough, it was easy to see that the monsters had mostly abandoned all other endeavors once they had an accessible target.

"Sonofabitch, you might be right about that," she conceded. "Still, banging on a pot and shouting for all the cryptid monsters to come get you doesn't strike me as the best plan in the world."

Taylor frowned. "Yeah, that's a good point. Still, drawing

them out does seem like a better plan than hunting them, mostly since shooting at and killing those we hunt will simply draw them out anyway. It's best to be prepared for anything, you know?"

"Sure, I guess that pans out," Vickie said. "That leaves the question of who you'll go in with."

He didn't have time to formulate a response. Niki had already shucked her jacket and placed it on the hood of the car.

"What?" she asked. "If you think I'll sit this one out while you try to run heroic bullshit on your own, you'd better think again—assuming that Neanderthal brain of yours is capable of that, of course."

Taylor laughed. "I didn't say anything. With that said, we should work under the assumption that our actions might not be enough to stop the monsters from getting out. We won't be able to act in time if some break away, which means we should leave functional suits out here in case."

Tanya looked up from where the paramedics applied a couple of splints to immobilize Bobby until they could get him to a hospital for proper treatment.

"Tanya, do you feel up to manning the defenses out here with Maxwell and Jansen?" he asked. He felt a pang of guilt. While asking her to sit another mission out might have a negative effect on her confidence—not only in him as a leader but also in her abilities— she would want to stay close to Bobby until such time as he was moved. Besides, the two bodyguards could be trusted to help her hold off an attack, and Niki would certainly not know what to do if there was a break from the lab.

She seemed to understand and there were no hard feelings evident when she nodded firmly. "I'll have my suit ready, just in case. Does Vickie know if there will be any kind of warning before the creatures break containment?"

"Vickie?" Taylor queried and waited for her to answer the question.

"Oh, don't worry about warning," the hacker replied. "There are big, blaring alarms set up in case the generators lose connection with the electromagnets on the doors. They should give you about a solid minute before the cryptids have a clear way out."

Tanya nodded. "So it would be best to have some of my suit out and ready, just in case."

"And the rest of the group here," Niki stated loudly and caught the attention of the military who were almost finished setting up their defensive positions. "Don't think that because you have superior firepower, you'll be able to contain the critters. All they need is one opening, and they'll tear into you motherfuckers. Stay alert and don't leave any part of the building unwatched, do you understand?"

"Yes, ma'am," one of the officers replied and relayed the orders down the line of defensive positions.

Taylor had to admit, she would have made a fantastic NCO in the field, although he wasn't sure if it was a compliment or not. The biggest assholes in the field were the best NCOs.

"Okay, Taylor, it looks like we have a battle plan," Niki said and turned to face him. "Did you bring my suit out for this or should I get used to using one of the others you brought?"

"Of course we brought yours," he retorted and indicated one of the crates with a gesture for her to start suiting up. His still had a couple of dents, but it would do for a fight against almost anything in this kind of situation. He would have second thoughts about heading into the Zoo with a suit in that condition but at the same time, it was likely to get damaged like this in the jungle and he would have had to deal with it.

Niki had clearly taken note of her training and she was quick to take the pieces out and join them together like the mechanical puzzle it was. She pulled on all the different chunks of armor and attached them with practiced precision before she finished with the helmet. The HUD would come online at that point and confirm if she had done a good job or advise her if any alterations needed to be made.

There were only a couple of small adjustments before she picked up the rocket launcher and assault rifle and attached the former to her shoulder and the latter to her right arm.

"Ready to roll," she stated, slapped the magazine in, and made sure a round was chambered before she turned her attention to him.

Taylor couldn't help a small grin as he refilled his stock of ammo and replaced the grenade he had used earlier. He had a tendency to hold off on using them until things were at their most dire. It often meant he held back on using them at all in his fights with the cryptids because he always waited for a bigger emergency.

He might have to work on that.

"Vickie, we'll work with you on this one," he stated as he

and Niki advanced toward the door of the lab. "Keep your ears and your eyes open."

"At the risk of repeating myself, no shit, Sherlock," she sassed in response.

Taylor grinned. He wouldn't give her or Niki any sign of the twists of anticipation mixed with a very natural fear of returning to the facility. They wouldn't understand or vaguely comprehend the concept of how much he relied on the burst of adrenaline that pumped through his system to survive.

Specialists would say he was broken. All he had to say was that he had adapted to survive.

CHAPTER TWENTY-FIVE

T he door opened and the two headed inside and made sure it was sealed before they began the tense walk into the depths of the facility.

Taylor wouldn't let himself relax, not until they were out the doors of the lab and perhaps not even then. He wouldn't let something like Bobby getting injured happen ever again.

He looked at where Niki stood, her gaze very clearly on the bodies of the monsters that had been killed in the atrium-like area at the entrance. The powerfully built wolves looked intimidating even in death.

"These things are the size of fucking bears," she noted and nudged one of them with her assault rifle. "Who the hell thinks that engineering monsters like this is a good idea?"

"The chances were they didn't know what they would get when they started the process," he replied. "Animal testing will always be preferable to human testing and for the most part, as far as I can tell, they simply pump these animals full of goop and record the results."

"The last place I visited actually planned genetic markers for the changes," she countered. "At least, that was what I understood from what Dr. Jacobs told me. He was furious about it too."

"Like it or not, there'll always be a huge market for pushing the limits of this kind of shit," Taylor agreed. "In the end, there are always people who will see the market with huge dollar signs in their eyes instead of realizing the dangers of what they try to do. Right up until it quite literally bites them in the ass, that is. And throat."

She chuckled as she pulled away from the dead cryptids. "Let's get moving. Vickie, what levels can we find these incredibly intelligent and bossy monsters on?"

"It would seem you can find them there on the first floor," the hacker answered. "Oh, you mean the cryptid monsters... Right. Those are currently on the twentieth level. That's almost at the bottom, by the way, and they're looking for something down there. They'll probably move up through the levels to find something electronic to sink their teeth into, or they'll leave that to other creatures. Oh, and if you encounter any, make sure to kill them quickly or they'll raise the alarm and the rest will rush to your position almost immediately."

"The twentieth level. Of course it's the twentieth level. It couldn't be somewhere a little more accessible." Niki scowled and glanced at Taylor. "Are you ready for this?"

"The fact that you have to ask is a little insulting, I won't lie. Realistically, though, these creatures have most likely infested the entire building. Smaller creatures will filter in and out of the tiniest of crevasses, which means we probably won't find them until they get big and strong enough to cause real problems. You should consider pulling a few strings with your army buddies and have them bomb the shit out of this place until there's nothing but a smoking crater left."

Niki studied him closely as they began to descend the stairs.

"What?" he asked.

"Nothing...but I've never seen you like this before. You're usually in a killer mood when you go after these fuckers, but this time you're... I'm trying to think of a better word than bloodthirsty."

"The bastards hurt Bobby badly," he said by way of explanation. "If this goop is anywhere near as intelligent as I think it is, I'll let that shit know it's a bad idea, from an evolutionary point of view, to fuck with my friends and see if it doesn't get a better idea."

Niki nodded. "Okay. I can live with that. But make sure that—"

"I may be in the mood to trash these sonsofbitches, but I still know how to work tactically in these situations. Don't be concerned about me."

"I'm not. Honestly, I'm more concerned about me."

"Don't be. You count as one of my friends too. I'll have your back, exactly like I always do."

Niki didn't look convinced. He wondered if he was reading too much into her body language since he couldn't see her face through her visor.

They continued their slow and cautious progress. He couldn't hear much of anything himself, but his suit identified movement and sounds he wouldn't have been able to detect on his own. They told him what he had already begun to suspect—that the cryptids were already spread throughout the building. Hunting them individually would be a dangerous exercise in futility. They would need to set explosives and blow the entire facility sky-high.

But only once the more intelligent of the creatures were dealt with.

"I'm picking up movement in the lower levels," Niki noted in a whisper that was more instinctive than necessary. "What's the plan of attack?"

"I only have the one plan," Taylor responded.

"Let me guess. Attack?"

"You've hung around me too long."

He checked his weapon yet again as they continued to move down the steps. The motion sensors told him a small group of creatures waited for them. It was impossible that they hadn't heard the heavy suits advancing in the stairwell, and the only real explanation he had to offer was that they had prepared for an attack.

Well, he'd make sure they had one.

He took one of the grenades from his belt, pulled the pin, and maintained his grasp on the lever for a few seconds as the HUD calculated where he was supposed to throw it to cause maximum damage.

"Fire in the hole," he muttered, lobbed it down the stairwell, and nodded as it bounced off the wall and to where the movement came from.

The four-second fuse felt like an eternity. Taylor felt afraid, sometimes, that the creatures would learn out how to throw the grenade back, but the seconds ticked past until the flash and bang of it were heard and almost felt, even through the suit. The sounds of pain and anger from below were impossible to miss and he focused on taking full advantage of the creatures' distraction after the explosion.

He was first down the stairs and his HUD immediately fixed on living, breathing targets for him to fire at. They looked like rats grown to the size of medium-sized dogs, and their tails worked to pull them up the walls with a small claw at the end. Even the sight of them was enough to make his skin crawl and he opened fire. Dozens of them skittered across the walls, but they seemed less interested in a fight than the rest of their fellows and tried quickly to retreat down the stairs. Below, a handful of larger targets began to push determinedly toward the sound of gunfire.

These looked a little familiar, almost like the large hyena creatures he remembered from the Zoo. They could almost have been imported from the jungle, and he would have suspected that if not for the fact that getting a live creature out of there was incredibly rare and had only been done a couple of times as far as he knew.

It seemed like the Zoo goop had found a design it liked.

The creatures were a little more athletic than he recalled. They twisted and climbed over each other before they bounded against the walls to try to strike at the two humans who advanced toward them.

Taylor opened fire but chose short bursts that allowed him to spare his ammo. Realistically, they would need to conserve what they had brought to make it last, which was why he had opened their engagement with the grenade. He had five more strapped to his belt, and Niki still had her rockets in case things started to go south and they needed to break an engagement. It wasn't an unlikely scenario, all things considered.

"Stop them from reaching our level!" he shouted and continued down the steps. "As long as we fire down at them, we'll always have the advantage."

"I thought our guns were what gave us the advantage."

"Sure, but using the guns right is the difference between killing and getting killed. Keep your shooting tight and let the suit do most of the aiming for you."

He wasn't telling her anything she hadn't heard before, especially during her training in using the suits, but it was still a good idea to remind her of it. As they drew closer to their adversaries, he drew himself away from her a little to give them a triangulated position to prevent the creatures from coming up to their level.

It wasn't long before the hyena creatures had enough. They weren't in the mood to keep fighting like the Zoo monsters, who tended to continue to attack until their numbers were decimated or they had overcome the invaders and killed enough of them. Taylor had never understood what kind of animal psychology went into abandoning all principles of survival instincts.

Then again, these creatures were a brand-new kind, even this long after the new monsters had first appeared on the biological map.

"Keep moving and don't let them regroup," he ordered and gestured for Niki to follow him. These were things he wouldn't have needed to tell Bobby or even Tanya, but he wasn't used to operating with her. He couldn't trust her to do what he expected her to do without having been told.

And given her lack of complaint about being ordered around, maybe she realized she still needed instruction.

He skirted the edges of the stairwell and remained alert for anything that might move around them. The hyenas continued to retreat.

His senses tingled before he saw a new threat. It crawled along the top of the walls—impossibly slowly like it tested the abilities of his motion sensors. The creature was long and thin and spread over the ceiling. It had six legs but there were two more limbs, long, agile tails with what looked like a scorpion's stinger at the ends. Those were what he saw at first. They swished from side to side as if to select a target.

"Get down!" Taylor shouted and followed his instruction as the first tail flicked into the arc of an initial strike. Venom dripped from the tip, primed and ready to punch into them, but it missed on the first attempt and the mutant skittered across the surface. It was twice as long as he was, but the thin structure as well as the hardened carapaces that armored it made it difficult to land a kill shot.

He growled with frustration as the mutant jumped from side to side, using the walls and ceiling as its tails flicked with deadly intent. He felt one of them strike his armor. It was only a glancing blow but enough for him to realize that they were going about this the wrong way. This creature was buying time for the other cryptids, whether intentionally or not, and he couldn't allow it to continue.

His mind made up, he advanced quickly but kept himself low and away from the shorter tails as they flicked from side to side and tried to target him. He waited for one of them to come in a little too close and tried to catch it.

The first attempt failed but he was rewarded with a second opportunity and took advantage, grasped hold of it, and held it motionless as he drew his knife from its sheath. A single decisive slice severed the stinger.

The creature hissed in pain and attempted to strike with the second tail, but he was waiting for it. He released the first and caught the second, yanked the mutant off of the ceiling, and forced it onto the stairs.

There was nothing he wanted to do more than to pump the monster full of holes but he elected to go a less wasteful route. He stepped closer to where it writhed in his grasp. His heavy boots crushed the carapaces easily and he ground them into the floor. It took a few steps to finally pin the head down but the pressure and weight of the suit were sufficient to end its struggles.

The body continued to twitch bizarrely, but it would clearly not get up again.

"Damn," Niki muttered and aimed her rifle's muzzle at the creature as she passed it. "That's some brutal shit right there."

Taylor smirked. "I decided we needed to treat it like a bug. This isn't the one we're looking for though. Right, Vickie?"

"That is correct," the hacker responded. "That one is still near the bottom level of the lab. Happy hunting!"

CHAPTER TWENTY-SIX

"That was an ugly motherfucker," Niki observed as they continued to move down the stairs. "I don't know why, but insects have always given me the creeps, ever since I was a kid. Them getting bigger doesn't help the feeling."

Taylor chuckled, even though he could more than sympathize with it. "It wasn't a pretty bastard but it's not the ugly bastard we're looking for. That one had only one tail that I saw, and it had enough power behind it to punch a hole in our armor, so keep your eyes peeled for it."

"Sure. I'll try not to get impaled by a super-intelligent boss creature with a long and nasty tail," Niki quipped.

"No...don't do it," Vickie all but yelled into the comm unit. "No...shit. Goddammit!"

"What's the problem, Vickie?" he asked as he continued his slow and wary descent.

"The critter found the circuit boards in the lower levels," she complained. "I think it was mocking me because it looked directly at the camera before it shoved its tail into the board. The electricity there is completely out."

"Are the seals still in place?" he asked to confirm what they could expect.

"Yep, the seals are still keeping the whole fucking place closed for now. But you'll be in the dark down there."

He nodded. As long as the facility remained sealed, they had time to hunt their target, even in the darkness. It wasn't like he hadn't gone hunting without natural light before. Most of his time in the Zoo had been spent relying on night vision with a mixture of UV light and motion sensors to give them an idea of what they were dealing with, even during the day.

That said, he wasn't sure how Niki would react to it. She had never been in the complete darkness he had almost grown used to. His grasp on the assault rifle tightened when he saw the murky, inky blackness spread below them.

Something instinctive drove him away from that place. It was like his whole body rejected the idea of heading in there, but he pushed the feeling away and turned on the night vision as he stepped away from the light.

"I guess me talking about how no one can hear us scream down here is probably not appropriate," Niki quipped as she activated the same software.

"No, it's rather appropriate in this case," Taylor muttered and kept his voice in a low monotone. "Something can probably hear us scream down here, but it probably won't help us."

He took slow, deep breaths, conscious of an anger building in him. The thought of facing the monster that had hurt his friend was enough to make his adrenaline pump, and his need for revenge drove him to put one foot in front of the other. The rage felt cold—icy, almost. It was a feeling he was more than used to and he had felt it many, many times before in the Zoo.

Slowly, he looked around. This was the area where most of the live test subjects were kept. The cages were a clear indicator, and it looked like the locks and seals had been broken, probably with a concerted effort from more than one creature. The question was, of course, which monster had been the first to break out.

Taylor had a good idea which one it was. In fact, if it was able to communicate with the other cryptids and issue orders, it could have happened with multiple monsters at the same time. They might well have broken out and over-whelmed their handlers in a single concerted action.

The absence of light made it difficult to see what exactly had happened to the people who had worked in the lower levels during the original breakout, but it wasn't difficult to imagine.

Besides, he doubted that there would be any evidence left except for blood spatters on the walls and the floor.

"There'd better not be another back door here," he muttered and studied the eerily silent section. The green lighting that gave him a view of the floor felt that much more chilling—like he literally walked through an alien world. It was helpful to prevent him from relaxing.

"What do you mean?" Niki asked.

"You know, like the other place had. Where the cryptids managed to dig themselves out of the lab and escape?"

"Oh...right. I'd forgotten about that. I don't think we'll

see the same thing down here. Wasn't the digging done by that huge badger cryptid that almost killed you?"

"Yes, and it was the reason why the rest of the cryptids didn't try to escape. It was different and very aggressive."

Niki chuckled but paused and peered at the floor. "Vickie, we don't see anything down here. Not even other creatures. I guess they all went into hiding when they heard us coming down the steps. Maybe the smarter monster realized what was coming down and these bastards really do have a decent idea of what revenge means."

"It doesn't matter," Taylor answered quickly. "If it's hiding in the air vents again, I'll tear this whole goddamn place apart, even if we have to go floor by floor to find that motherfucker."

She sighed. "I really, really hope it doesn't come to that."

Although she tried to sound tough and acted like the situation didn't unnerve her, he could hear a tremble in her voice. Her whole body had gone into overdrive, everything ticked at the limit of her control, and any sound was almost enough to make her open fire. He wouldn't tell her she was wrong to feel that way and he had seen that kind of reaction from almost every single person he had gone into the Zoo with. Everyone reacted that way during their first time in the jungle.

Maybe this meant that she would be better prepared than most of the recruits who were sent into the Zoo for the first time. Assuming, of course, that she ever ended up in the nightmare jungle.

His gaze scanned the area in search of any evidence of movement around them but found nothing. Either the creatures had left or they were incredibly careful about their movements.

"I'm not sure how it's possible, but this green worldview is even creepier than the pitch black," Niki commented. She was openly nervous now, and Taylor couldn't help but share the sentiment. It was the kind of tension that came to him when he was about to step into an open, pitched battle against the creatures, the calm that came before a storm.

"I know the feeling," he muttered. "Vickie, do you have any updates for us?"

"Not...not really. I still don't have any eyes down there and the bastard doesn't appear on any of the eyes I do have. Not that this is any kind of news."

It wasn't a good sign. That the creature had the presence of mind to turn the lights off before they arrived was worrying enough and now, there was no sign of it anywhere. Had it escaped? Or was it waiting to snap the jaws of a trap shut on them like it had when he and Bobby had helped the civilians to escape?

He'd barely considered the possibilities when something darted into his field of vision. It was massive and long and sinuous like a snake, but it extended into a four-legged creature. The speed at which it moved made it difficult for him to find a shot.

He knew immediately that this was the creature he was there for.

"Come on, you ugly piece of shit!" Taylor bellowed. "Let me show you what happens when you fuck with a friend of mine."

The creature roared in response.

"Taylor, look out!"

Niki's warning came barely in time. The cells they had thought were empty suddenly surged with life. The bars and Plexiglas walls were enough to hide the creatures within them that now surged into the attack from all sides.

She opened fire and the flares of her rockets illuminated the room for a quarter of a second before they flashed with brilliant light. Thankfully, they were the smaller versions that delivered significant damage but wouldn't annihilate everything—themselves included—in the confined space. Screams of pain issued from the cryptids and spurred him into action.

Taylor took the grenades from his belt, two at a time, and lobbed them into the attacking mutants before he readied his assault rifle and switched to full auto. With the creatures bunched together as they were, there was no way he could miss. The only danger was that he would accidentally shoot Niki.

He turned his back and trusted her to keep him safe as he continued to fire. The weapon clicked empty and instead of reaching for his sidearm, he drew his knife. His roar of rage drowned out their screams as he hacked into the creatures, pounded them with his fist, and crushed them underfoot. A few of the hyenas tried to pounce and pin his arms and a laugh bubbled up. In response, he simply drove them into the wall and crushed them between it and his suit while his assault rifle reloaded.

More flashes of fire were almost blinding in the pure darkness and made it difficult for the night vision software to cope. He continued to shoot for a few seconds until he realized there was nothing left to target.

"Did we get it?" Niki asked and sounded breathless. "Did we kill the fucker?"

Taylor studied the bodies as he brushed idly at the blood and gore that had accumulated on his suit. "I...I don't think so. It disappeared when the shooting started. I can't see it."

"Dammit!" she snapped. "It probably retreated and has gone to choose more friends to ambush us with."

That sounded about right. It had probably snuck into the ventilation shafts again and moved to another floor, where there were more of its comrades.

"We'll take this place floor by floor," he announced and turned to head the way they'd come.

He registered that something was wrong almost immediately, but he couldn't tell what. Something nagged at the back of his mind and instinct dug into his gut and told him to freeze in place.

"Look out!"

Niki had seen what he had only a feeling about. Instantly, he realized that blood dripped from the ceiling above him. It was barely picked up by the motion sensors and it wasn't from the fighting. Something alive and bleeding waited for him.

He tensed as the long, snake-like tail with the claw arced toward him. It had learned from its attack on Bobby, and the talon-like weapon aimed at his stomach, away from the thicker armor around his chest.

Instinctively, he swung his rifle up but it felt like he was caught in molasses and moved in slow motion.

Blasts and gunfire penetrated his awareness, not his own but coming from behind him. Niki had acquired her target already and the gunfire didn't stop at a three-round burst. She had set it on full auto. He wasn't sure how she had reacted so quickly, but a few seconds ticked past until her rifle clicked empty. The tail dropped away, but Taylor wasn't done with it.

He delivered a sustained barrage until he'd emptied his magazine and the creature tumbled to land near his feet. It writhed for a few seconds until it finally went still, although blood still oozed from its numerous wounds.

The seconds of silence ticking away were deafening as he stared at the corpse in front of him.

"Nice…nice shooting," he muttered and finally glanced at Niki.

"Thanks," she whispered breathlessly.

CHAPTER TWENTY-SEVEN

Other teams had moved in. Vickie had alerted them to how the rest of the animals lost their coordinated hunting for the electronics once the tailed creature was dead, which left them vulnerable. It could all be handled by someone else.

Taylor and Niki made their way out and eliminated a couple of stragglers that were more interested in running away than putting up a fight.

Still, it looked like his advice was listened to. Massive charges were set to be delivered into the lab below. They would transform the whole facility into a smoking crater and even then, the troops would wait outside in case something tried to climb out of the rubble.

It wasn't like their team was needed anymore. The real threat had been handled, and the military—who also had suits and men trained in using them—could head in to deal with the creatures that remained and might pose a threat to the bomb specialists who were preparing the explosives.

"Honestly, if they have people of their own, I don't

know why they need our help," he muttered as he watched the troops prepare to head in. "You have to think that going in there with a whole platoon has to be better than sending one or two people in there to deal with it, right?"

He expected Niki to offer him some kind of quick-witted response like if the military folks were all that was needed, maybe she didn't have to deal with his abrasive nature anymore. Or she would since there were many of his kind in the armed forces but she would expect less backtalk since she was technically a superior, even if she was a civilian.

But he waited a few seconds and nothing followed. There was not a single word from the woman. He turned to investigate the lack of a response from her, and it didn't look like she had paid attention to a word he'd said. Her eyes stared off into the distance, and she clasped her hands together in an effort to keep them from shaking.

She failed miserably.

He'd seen the symptoms before. Hell, he'd felt them himself on more than one occasion. The effects of adrenaline on the system—and more importantly, leaving the system—were terrifying. People called it the thousand-yard stare. She was processing the fact that she had escaped a life-threatening situation.

There was no way he could even try to imagine what was going through her head. All he could bring himself to do was drop into the seat next to her. There wasn't anything he could say that would help her process it all. She had probably been in life-threatening situations before, working with the FBI as she had. By now, she had to know the symptoms, even if she felt them herself.

She had needed help to climb out of her suit and had acted in an uncoordinated way which had been made worse by the exaggerated response from the power armor. The paramedics had checked her to make sure there was nothing wrong.

They had said that there was nothing physically wrong with her except for something called Combat Stress Reaction, which was common in soldiers post-combat. Taylor had heard the term before, of course, and even heard himself diagnosed with it.

But it looked like Niki hadn't heard what they said either.

Her hands were shaking again, and moisture brimmed in her eyes. He didn't know what else to do so simply wrapped his arms around her shoulders and pulled her in close to him. Part of him expected her to pull away, laughing at him for being a sentimental sap, but to his surprise, she leaned into him and pressed the side of her head into his shoulder.

"Are you okay?" he asked. It was a stupid question and he realized it the moment the words left his lips.

She didn't reply and simply shook her head and leaned a little closer to him.

"You know, the first time I went into the Zoo, I felt sick for a week after coming out," Taylor said, not sure why he was talking but going with the instinct. "I wasn't able to keep anything down and wasn't even thirsty during all that time. Doctors in the base said it was the same thing—this CSR—and told me I needed to look into getting treatment. They suggested I talk to a shrink and maybe take a few pills for it. The truth was, they wanted me back in a suit and heading out as soon as possible. I guess people don't care if you're not in the mood to head into the death jungle after a little while."

Niki snorted but remained pressed against him.

"In my defense, my first time in was kind of a trial by fire. Tons of guys were killed and I barely got out with my life. I'd been in combat innumerable times before, but there's nothing quite like the experience of looking into the eyes of that kind of...alien hatred. I'm not sure why I'm telling you this. Maybe it's simply to let you know that... well, you're not alone in this. Even this Neanderthal has felt the same way you feel right now. It took me five or six trips into the Zoo to get past it, and I'm still not sure how it happened or when."

She looked at him and smiled. He realized that she was no longer shaking, and while there were still a few tears on her face, they looked like they wouldn't last very long.

Suddenly, she looked around and realized they were still near the lab where dozens of men and women in military garb continued to work.

"Hey," Taylor said when he saw where her mind was going. He withdrew his arms from her as she pulled away. "This never happened."

Niki stood quickly, straightened her clothes, cleared her throat, and wiped the tears from her cheeks. "Did anyone see that? Is anyone listening in right now?"

He shook his head. "No one was watching and I turned the comms off when we got out of our suits so no one's listening in either."

She nodded and dropped quickly into the seat beside him again. He simply waited while she cleared her throat a few times before she spoke again. "Well, let it be known, Taylor McFadden, that a woman expects a nice dinner when you hold her like that. I expect a date request soon. And try not to be a dick about it."

Taylor doubted that she was joking, even if she did sound a little amused as she stood again, brushed her clothes off, and stepped out of the first aid tent where they had been seated. A few seconds ticked past before she poked her head in.

"Stop gawking, you big dummy," she said with a grin. "And snap that mouth shut before it catches flies. Get off your ass and let's get moving. I wouldn't want you to be killed by a cryptid we missed until after that date you owe me."

He didn't even think before he did as he was told, stood quickly, and followed her out of the tent. They wandered to the vehicles that waited to transport them to the airstrip.

Finally, he pursed his lips and studied her closely as they walked. "I usually expect to negotiate what is on and off the table—or bed—before we go on a date so I know how to act."

She nodded firmly. "I expect to be the focus of your attention until we agree otherwise, and I suppose it depends on where you take me to impress me."

"Expensive as hell, gotcha." It sounded like a decent enough date. Il Fornaio was probably off the table until after they were past the first date, but that would be a topic for later.

He realized he was walking fairly rapidly and motioned for her to pick up the pace. "Don't you think you should go first? You are team leader, after all. It's my job to watch your back now, right?"

"I'm more worried about you watching my ass than my back."

"Shit." He huffed and moved in front of her. "You know me too well."

"Yes," she admitted as she followed him. "This way, I get to watch yours."

Taylor opened his mouth to reply but he honestly had nothing to say to that. If she was going to be that open about what she wanted, there was little he could do to say otherwise. He merely wasn't sure how to respond. This new Niki was something he wasn't used to and as he now entered into uncharted territory, he didn't want to fuck anything up.

He let her hang back to ogle him, by her own admission. Bobby and Tanya had already been ferried to the nearest medical base to have the man examined, which left little for the two to do except climb into their transport with Jansen and Maxwell and return to the plane. Niki would have to work out a way to transport the others once they were finished with their hospital visit.

At least once she was finished checking him out. Not that he minded. It was a nice ass she was looking at.

AUTHOR NOTES

MAY 12, 2020

THANK YOU for reading our story!

We have a few of these planned, but we don't know if we should continue writing and publishing without your input.

Options include leaving a review, reaching out on Facebook to let us know, and smoke signals.

Frankly, smoke signals might get misconstrued as low hanging clouds, so you might want to nix that idea...

Coke and Pepsi

So, there is a podcast I do with Craig Martelle called the C&M Show...podcast? Something. I really don't know because Craig names the stuff.

Anyway, there are usually a few dozen authors who watch it live-stream and many others who will eventually watch it on the YouTube channel or on Facebook.

This last Saturday, I had to admit I will drink a Pepsi if forced.

I know, right?

Pepsi is not my preference, but here in Vegas, I feel like I'm living in a town of pushers. "We don't serve Coke, will Pepsi be ok?"

I've been told you don't snark back at the messenger. I respect my waiters/waitresses, and I do my best. When they see my answer on my face, they often lean in, their eyes casting about, and whisper, "I completely understand. It wasn't my choice!"

What does a person say after that?

I've learned to drink Dr. Pepper and non-cola sodas. However, sometimes caffeine is exactly what I need, and water won't do. Since I don't drink coffee...

That leaves only one choice here in Vegas. *And that is Dr. Pepper.* If they don't have the doctor, that means the only *other* choice is Pepsi.

I know the saying that drinking while dancing might make you wake up with someone next to you who looked a lot nicer the night before, but sometimes caffeine makes you do stranger things.

And you do them sober.

Diary for May 10th to May 16th

So last week, I blamed Ramy Vance for messing up my office in the virtual world with a bunch of gnome "stuff."

Unfortunately, I blamed the wrong person! Not only did I blame the wrong person, but I also got the right person upset by not giving her credit in the first place.

I can't make this up, people. (Well, ok, I could, but it wouldn't normally come to mind.) It seems that Elaine Bateman, and more importantly, Sarah Noffke, were the people responsible for putting up all the gnome stuff around my office.

It seems that Sarah was cheerleading Elaine the whole time. So, between the two of them, my virtual office was essentially TP'd. Thinking that Ramy Vance, who had been talking to me about samurai and vampires, was responsible, I gave him credit last week.

FOR THE RECORD, it was Sarah and Elaine. Ramy has been exonerated, but I'm still not doing the Samurai / Vampire effort. But, you know it's "never say never."

(*Editor's Note: If you do it, make sure you get the samurai armor right. Editors know these things. No pressure.*)

VEGAS IS OPENING BACK UP SLOWLY

A couple of days ago, I was able to have a dining experience with Mike Bray of Wolfpack Publishing. On Saturdays, we normally eat at the Las Vegas golf club and enjoying chicken fried steak and hash browns. Little did I know this restaurant was the *only one* that had their dining room open at the moment.

It seems most of the other restaurants I enjoy don't have dining in yet.

I'm still starving for Chinese food, but the best Chinese restaurant I know of around Vegas is still closed. Ping Pang Pong is inside the Gold Coast Casino and won't be available for at least another five weeks.

Minimum

Do any of you remember when folks would pop up tents outside of Apple stores to get the latest iPhone when they went on sale? That might be my plan for when Ping Pang Pong opens again.

Did I mention I am still hungry for Chinese?

Oh, and chili. Maybe once the hotels/motels re-open, I can rent one with a kitchenette and make chili properly (which requires time, proper ventilation, and me not being at home where my wife smells it cooking.

(Editor's note: We are here for you any time, big guy, have fabulous ventilation, and we have Mexican Cokes. Plus, Marc loves chili! Bring Mike Bray! Only a short, scenic drive from Vegas.)

THE KURTHERIAN GAMBIT

On the Author side of things, I have great news for people who enjoy audiobooks. We signed a contract last week to publish the Kurtherian Gambit first twenty-one books and the four books from the *Dark Messiah* series with RB Media, a multi-cast audio publisher.

I remember driving back and forth to work, listening to a couple of my favorite stories on Audible with multi-cast narration. To this day, I still hear the sound effects in the ships when opening doors inside, or the blast of their engines as the spaceships rose out of the water, heading to the deep dark of space.

To know that my own *Kurtherian Gambit* series is heading for multi-cast is a really cool feeling.

That's it for the diary entry for this week. I hope you have a fantastic week and weekend coming up!

Ad Aeternitatem,

Michael Anderle

Have you read *The BOHICA Chronicles* from C.J. Fawcett and Jonathan Brazee? A complete series box set is available now from Amazon and through Kindle Unlimited.

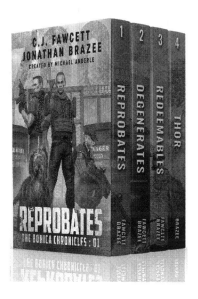

Kicked out of the military for brawling, what can three friends from different countries do to make some needed money?

Grab your copy of the entire BOHICA Chronicles at a discount today!

Reprobates:

With nothing in their future, Former US Marine Charles, ex-SAS Booker, and ex-Australian Army Roo decide to give the Zoo a shot.

Without the contacts, without backing, without knowing what they are getting into, they scramble to get their foot in the door to even make rent in one of the most dangerous areas in the world.

With high rewards comes high risk. Can they learn on the job, where failure means death?

Relying on their training, they will scratch, claw, and take the most dangerous jobs to prove themselves, but will it be enough? Can they fight the establishment and the Zoo at the same time?

And what the heck's up with that puppy they found?

Degenerates:

What happens when you come back from vacation to find out your dog ate the dog-sitter?

And your dog isn't a dog?

The BOHICA Warriors have had some success in the Zoo, but they need to expand and become more professional to make it into the big time.

Each member goes home to recruit more members to join the team.

Definitely bigger, hopefully badder, they return ready to kick some ZOO ass.

With a dead dog-sitter on their hands and more dangerous missions inside the Zoo, the six team members have to bond and learn to work together, even if they are sometimes at odds with each other.

Succeed, and riches will follow.

Fail, and the Zoo will extract its revenge in its own permanent fashion.

Redeemables:

NOTHING KEEPS A MAN AND HIS 'DOG' APART...

But what if the dog is a man-killing beast made up of alien genetics?

Thor is with his own kind as they range the Zoo, but something is missing for him. Charles is with his own kind as they work both inside and outside the walls of the ZOO.

Once connected, the two of them are now split apart by events that overcame each.

Or are they?

Follow the BOHICA Warriors as they continue to make a name for themselves as the most professional of the MERC Zoo teams. So much so that people on the outside have heard of them.

Follow Thor as he asserts himself in his pack.

Around the Zoo, nothing remains static, and some things *might converge yet again if death doesn't get in the way.*

Thor:

The ZOO wants to kill THOR. Humans would want that as well, but they don't know what he is.

What is Charles going to do?

Charles brings Thor to Benin, where he can safely hide out until things calm down. Unfortunately for both of them, that takes them out of the frying pan and into the fire.

The Pendjari National Park isn't the Zoo, but lions, elephants, and rhinos are not pushovers.

When human militias invade the park, Thor and park ranger Achille Amadou are trapped between the proverbial rock and a hard place. How do you protect the park and THOR Achille has to hide just*what* **Thor is...**

Can he hide what Thor is when Thor makes that hard to accomplish?

Will the militias figure out what that creature is that attacks them?

Available now from Amazon and through Kindle Unlimited.

CONNECT WITH THE AUTHORS

**Michael Anderle Social
Website:
http://lmbpn.com**

**Email List:
http://lmbpn.com/email/**

**Facebook Here:
https://www.facebook.com/groups/lmbpn.thezoo/**

https://www.facebook.com/LMBPNPublishing/

One Crazy Set Of Stories (12)

SOLDIERS OF FAME AND FORTUNE

Nobody's Fool (1)

Nobody Lives Forever (2)

Nobody Drinks That Much (3)

Nobody Remembers But Us (4)

Ghost Walking (5)

Ghost Talking (6)

Ghost Brawling (7)

Ghost Stalking (8)

Ghost Resurrection (9)

Ghost Adaptation (10)

Ghost Redemption (11)

Ghost Revolution (12)

THE BOHICA CHRONICLES

Reprobates (1)

Degenerates (2)

Redeemables (3)

Thor (4)

Printed in Great Britain
by Amazon